SUDDENLY AT HOME

SUDDENLY AT HOME

A Brock and Poole Mystery

Graham Ison

This first world edition published 2016
in Great Britain and the USA by
SEVERN HOUSE PUBLISHERS LTD of
19 Cedar Road, Sutton, Surrey, England, SM2 5DA.
Trade paperback edition first published
in Great Britain and the USA 2016 by
SEVERN HOUSE PUBLISHERS LTD

Copyright © 2016 by Graham Ison.

British Library Cataloguing in Publication Data
A CIP catalogue record for this title is available from the British Library.

ISBN-13: 978-0-7278-8641-5 (cased)
ISBN-13: 978-1-84751-742-5 (trade paper)
ISBN-13: 978-1-78010-807-0 (e-book)

Typeset by Palimpsest Book Production Ltd.,
Falkirk, Stirlingshire, Scotland.

ONE

It was the hottest day of the month so far, although there were still five more days of July remaining. But the forecast suggested that August would be no cooler.

I was sitting in my office above Belgravia police station in central London, with a cup of fresh coffee in front of me and beside it a completed report for the Crown Prosecution Service. My in-tray was empty and the commander had taken the day off. My jacket was hanging over the back of my chair, and I was contemplating the possibility of actually having a weekend off to do exactly as I pleased. And that was to do nothing. What could be better than that?

Unfortunately what we anticipate rarely occurs, and it is particularly foolish for a detective chief inspector who is attached to the Homicide and Major Crime Command of the Metropolitan Police to think such things. Especially at half past two on a Friday afternoon.

'Excuse me, sir.' Detective Sergeant Colin Wilberforce, the incident-room manager, appeared in my office doorway. Colin is a mild sort of guy who's happily married to Sonia, has three children and lives in Orpington. But this gentle giant becomes a ferocious rugby player when he turns out for the Metropolitan Police and has a cauliflower ear to prove his on-field aggressive qualities.

'What is it, Colin?' I was disconcerted by the expression on Wilberforce's craggy face. It had a certain triumphant look about it, and I imagined it was the sort of triumphant look that appears on his face when he's barged his way through the opposing players and is in sight of a touchdown.

'We've got one, sir, and Mr Dean has given it to you.'

'By which I take it that, in his infinite wisdom, Mr Dean has decided to ruin my weekend.' But I couldn't really complain, Patrick Dean was the detective superintendent in charge of our bit of HMCC and his allocation of cases was always scrupulously fair.

'Yes, sir,' said Wilberforce, his face not betraying the slightest amusement, even though I knew that inside he was laughing like a drain. It was all right for him: he had the weekend off. 'What's the SP?' I asked wearily, as I stood up and put on my jacket. Short for starting price, SP is a bit of terminology the police have lifted from the sport of kings, but to CID officers it's a desire to know what's happened so far.

Wilberforce glanced at some sort of electronic gismo he was holding in his hand. 'The body of a deceased male was found in Apartment E, Cockcroft Lodge, Cockcroft Grove, North Sheen, sir. First officers on the scene were told that it was the deceased's home address.' After grinning owlishly, he added, 'It would appear that he'd been shot, sir.'

'Has he been identified?'

'Sort of. His name's Richard Cooper according to the man who called the police.'

'And who was that?

'A man by the name of Dennis Jones who claims to be a friend of Cooper. He's been detained at the apartment pending interview.'

'When did this drama unfold, Colin?'

Wilberforce glanced at his gadget again. 'It was approximately thirteen thirty hours when Jones found the body, sir.' And anticipating my next question, he added, 'Dave Poole is in the car park ready and waiting, and Miss Ebdon is assembling the rest of the team.'

Detective Sergeant Dave Poole is my black bag carrier. And to clear up any ambiguity, it is Dave who is black not the bag. In point of fact there isn't a bag any more, but the term has stuck. Of Caribbean descent, his grandfather arrived in the 1950s and set up practice as a medical doctor in Bethnal Green; his father is a chartered accountant, but Dave, after obtaining a good English degree at London University, claims that in a moment of insanity he joined the Metropolitan Police until he could find a proper job. And I can honestly say that he's the best assistant I've ever had working with me. What I forget, he remembers.

Adopting a mock West Indian sing-song accent in place of his native cockney, Dave frequently refers to himself as the black sheep of the family, thus alarming the more sensitive of those among our hierarchy who consider racial diversity to be far more important than fighting crime. But there's not a lot they can do about Dave making racist remarks about himself, especially when doing so he adopts a sort of downtrodden expression.

I made my way to the car park, where Dave was waiting with the engine running.

The distance to North Sheen from Belgravia is about ten miles, but given that London is probably the most congested city in Europe, Dave did well to get us there in slightly less than forty-five minutes, by dint of what he calls positive motoring.

One glance at the exterior of Cockcroft Lodge was enough to confirm that it comprised a series of upmarket apartment blocks. Looking at the pristine lawns and delicately playing fountains in the gardens, I guessed that my salary wouldn't even cover the maintenance. And that was before I discovered that underground there existed a swimming pool, a gymnasium and a squash court and that there were tennis courts in the gardens at the rear. All of which pointed to the residents being seriously rich people.

A youthful inspector, clutching a clipboard and looking terribly important, stood in the main entrance to the nearest of the three apartment blocks. He raised his pen and opened his mouth as I approached, but I answered the question I knew he was going to ask before he'd uttered a word.

'DCI Harry Brock, HMCC.'

'Thank you, sir,' said the inspector, and waggled his pen at Dave with an officious sort of flourish.

'Colour Sergeant Poole, ditto, sah!' Dave, having guessed that the inspector was one of the aforementioned diversity worriers, adopted his West Indian sing-song accent and contrived to look like a recently emancipated slave.

The inspector gulped and scribbled on his clipboard. So far he had remained silent, but as he probably hadn't anything useful to contribute that was undoubtedly for the best.

A uniformed constable whose ravaged and weary seen-it-all face gave him the appearance of one old enough to be the inspector's father smirked and lifted the blue-and-white tape. 'First floor, guv. The hat inspector's there.'

The HAT inspector is so called not because of a propensity for eccentric headgear or, for that matter, any sort of headgear. The acronym HAT means Homicide Assessment Team, a roving band of detective inspectors, male and female, who are called upon to determine if a suspicious death is a homicide. And if it is, that's where I come in. There was a time when the Murder Squad at Scotland Yard was so small that its members knew each other, but now there are over seven hundred of us. Nevertheless, we're told by the inhabitants of that self-deluding dream factory known as the Home Office that incidents of major crime are on the decline.

Dave and I took the stairs to the first floor. I have a negative attitude towards lifts; they tend to malfunction when you're in a hurry, and it's embarrassing if you get stuck in a lift when you're on your way to investigate a murder. It happened to me some years ago, but I can still recall the collective sniggering of the firefighters who eventually liberated me.

'Afternoon, guv.'

'Still not doing me any favours, then, Jack.' I had first met Jack Noble, the HAT inspector, at the scene of a murder one snowy February morning in Chelsea.

'Sorry about that, guv'nor. People will go about getting topped, but at least the weather's better. To get down to business, Dennis Jones, the guy who found Cooper's body, is inside. He'll tell you the tale, and it all sounds pretty sussy.'

'How so?' I asked.

'He struck me as being a bit iffy, and he's a wimp. I didn't question him, of course, but what he told us when we arrived didn't seem to ring true.' Noble shrugged. 'You might take a different view, though.'

'Thanks for the heads-up, anyway, Jack.' Most CID officers will tell you that the view of the first detective on the scene is invaluable.

There was little doubt that Richard Cooper's apartment was expensive, but it was not to my taste. It was what I think the chattering classes call minimalist, which is another way of saying you don't have much furniture and excuse its absence by pretending that it's very much the trendy way to live.

Or in Richard Cooper's case, die.

The body was sprawled face up, arms outstretched, on the floor of the living area. I deliberately didn't use the term 'living room' because there was no easy way of working out where the various functions began and ended. Imagine a sitting area with a large uncomfortable sofa, a dining area with a glass-topped table and uncomfortable chairs, and a sort of kitchenette arrangement. All merged into one huge space that seemed, at first glance, to be about half an acre. And large picture windows affording panoramic views of . . . well, Hounslow. Pollution permitting.

My first impression of Richard Cooper was that he was about thirty-two years old, but I later learned that he was thirty-five. And he was prematurely bald. He was dressed in light-blue linen trousers, Gucci suede loafers and a white silk shirt. At least, it had been white when he put it on, but there was now a large bloodstain across the front and several holes in the material near the location of the heart.

'That's no way to treat an expensive shirt,' observed Dave.

'Where's this Dennis Jones now, Jack?' I asked, seeing that he wasn't in the living area.

'I've put him in one of the bedrooms,' said Noble. 'Mrs Maxwell – she lives in Apartment F opposite – offered to look after him until you arrived, but she could be a material witness so I've kept them apart. Jones has obviously had a touch of the vapours, but the first officers on the scene said he refused medical assistance.'

'You say that this Maxwell woman could be a material witness?'

'Yeah. When police arrived, she was standing outside her front door and volunteered the information that she'd heard two or three loud bangs at around one o'clock.'

'Don't tell me, she thought it was a car backfiring.'

'No,' said Noble with a laugh. 'Strange to relate, she thought they were gunshots. Being a hot day, most people have got their windows open – there are another two apartment blocks behind this one – and she couldn't make out where the noise had come from. She eventually put it down to someone watching an American cop show on television. Then, about half an hour later, this Jones guy banged on her door and asked her to call the police and an ambulance, which she did, and suddenly there were coppers running about all over the place. Her words, not mine,' he added, smiling. 'The skipper on the Q car, who was first officer on the scene, straight away sussed out that it was a murder and called me.'

'I'll have a word with Jones while we wait for the cavalry to arrive. Who's the pathologist?'

'Doctor Mortlock. He was complaining that he had to come from Chelsea, but he should be here any minute. I suppose he's dealing with another dead body.' Noble sighed. 'Never rains but it pours,' he said.

'Chelsea's where Dr Mortlock lives, and he's always complaining about something.' I shook hands with Noble. 'Thanks, Jack.'

'Be lucky, guv,' said Noble, and went on his way.

The rest of the supporting cast arrived together. Detective Inspector Kate Ebdon headed the team of detectives that always worked with me; and Linda Mitchell, the crime-scene manager, was accompanied by a band of murder technicians bearing the tools of their trade. DI Len Driscoll would be back at the incident room, ready to deal with anything that needed a bit of weight.

'I'll leave you to oversee the scene, Kate, and the usual local enquiries; you know the form,' I said, 'while Dave and I interview the guy who found the body. But leave Mrs Maxwell in Apartment F opposite. I'll speak to her.'

I left Kate to organize her officers into doing what was necessary in a murder investigation, such as starting house-to-house enquiries. Or in this case, apartment-to-apartment.

The bedroom was large and was dominated by a huge bed. I knew about king-size beds, super-king-size beds and even emperor-size beds, but this one was even larger. One wall was covered with mirrored sliding doors, behind which, doubtless, was a wardrobe full of expensive suits, shirts and ties. Assuming he was someone who wore a tie. There aren't many of us left.

I glanced at the man slumped in one of two armchairs, both of which were skeletal in design and looked as though they were only half finished.

'Dennis Jones?'

'Yes, that's me.' Jones struggled to stand up, but I waved him down.

By the look of him Jones was probably around thirty years of age. He had large owl-like spectacles through which he blinked repeatedly. His pale face may have been the natural complexion of someone who spent his whole life indoors, or it may be that he was still in shock. Nevertheless, it was a face that betrayed an overall weakness of character. He was curiously dressed, at least by my standards: a pair of the ubiquitous blue jeans and a dark-blue shirt, the collar, cuffs and patch pocket of which were pale blue. This bizarre ensemble was completed by a pair of light-blue shoes with thick white-rubber soles. I imagined this to be his idea of what the modern man-about-town should wear.

'I'm Detective Chief Inspector Harry Brock, Mr Jones, and this is Detective Sergeant Poole. Just relax and tell me what you know about this business.'

'You wouldn't happen to have a cigarette, would you? I've been trying to give up, so I haven't got any with me.'

'I'm afraid you'll have to wait until you're out of here,' said Dave. 'This whole area is a crime scene and we don't want it contaminated.'

'Oh, I see. I didn't understand that.' Jones's hands were shaking so much that he eventually pushed them into the pockets of his jeans. 'It's the first time I've ever seen a dead body.'

'I guessed that,' I said, but didn't feel a great deal of sympathy. One of the regrettable facts of life – or should that be death? – is that coppers very quickly become inured to the sight of what man can do to his fellow man. 'I understand that it was you who found Mr Cooper.'

'Yes.'

'Why did you call on him?' asked Dave.

'He asked me to.'

'Why did he ask you to call on him?' Dave was being extremely patient, but he knew that a nervous witness was unlikely to respond if an investigating officer pushed him too hard.

'He was scared.' Jones flicked his long blond hair out of his eyes. It was a habit that was to be repeated frequently during the course of our conversation.

'What was he scared of?' I'd been tempted to say that he apparently had good reason, but this wasn't the time for flippant remarks.

Jones looked nervously in my direction and began to blink through his glasses again. 'All he told me was that someone had threatened to kill him. In fact, he'd taken the threat so seriously that he'd moved out of his apartment and was staying in a hotel.'

'D'you know the name of the hotel?' I asked.

'No. He said it was better I didn't know.'

'What was he doing back here, then?' Dave glanced up, a suspicious expression on his face.

'He'd come back to get a change of clothes and to pick up some papers connected with his work.'

'How d'you know that's why he was coming back?'

'Because he rang me and asked me to meet him here. He didn't want to be here on his own in case this person turned up.'

'What time did he ask you to meet him?' I asked.

'At about one o'clock.'

'And when did you get here?'

'About half past one, I suppose it must've been. There was an accident on the M4 and I got held up.' Jones shook his head. 'If I'd been here, this wouldn't have happened.'

'If you *had* been here, you'd probably have been shot as well,' commented Dave cynically. 'What d'you know about this person who was threatening Mr Cooper?'

'Nothing,' Jones said. 'Dick wouldn't tell me. He said that if I knew, it would put me in danger as well.'

'You said he'd come back for a change of clothing and to pick up some papers connected with his work,' said Dave. 'What was his job?'

'I don't know,' said Jones. 'But if this flat is anything to go by, it pays well.'

'I think that'll be all for the moment, Mr Jones,' I said, 'but we'll need to speak to you again before you leave. In the meantime, perhaps you'd give your details to my sergeant here.'

'Have you got any evidence of identity on you, Mr Jones? Your passport or a driver's licence?' Dave had no intention of accepting this man's word for his name and address. Vital witnesses – who later proved to be suspects – had been known to give the police false details before disappearing, never to be seen again. Dave was making sure it wasn't going to happen this time.

'I've got my driver's licence.' Jones opened his wallet and handed Dave the small plastic card. I got the impression that he did so reluctantly, but it was only later we discovered the reason.

'That'll do for a start.' Dave copied the details into his pocketbook. 'You're still residing at this address in Petersham, are you?'

'Er, yes.' Jones hesitated, and flicked his hair back again before answering.

'And your phone number?'

'I can never remember the number of my mobile,' said Jones, taking the phone from his pocket. 'That's why I've written it down.' He took out a pocket diary and thumbed through its pages. Eventually finding what he was looking for, he gave Dave the necessary information.

'As a matter of interest, why did you knock on the door of the flat opposite and ask the occupant to call the police and an ambulance when you'd got a phone with you?' Dave rested his pocketbook on his knee, gazed at Jones with a thoughtful expression and waggled his pen. I'd seen him do this quite often and it always had a disturbing effect on witnesses.

'Er, I never thought of it,' said Jones nervously. 'When I came across Dick's body, I just panicked. I rushed across the hall and banged on the nearest door.'

'But even if you didn't use your own mobile phone, there's a landline in this apartment. You could have used that.'

'I never thought,' said Jones lamely.

'I'll get someone to take a statement in a minute, Mr Jones,' I said, and Dave and I returned to the main area of the apartment. 'What d'you think, Dave?'

'I don't fancy him at all, guv. This panic-stricken rush across the hall and making a song and dance about calling us and a meat wagon could all be a load of old moody. And we don't know that he arrived when he said he did. He could've murdered Cooper and then hung about for half an hour before putting on his face-saving performance.'

'Interesting,' I commented. 'Jack Noble thought he was a bit iffy. On the other hand, his story might be genuine. Nobody but a complete idiot would make up a story like that unless it was the truth. We'll see if Mrs Maxwell can shed any light on it.'

TWO

The woman who opened the door to Apartment F was some five ten in height with short brown hair and a buxom figure that was attractively well-rounded. I reckoned that she was in her mid-thirties. Her faded blue jeans were rolled to mid-calf, and she was wearing deck shoes. That together with her Breton sweater gave the overall impression of someone who had at that very moment stepped off a yacht, though to the best of my knowledge there isn't a yacht marina in the North Sheen area.

'Mrs Maxwell?'

'Yes, that's me,' the woman said, smiling.

'I'm Detective Chief Inspector Harry Brock, Mrs Maxwell. I'm in charge of the investigation team from Scotland Yard that's dealing with this case. And this is Detective Sergeant Poole.'

'Oh, please call me Lydia, and come in and make yourselves comfortable.' Mrs Maxwell spoke in a breathless, husky voice that sounded sexy, although it may have been the result of too much smoking. But that's what comes of being a cynic: I try hard not to see the best in people when I'm investigating a murder. I later found out that she didn't smoke and never had.

As I'd expected, the layout of Lydia Maxwell's apartment was a mirror image of the one Dave and I had just left, but was furnished more warmly than Cooper's. 'Would you gentlemen like a cup of tea? I'm just about to make one. And do take a seat.' She pointed at a pair of white leather settees that had probably cost the earth, but still managed to look cheap. As Dave often said, it's all a matter of taste, whatever he meant by that.

'Perhaps you'd start by telling us what you know of this matter, Lydia,' I said, once she'd poured the tea and sat down on the settee opposite us. 'Right from the beginning, if you would.'

'I was actually starting to make myself a pot of tea over there.' Lydia waved vaguely at the kitchen bit of her all-in-one living space, and then smiled guiltily. 'Actually, I was being

lazy and I put a tea bag in a mug of hot water. It was then that
I heard gunshots. Well, at first I thought that someone was
watching one of those awful cop shows on the television.'
She paused to put a hand to her mouth. 'Whoops! No offence,
Mr Brock. I meant that the shows were awful, not the cops – er,
the police.'

'I should give up while you're still losing, Lydia,' said
Dave, 'but I agree with you that they're pretty awful. It wouldn't
be so bad if they were anything like the real thing.' He paused.
'But then I suppose they'd be boring.'

'I can't believe that.' Lydia shot Dave a lingering smile that
hinted at availability, but mature women always seem to smile
at him like that. And he never seems to notice.

'Please go on,' I said. 'Where did this sound come from?
Could you tell?'

'No, I'd no idea,' said Lydia. 'Being such a hot day, most
people had their windows open, me included.'

'And this was what time?' asked Dave, glancing up from
taking notes.

Lydia considered the question for a moment or two. 'About
one-ish, I suppose. Yes, that'd be right because I'd just watched
the news headlines on the TV.'

'But you still managed to hear the sound of what you thought
was gunfire over the sound of the television?' Dave raised a
quizzical eyebrow.

'Oh, I'd turned it off by then. As I said, I'd only switched it
on for the headlines. It's never very interesting and you get the
same stuff over and over again, until there's another crisis to
take their minds off the last one. But I like to keep up with
what's going on, if you know what I mean.'

'It was just after one, then,' suggested Dave. 'A few minutes
perhaps?'

'Yes, that would be about right.'

'What happened next?'

'Well, the next thing,' continued Lydia, the tone of her voice
dropping as though she was about to share a confidence, 'was
that someone was hammering loudly at the door. I opened
it and there was this agitated man standing there. He was in
a terrible state, all flushed and shaking, as though he'd seen a

ghost. I wondered what on earth was wrong with him. Then he asked me to call the police and an ambulance because there'd been a terrible accident in the apartment opposite.'

'Were they the words he used, Lydia?' I asked. 'A terrible accident?'

'Yes, a terrible accident. Those were his exact words. And then he said he thought the man was dead.'

'And what time was this?'

'It must've been about half past one by then, I suppose.'

'That would be right, sir,' said Dave, turning to me. 'The ambulance service logged the call at thirteen thirty-four and the police received the call two minutes later.'

'Where did this man go next, Lydia?' I asked.

'Back across the hall, I imagine.' For a second or so, she seemed uncertain about what had happened, but I put that down to excitement. 'I was too busy phoning for the police and the ambulance to see exactly where he'd gone. But after I'd put the phone down, I opened my front door—'

Again she paused. 'Come to think of it, he'd actually left my door open. The man, I mean. And the door to Mr Cooper's apartment – that's the one opposite – was ajar. It was then that a number of policemen came up the stairs and went into that apartment.'

'It will be necessary for you to be spoken to again at some time, Lydia,' I said. 'Either by me or one of my officers. We'd like to know how much you knew about Richard Cooper, because this is a murder enquiry.'

'He's been murdered?' said Lydia, a little too innocently I thought, and put a hand to her cheek. 'Oh my God! How awful. Poor Mr Cooper. But the man who knocked on my door said it was an accident.'

'Do you have a key to Mr Cooper's apartment, Lydia?'

'No. Why on earth would I have a key?'

'Neighbours sometimes exchange keys in case they lock themselves out,' I said.

'Oh, I see. Well, Mr Cooper and I didn't have keys to each other's apartment.'

'I'll leave Sergeant Poole here to take a brief statement from you,' I said, unwilling to go into details, 'but as I said, someone will see you again in the near future.' I thanked her for the tea and returned to the crime scene to see what Linda Mitchell and her experts could tell us.

The pathologist had finished his initial examination, and the machinery of scientific murder investigation was in full swing throughout the apartment.

'I've made a cursory examination of the cadaver, Harry.' Dr Henry Mortlock levered himself out of the uncomfortable settee and adjusted the pince-nez he had lately taken to wearing in place of the old-fashioned wire-rimmed spectacles that had always seemed to be a part of his rounded face – almost as if he'd been born wearing them. Henry Mortlock was a difficult man to get to know personally, so much so that I wondered if he deliberately kept himself aloof from personal relationships. Consequently I didn't know very much about him, even though we'd been professionally acquainted for years. I did know that he played golf, because he was always complaining that my dead bodies were interfering with an important game. Natural enough, I suppose, because he seemed to play a lot of important games and I seemed to attract a lot of dead bodies. He was rather short, about five foot seven and had the sort of shape that my ex-wife would've described as cuddly. In his case sartorial elegance was non-existent and his suits, even when new, looked as though they'd been lived in for some time. Or even slept in. That, together with his trademark spotted bow tie, a watch chain strung between the pockets of the waistcoat he wore all year round, and now the pince-nez, lent him a vaguely Dickensian look that I suspect he nurtured.

But the overtly avuncular disposition, similar to that of a family doctor in whom one felt one could confide, was misleading and he could become noticeably short-tempered when anyone got in his way while he was conducting an examination, or if they started asking stupid or ill-formulated questions. He also had a sarcastic and acerbic wit, but that perhaps was the result of a professional lifetime mixing with cynical coppers like me. He's frequently mentioned a wife, but never by name, and I've no idea if he's got any children. And that really sums up all I know of the man.

'And your diagnosis, Henry?'

'Oh, dead, Harry, dear boy. Quite definitely dead.' Mortlock began to pick up his various pieces of equipment and pack them into his bag.

'Good gracious! Surely not! Any thoughts on how he came to be in that parlous state?' I asked, playing along with what in his case passed for witty repartee. Forensic pathologists, especially first-class ones like Henry Mortlock, have a sense of humour that swings between the macabre and the puerile and back again. All within a matter of seconds.

'Shot,' said Mortlock tersely, but then, tiring of trivial banter, he switched to his professional mode. 'As far as I can see without having him on the slab, Harry, several shots to the chest, rather than stab wounds.' He picked up a stethoscope, stared at it as though wondering why it was there, and tossed it into his bag. 'They appear to be close to the heart, assuming that his heart is where it should be. I once performed a post-mortem on a Latvian seaman and found that all his organs were on the wrong side of his body.' He sniffed contemptuously. 'Very inconsiderate for pathologists working every hour that God gave trying to scrape an honest crust.'

Dave had returned from taking Lydia Maxwell's statement in time to hear the last part of Mortlock's story. 'My heart, which is in the *right* place—' he began.

'You could've fooled me,' commented Kate Ebdon quietly.

'As I was about to say before my revered inspector interrupted me, Doctor,' said Dave, 'my heart, which is in the right place, bleeds for you.'

'Shut up, Sergeant Poole!' said Mortlock.

'Time of death?' I queried, cutting across the badinage that seemed always to take place in the presence of violent death.

'Your aforementioned young and attractive lady inspector,' said Mortlock, and pointed a large rectal thermometer at Kate Ebdon before putting it in his bag, 'said that a witness heard gunshots at about one o'clock, and my initial findings would seem to indicate that to be the case. Mind you, the fact that the windows were all wide open and that it's a hot day may make a substantial difference, so I might change that view. However, further and better particulars will be forthcoming in due course.'

He closed his bag, but as usual had left his options open before striding out of the room.

'That's strange,' said Dave. 'He usually hums a bit of classical music when he leaves a crime scene, but not this time.'

'You must've upset him with that smart remark,' said Kate.

'It's more likely that he doesn't like North Sheen, ma'am,' suggested Dave, and paused. 'But going back to the time of death and what Dr Mortlock said about its uncertainty,' he continued, addressing both of us, 'we've only got Mrs Maxwell's word for the time of the murder. For all we know, the shots she heard might really have been on someone's television. It's just as likely that the killer could have arrived earlier or later and shot Cooper with a firearm fitted with a suppresser. Although that doesn't reduce the noise by much.'

'You've still got a suspicion that Jones might be the murderer, haven't you?' I said.

'Well, what d'you think, guv?'

'I must admit it's a possibility, Dave, but he seemed genuinely shaken when we spoke to him.'

'I imagine he would be if he'd just murdered someone, particularly if he did so in the heat of the moment,' said Dave bluntly. 'Either that or he's a good actor. But think on this for a plan: Jones turns up with a firearm fitted with a silencer, shoots Cooper at half past one, and then goes screaming across the hall to Lydia Maxwell's drum so that he's got a witness to his panic attack. He admitted to having a mobile phone, so why didn't he use it? I don't believe this nonsense about being so confused that he forgot he'd got a phone in his pocket. Everyone carries a mobile these days and it's second nature to use the bloody thing. Especially in an emergency.'

'Jones could be a good actor,' suggested Kate.

'I just said that, *ma'am*,' commented Dave, but was ignored by Kate.

'There's only one flaw in your argument, Dave,' I said. 'Where's the firearm now, given that Jones was searched by the first police on the scene?'

'He might've tossed it out of the open window intent on collecting it later.'

'We'll soon find out,' I said. 'We've got a team searching

the grounds. I suppose there might be some profit in checking the television schedules to see if there was a cop show on at around one o'clock.' I was actually thinking aloud, but Dave scuppered that idea immediately.

'There are hundreds of channels on the box now, *sir.*' Dave always called me 'sir' when I made a fatuous comment or came up with a stupid suggestion. 'And I've no doubt whatsoever that there's almost bound to have been one at that time, probably on several channels at the same time.'

'Yes, I suppose you're right, Dave.'

'Yes, sir,' said Dave.

I was also harbouring a few doubts about Lydia Maxwell's part in all this. Her story about hearing a police show on TV was just a little too pat for my liking. That said, however, people do react in different ways when witnessing or being close to a murder, and sometimes say very silly things if they're in shock. Not that the Maxwell woman seemed likely to be shocked that easily.

'Would you like me to have a word with Jones, guv?' asked Kate.

Detective Inspector Kate Ebdon is a subtle and tenacious interrogator, and in the past one of her 'words' had often elicited a confession. Right now, I think all three of us had grave doubts about the veracity of what Jones had told us.

Kate Ebdon is an attractive thirty-something flame-haired Australian who had left her native Port Douglas in Queensland at the age of seventeen. She frequently talks about her home on the coast of the Coral Sea, and unashamedly boasts that she enjoyed skinny-dipping there. Following a few false starts as a layout artist with an advertising agency and then a spell as a clerk in hospital administration, she had joined the Metropolitan Police.

After two years' street duty in Hoxton, she was selected for the CID and served in London's East End. Proving herself to be a good thief-taker, she was rapidly promoted to detective sergeant and served for a few years on the prestigious Flying Squad. Somewhere along the way she'd found time to acquire a black belt in judo, and I once saw her put a six-foot villain on his back with about as much effort as she would've used to swat a fly.

'Yes, have a word with him, Kate, and take Dave with you. See if Jones will open up. And I think you should interview him at the local nick so that you can record what he says.'

'Shall I dust him with the frightening powder, guv?' queried Dave, raising a quizzical eyebrow. 'Or on the other hand take a statement under caution?'

'Depends what he says, Dave. You know the rules. If he coughs, caution him and give me a ring and I'll decide what to do next. Meanwhile, I'll stay here and follow up on anything Linda finds, but I'll probably be back at Belgravia by the time you've finished with Jones at Richmond nick.'

A few moments later Dennis Jones, a worried frown on his white face, was escorted from the bedroom where he had been waiting and taken down to one of our cars.

'I don't suppose you've been lucky enough to come across a firearm of any description, have you, Linda?' It was a jocular question – the only occasion I'd found a firearm at the scene of a murder was when the killer had tried to make it look as though the victim had committed suicide and the weapon had been in plain view.

'No such luck, Mr Brock.' Linda Mitchell turned to face me, and afforded me one of her impish smiles as if to suggest that I'd just asked a stupid question.

'When are you likely to be finished here?'

'We'll probably be here until midnight. And very likely again tomorrow, I should think. There's a host of fingerprints that'll take some time to process. There was no sign of forced entry, so I imagine that the killer was known to the victim and was admitted by him.'

'Or maybe was here first.'

'Provided he or she had a key,' said Linda. 'I'll come and see you when I've got something to tell you, but I can't promise a time.'

'Of course. Whenever suits you.' There was no point in attempting to rush Linda. She was a painstaking expert and I knew that if there was anything of evidential value to be found, she would find it. 'In the meantime, Linda, I'll have a word with the concierge.'

According to Detective Constable Sheila Armitage, one of

Kate's house-to-house team, the Cockcroft Lodge concierge's name was Mark Hodgson. She had spoken to him briefly during the course of the original canvass and had marked him up as worthy of further interview. Given that concierges are often a mine of information, I chose to speak to him myself, rather than let one of the team take a statement.

The concierge's lodge was in a strategically advantageous position near the main entrance to the estate and had windows on three sides. There was a rising ramp set into the road and a stand-alone card reader that allowed residents to gain access by inserting an authorization card. I was pleased to see that focused on the entrance there were CCTV cameras which I hoped might assist in our investigation.

'Good afternoon, sir. How can I help you?' The concierge's voice was firm and gave the impression that he was a man with whom it would be unwise to trifle. I guessed that he was not much older than forty; and his immaculate appearance, in a navy-blue uniform with crossed keys on the collar and a short, neat haircut, seemed to indicate a military background.

'I'm Detective Chief Inspector Brock of the Murder Investigation Team.' I showed the concierge my warrant card before he had a chance to ask for it. He was the sort of man who undoubtedly would want to see some identification before answering any of my questions.

'Please take a seat, sir.'

'My DC Armitage said that your name is Hodgson. Is that correct?' I asked, as I seated myself in the chair in front of his desk.

'That is so, sir. Mark Hodgson, late of the Royal Military Police,' the concierge said, confirming my belief that he was an ex-soldier.

'You obviously know that I'm investigating the murder of Richard Cooper, who lived in Apartment E.'

'A strange man was Mr Cooper, sir.'

'In what way strange?'

'In the army he'd have been known as a loner. Very polite – couldn't find fault on that account – but he never opened up, if you know what I mean. Now, many of the residents here,' said Hodgson, waving a hand at the window as if to encompass all the inhabitants of Cockcroft Lodge with the gesture, 'are usually very chatty. You get to know an awful lot just by listening. But Mr Cooper would just pass the time of day, and that's all.'

'I take it you didn't have much to do with him, Mr Hodgson.'

'Hardly anything, sir. A lot of the people here are at work all day, and if any deliveries or registered letters or the like come for them I take them in and they collect them when they get home. But Mr Cooper didn't have anything to pick up. Mind you,' Hodgson added thoughtfully, 'he seemed to be at home most of the time during the day. Of course, that's not unusual because a fair number of the residents work at home. You get security firms delivering data and that sort of thing. Mr Cooper would go out in the evenings quite a lot, but his car rarely left during the day.'

'His car? Any idea where it is?' None of the house-to-house team appeared to have picked up that Cooper had a car.

'In the underground car park, sir.' Hodgson's expression implied that that was the obvious place to find a car. 'D'you want to inspect it?'

'I don't suppose you've got a key?'

'No, sir, Mr Cooper declined to leave one with me. It's purely optional, but we ask the residents if they'd care to leave a key here, in the lodge, in case of fire or in case their car alarm goes off. Those alarms sometimes go off for no apparent reason. Mind you, quite a few of them that live here have refused to leave keys so Mr Cooper wasn't the only one.'

I rang Cooper's apartment and got hold of DC Appleby, who was standing by in case any immediate evidence needed to be 'bagged and tagged'.

'It's Brock, John. Have a look round and see if you can find a car key.'

'There's one on a hook in the kitchenette, sir.'

'Good. Bring it down to the concierge's lodge as quick as you can.'

Five minutes later, a breathless Appleby appeared in the doorway and handed me the key to a BMW.

'Before we go, Mr Hodgson,' I said, 'do you know if Mr Cooper was away for any length of time recently?'

'Soon tell you, sir.' The concierge turned to a desktop computer. 'Yes, sir,' he said, moments later. 'He drove his car out of the gate at ten forty-three hours on Wednesday the tenth of July and returned at twelve fifty-seven hours on Friday the twenty-sixth of July.' He looked up. 'That's today, of course. That's all the CCTV cameras tell me, but there's nothing to say he didn't go out on foot at other times. There'd be no record of that unless he happened to call in here, in which case I'd make a mental note, so to speak, but we don't log the comings and goings of the residents, only their cars.'

'What about CCTV cameras?'

'Yes, pedestrians might be picked up coming and going. And there are cameras on each of the block entrances and in the lifts. I'll arrange for the tapes to be ready for you whenever you need them, but we only keep them for two weeks, otherwise we'd be snowed under. I'm afraid that we won't have anything before that.'

Hodgson looked into a back office to tell his deputy to take over the desk, then escorted Appleby and me to the underground garage. Once there, he led us straight to a black BMW Gran Turismo saloon. I surmised that Cooper wouldn't have got much change out of forty grand for that little beauty.

Donning a pair of latex gloves, I opened the driver's door, but only to make sure that this was Cooper's car, or at least the car for which Appleby had found a key.

Locking the car again, I gave the key back to Appleby. 'Ask Mrs Mitchell to get one of her people to examine this vehicle as a matter of urgency, John, if you please.'

'Anything else I can help you with, sir?' asked Hodgson, once we were back in his office.

'Yes. Would you know if any non-residents who drove in here were visiting a specific resident?'

Hodgson looked mildly affronted. 'Absolutely, sir. They're not allowed in until we've communicated with the resident in question and got his or her clearance. Then we log it,' he added smugly.

'Is it possible that you could tell me if Mr Cooper had any such visitors recently?'

'Again I can only go back two weeks, sir,' said Hodgson

triumphantly. 'I'll print the details and give you a bell if you'd like to leave me your phone number. And I'll have sorted out the relevant CCTV tapes by then.'

'Excellent,' I said. 'I'll get one of my people to collect them. How long will it take, d'you think?'

'About half an hour, sir,' said Hodgson, glancing at the clock on the wall. 'And there's one other thing before you go, sir. Mr Cooper issued permits to two friends of his to use the swimming pool. Personally I don't think it's a good idea, but I can't argue with the directors.'

'D'you know the names of these friends of Mr Cooper?'

'The only ones I have listed are a Mr Dennis Jones and a Miss Chantal Flaubert.'

'You've got a good memory.'

'Not really, sir,' said Hodgson, with a sly grin. 'I guessed you'd come to see me at some time, so I looked it up.'

THREE

'**W**e are recording this interview in order to establish the facts while they're still fresh in your mind, Mr Jones.' Dave Poole switched on the tape recorder. 'Present are Dennis Jones, Detective Inspector Kate Ebdon and Detective Sergeant David Poole. The time is sixteen fifteen hours and the date is Friday the twenty-sixth of July.'

'Should I have a solicitor here?' asked Jones nervously, obviously disconcerted by the formality of Dave's introduction to the tape. In addition, he was noticeably overawed by the stark surroundings of the interview room in which he now found himself. Kate thought that it was probably the first time he'd ever been in one.

'Why, Mr Jones? Have you committed a crime?' Dave adopted his innocent expression.

'No, of course I haven't,' said Jones, 'but why have you brought me to a police station and why are you recording everything? I've already told you all I know about this dreadful business.' His face took on an even more worried expression than hitherto; more, Kate thought, than making a witness statement warranted, albeit a recorded one.

'I think you ought to be clear about one thing, Mr Jones,' said Kate. 'We are dealing with a murder, and when eventually we make an arrest and go to trial everything has to be as right as it's possible to get it. What you tell us could be vital, and that's the main reason we're recording it. If we then decide to take a written statement, Sergeant Poole will put it down in writing and ask you to sign it.' Her quietly spoken but uncompromising attitude did little to afford Jones any comfort.

'Oh, I see.' It was the first time Jones had heard Kate Ebdon say anything more than a few words, and he was obviously surprised to hear that she was Australian. He could see that she was an attractive woman, but was taken aback by her sexy outfit: skin-tight jeans and a white shirt. It was a style of dress that didn't accord with his pulp-fiction idea of what a detective inspector should look like, and it certainly didn't accord with what the HMCC's stuffy commander thought a 'lady inspector' should wear. Despite his wimpish appearance, Jones imagined himself to be quite the ladies' man, but if he thought for one moment that Kate would succumb to his charms and be a pushover he was sadly mistaken. She was very good at countering sexism.

There was a story going back to her days as a uniformed constable when an inspector had cornered her in an office one night duty and started physically to come on to her. She told him very calmly and very quietly that if he persisted or ever tried it on again, she'd rip open her blouse, run out of the office and scream rape at the top of her voice. 'After I've kneed you in the balls, sir,' she added, to emphasize her point.

The inspector rapidly retreated and was very careful to make sure thereafter that he only spoke to her when other people were present. As he was an unpopular officer, the story had not only quickly circulated around the station but, thanks to the social media, it went 'viral' throughout the Force. From then on, Police Constable Kate Ebdon was treated very respectfully. Employment tribunals or official complaints of sexism were not for her; she had her own methods, and whingeing to authority wasn't one of them.

'Let's begin at the beginning, then.' Kate pulled her chair closer, linked her fingers and rested her arms on the table as though about to start a cosy chat. 'Tell me exactly what happened, starting with when and how you came to meet Richard Cooper.'

'It was about a year ago, I suppose.' Jones looked into the middle distance as he thought about what he had just said. 'Yes, it must have been about this time last year. Actually, I think it was June.'

'How did you meet?'

'At a swimming pool.'

'Which one?'

Jones paused again. 'It was a private one in Richmond, part of a health club, but it's closed now. I think it was bought by some property developers, but I don't know if that's true.

But by then Dick had moved into his apartment at Cockcroft Lodge. There's an underground pool there and he invited me to make use of it as often as I liked. He told me that the residents are allowed to give two named guests admission cards.'

'Where did Mr Cooper live before he moved in to Cockcroft Court?' Kate asked.

'I don't know.'

'Where d'you live, Mr Jones?' asked Dave.

'Munstable Street in Petersham, but I told you that. I showed you my driving licence. It's only about five or six miles from here.'

'Are you married?'

There was a distinct pause before Jones spoke. 'No.'

'Were you in a homosexual relationship with Mr Cooper, then?' Dave asked the question suddenly and bluntly.

'Certainly not.' Jones replied with a vehemence that bordered on outrage. It may have been contrived or, as Kate and Dave had each suggested, he was a good actor.

'There's no need to get so excited, Mr Jones. It's not uncommon these days.' Nevertheless, Dave wondered if Jones was protesting too much.

'Well, I'm not.' Jones reacted like a spoilt schoolboy who'd just been falsely accused of committing some transgression of school rules.

'Was Richard Cooper in a relationship?'

'He never mentioned having a girlfriend, if that's what you mean, but I don't think he was gay.'

'But you don't know for certain.' It was a statement not a question. Dave was slowly discovering that for someone who claimed to have known Cooper for a year, Jones knew remarkably little about his so-called 'friend'. And that increased Dave's suspicions.

'You said that Richard Cooper was allowed two named guests who could use the swimming pool downstairs. Who was the other one?'

'I've no idea. I don't even know if there was another one.' Jones obviously hadn't met Chantal Flaubert, the other pass holder.

'Can we now get to today's events, Dennis? You don't mind if I call you Dennis, do you?'

'No, of course not.'

'You told Mr Brock and me earlier what had happened, but perhaps you'd repeat it for the benefit of my inspector.'

Jones recounted, with no variation from what he had said previously, his version of events prior to the arrival of the police.

'Mrs Maxwell, the woman in the flat opposite,' said Dave, 'told me that you'd banged on her door and said there'd been a terrible accident.'

'Yes.'

'But surely it must have been obvious to you that a dead man with blood all over his shirt front had been murdered.'

'Well, I thought it was an accident.'

'What sort of accident, Dennis? What sort of accident results in a man dying in his own home with blood all over his shirt?'

'I don't know.' Jones began to look decidedly shifty. 'You're trying to confuse me.'

'So to summarize,' said Kate Ebdon, when Dave had finished labouring the matter of Jones's description of Cooper's murder as an accident, 'you met Richard Cooper at a swimming pool that no longer exists. You've no idea what he does for a living, you don't know whether he's in a relationship, and you've no idea who this person is who was so dangerous that Cooper claimed he was in fear of his life. Finally, he asked you to meet him at his apartment at one o'clock, but you didn't turn up until half past one. And you've known each other for a whole year.' She made no attempt to hide the cynicism in her voice. 'Is that about the strength of it, mate?'

'Yes, but I was held up by an accident on the M4.'

'Did you see this accident?'

'No, not exactly, Inspector,' said Jones and smiled at Kate in what he believed to be a beguiling way.

'Meaning?'

'Well, I assumed it was an accident. That's what usually causes hold-ups, isn't it?' Jones stared at Kate, the expression on his face imploring this tough Australian inspector to believe the implausible. He didn't have long to wait to realize it was a vain hope.

Kate scoffed. 'D'you seriously expect me to believe any of your story, Dennis? Because frankly I don't.'

'It's the truth. Honestly, that's what happened, Inspector.' Jones's voice was reaching an almost hysterically high pitch of desperation now as he realized that Detective Inspector Ebdon was not susceptible to what he believed to be his irresistible charm.

'I'll tell you what I think is the truth, Dennis,' continued Kate relentlessly. 'I don't think you've known Richard Cooper for as long as you say. You knew he had a lot of money, that would have been apparent from the apartment he lived in; and having formed a homosexual relationship with him, he then tired of you. But you knew he was a rich man, probably with a good job, and you started to blackmail him. When he said that he wouldn't pay any more and threatened to go to the police, you lay in wait for him in his flat, to which you had a key, and you murdered him. What did you do with the gun, Dennis?'

Dennis Jones blanched and his jaw dropped at the magnitude of the allegation. He gripped the edges of the table, and for a moment Kate thought he was about to faint or be sick. 'I wasn't in any sort of relationship with Dick, and I didn't kill him. And I don't have a gun. I hate guns.' His throat was now so dry with the fear that he was about to be charged with murder that he was able only to croak his reply. 'Could I have a glass of water, please?' he asked, still slack-jawed and sweating.

Dave leaned across to take a plastic bottle of water from a shelf and handed it to Jones. 'What d'you do for a living, Dennis?' he asked, almost conversationally.

Jones took a swig of water. 'I'm a project manager in an advertising agency.'

'And how old are you?'

'Thirty.'

'You deny being in a homosexual relationship with Cooper, so does that mean you have a girlfriend?'

'Not at the moment; we split up. But what has any of this to do with Dick getting shot?'

'You just heard my inspector say she doesn't believe you, Dennis, and neither do I. That means that we're going to do a lot of checking. So, write down your date and place of birth, your full address, telephone number, your ex-girlfriend's name and address, and finally the address of this defunct swimming pool where you claim to have first met Richard Cooper.' Dave pushed a pad across the table and tossed a ballpoint pen on top of it, almost contemptuously.

'And if I refuse?' Suddenly Dennis Jones developed some spirit, but he was not the first man to underestimate Kate Ebdon.

'I shall arrest you on suspicion of murdering Richard Cooper and you'll be locked up in this police station while we make our enquiries the hard way.' That Kate spoke quietly and calmly made her statement sound even more menacing. 'And that could take a long time.' However, it was all bravado; there was not a vestige of evidence that Jones had murdered Cooper, but Kate was going to make certain of it one way or the other.

With a shaking hand, Jones wrote down everything that Dave had demanded and handed the pad back to him.

'Seems to be everything we need, ma'am,' said Dave, having scanned the details, and pushed the pad across to Kate.

'That'll do for the time being, Dennis,' said Kate. 'You will be admitted to police bail to return here in one month or sooner if we send for you.'

'Just now you said you might want me to make a written statement.'

'I've decided we don't need one at this stage. We've got all the details on tape. We'll see you another day to take a statement.' Kate's decision to take a statement later was intended to see if Jones's subsequent version would be the same as the one that had just been recorded. Or whether there would be inconsistencies that pointed to his culpability.

'Before you go, Dennis,' said Dave. 'You said you were delayed by an accident on the M4. Where was this?'

'Near West Drayton, I think it was.'

'What were you doing there when you live in Petersham and were on your way to North Sheen?' Dave looked suitably bemused, as though he was trying to work out an intriguing puzzle.

Jones hesitated for a few long moments and then said, 'I'd been to Heathrow Airport for a conference with an airline about an advertising campaign.'

'Write down the name of the company you visited and the person you saw.' Dave pushed the pad back towards Jones.

After some considerable thought, Jones eventually scribbled a name and a company address.

Once Dave had arranged bail and escorted Jones from the police station, he returned to the interview room.

'What d'you reckon, guv?'

'He didn't do it, Dave,' said Kate. 'He hasn't got the bottle.'

'Maybe,' said Dave thoughtfully, 'but I agree he's a wimp. What the hell does a project manager do in an advertising agency anyway?'

Kate laughed. 'I used to work in an ad agency, Dave, and the answer to your question is not a lot.'

I was back in the incident room at Belgravia when Kate Ebdon and Dave Poole returned from Richmond police station.

'What did you make of Jones, Kate?'

'He's a galah, guv, and he chucked a nervy when I suggested he'd topped Cooper.'

Dave made a great show of pulling out his diary and thumbing through it as if it was a pocket dictionary. 'The inspector wishes you to know, sir, that in her opinion Jones is a fool and that he came close to a nervous breakdown when she suggested he had murdered Cooper.'

'Thank you, Dave,' I said, 'but I've now got a fairly good grasp of Strine, as Miss Ebdon sometimes calls it.'

'I'll speak to you later, Sergeant,' said Kate, attempting a serious rebuke, but she couldn't maintain a straight face and finished up convulsed with laughter.

It was around seven o'clock that evening by the time the rest of the team returned to Belgravia police station and assembled in the incident room.

While the legwork had been going on out at North Sheen, Colin Wilberforce had been organizing the administrative side of the enquiry, a task at which he excelled. When it comes to paperwork, he is an administrative genius. Dave Poole, who describes himself as an action man rather than a desk jockey, once sarcastically commented that if there was a degree in origami Wilberforce would have achieved first-class honours.

The computer that would record the details of day-by-day actions and draw together the disparate elements of a murder investigation had been set up. That comprehensive system would record the sequence of events, contain an index and facilitate the cross-referencing of all the information. Consequently, whenever any of us asked for a particular name or piece of information, Wilberforce would be able to produce it instantly. In fact, he'd have the answer to *any* query within minutes. And he always seems to make it appear effortless.

But to interfere in his empire is a very dangerous thing to do, and that goes for everyone from the commander downwards. And God help the cleaner or the night-duty incident-room manager if ever Wilberforce arrives in the morning to find that so much as a pencil is out of place on his desk.

It is said that no one is indispensable, but that may not be so in Wilberforce's case. However, he seems to have no desire for further promotion, which somewhat selfishly I am pleased about. His family and rugby football seem to be all he wants out of life, and for that he is to be envied.

No matter what fables you may have heard about the 'paperless society' that the advent of computers was supposed to have brought about, such a concept has yet to filter through to the Metropolitan Police. Consequently, Wilberforce had prepared lever-arch files in which to keep all the written statements that would inevitably be taken before we finished our enquiries and, it is to be hoped, had Richard Cooper's killer in custody awaiting trial.

And even if it wasn't the Crown Prosecution Service demanding more and more unnecessary paper, our beloved commander most certainly would. He adores paperwork – seeks it out, in fact – and the more of it that comes his way the more he enjoys it. Given his propensity for charging headlong into indecision, 'paper tiger' is an apt description of him. To secure a positive direction from the commander is virtually impossible.

'Could you find out if there was an accident on the M4 somewhere near West Drayton at about midday today, Colin?' asked Kate Ebdon.

'Certainly, ma'am.' Wilberforce regarded a computer as a tool, nothing more, and if a pen and paper was quicker he'd use it.

He certainly wasn't like the IT enthusiasts who believe the world begins and ends on a computer screen, and that if the answer isn't there then there isn't one. He seemed to have contacts in all the right places and would cut corners by speaking to one of them in order to get the information he needed. Tapping a number into his telephone console, he spoke to one such contact in the traffic control room responsible for overseeing the M4. 'No accidents reported, ma'am,' he said, when he'd finished his brief conversation, 'but traffic was slow-moving due to what the Black Rats call SWOT.'

'What on earth are you talking about, Colin?' demanded Kate, whose bemused expression indicated that she'd hardly understood a word he'd said.

'The Black Rats are what the CID calls the traffic units, ma'am, and SWOT is an acronym for "sheer weight of traffic". Or to put it another way, they haven't a clue why it happened.' Wilberforce had a wry sense of humour and would occasionally avenge Kate's frequent use of Australian argot by using the more obscure Metropolitan Police jargon or even cockney rhyming slang.

'Did you have any luck locating this redundant swimming pool that Dave phoned in about, Colin?' I asked. 'The one where Dennis Jones claims to have met the victim.'

'Yes, sir.' A slight frown settled on Wilberforce's face, as though he found the term 'luck' distasteful. In his case, luck didn't enter into such enquiries. 'As the witness said, sir, it's ceased to exist and the site's being redeveloped. I've given all the details to Dave. Unfortunately, the building firm's offices are closed on Saturdays and Sundays.'

'We'll pay them a visit on Monday morning, Dave.' I turned to Detective Sergeant Tom Challis. 'Tom, the concierge told me that there are CCTV cameras all over Cockcroft Lodge, and even in the lift in Cooper's block. He's looking the tapes out and he said he'd give us a bell when they were ready for collection.'

'Yes, guv, they've been picked up and I've been going through them. But he only had the past two weeks.'

'Yes, he told me that's all that was kept, but it should be good enough. I'll have a look at them sometime tomorrow.' I

gazed round the incident room for DS Flynn, the ex-Fraud
Squad officer. 'Charlie, where are you?'

'I'm here, guv.' Flynn waved an arm.

'I want you to look into Richard Cooper's finances, Charlie.
He's obviously got a lot of money to be able to live in a place
like Cockcroft Lodge. Find out where it came from, and if he's
given any large sums away and if so to whom.'

Flynn nodded and made a note in his pocketbook. 'Are you
thinking fraud, guv?'

'No, Charlie. From what Miss Ebdon suggested, I'm
thinking blackmail. But until we know a bit more about his
lifestyle and what he did for a living and who his friends were,
we've not got much to go on. And that reminds me.' I glanced
across at DC Appleby. 'John, liaise with Sergeant Wilberforce
and do a birth search on Richard Cooper at the General Register
Office in Southport. And while you're about it, see if he's
married.'

'I've done that already, sir,' put in Wilberforce, 'but without
a date of birth we're not going to get very far. There are liter-
ally hundreds of Richard Coopers in the GRO indices.'

'What've you got lined up for me, guv?' asked Kate Ebdon.

'Tomorrow morning, if you would, take your team back to
Cockcroft Lodge and do a thorough search of Cooper's apartment. Documents, laptop computers, a passport. In fact,
anything that'll tell us more about this guy. And canvass all
three apartment blocks to see if anyone knew Cooper or what
he did, or whether he had visitors.'

'Yeah, I know the drill, guv,' said Kate, a little sharply.

'Sorry, Kate. Of course you do. I'll meet you there.' I
assigned tasks to Kate in exactly the same way as I would to
any one of my officers. On several occasions she and I had
been away on enquiries and it was, I suppose, an attempt on
my part to counter any suggestion that we enjoyed more than
a working relationship. The rumour mill of the Metropolitan
Police works overtime.

On one occasion recently, Kate and I had spent a couple of
days in Paris in connection with a murder enquiry. In the evening
of our stay we'd enjoyed a pleasant dinner at the apartment of
my old friend Henri Deshayes, a commandant in the Police

Judiciaire, and his charming wife, Gabrielle. Henri had been more than generous with the wine and, tough Australian though she is, I belatedly discovered that Kate couldn't handle it. She had almost collapsed as we returned to the hotel where we were staying, and I half carried her to her room.

There is no denying that she is a very attractive woman, but an intimate relationship would undoubtedly endanger our professional one, and that would have made our working relationship very difficult. It has happened between police officers of differing ranks before, often with disastrous results. If not work-related, certainly domestically.

FOUR

On Saturday morning, Dave and I joined Kate and the rest of team at North Sheen. To my surprise, Linda Mitchell was there too, but she was no longer wearing the shapeless coveralls and cap in which she was usually seen. It was a sure sign that there was now no risk of scene contamination. Instead, she was attired in a flattering grey trouser suit and heels, and her long black hair was loose. With her youthful figure and quirky sense of humour, I'd always thought of her as an attractive 'girl' rather than a mature woman – especially when, as now, she was out of her working gear – but to my astonishment I'd recently learned that she was a grandmother.

'Linda and I are still going through the apartment, guv,' said Kate, 'but that's the correspondence we've found so far.' She pointed at the dining table. 'I haven't been through it thoroughly yet, but what I have seen looks pretty innocuous and seems to come from women.'

'Jones claimed that Cooper said he was coming home for a change of clothing and to collect some papers connected with his job. Have you come across any work papers, Kate?'

'No, none at all. However, the contents of the bedroom will probably interest you more.'

'Don't tell me. He has a wardrobe full of Savile Row suits.'

'No, there are two or three off-the-peg lounge suits, but they were purchased in England, except for one that has a label in it that shows it came from a firm called Verbeke in somewhere called Ieper. Wherever that is.'

'It's better known as Ypres and it's in Belgium, ma'am,' said Dave, delighted at being able to tell the Australian DI something that he thought she should have known. 'A lot of your countrymen died there during the First World War.'

'What's he doing with a Belgian suit, I wonder?' I asked of no one in particular.

'He might've visited there,' volunteered Dave. 'A lot of people go to see the battlefields and the cemeteries. I took Madeleine a couple of years ago.' Madeleine was Dave's wife, a principal ballet dancer with the Royal Ballet. She was petite and a foot shorter than her hefty husband. There was a rumour that she occasionally attacked Dave physically, but having met her I dismissed that story as canteen scuttlebutt, even though ballet dancers are pretty powerful physically. It seemed that Dave and Madeleine were as happily married as Colin and Sonia Wilberforce.

'But more interesting than a Belgian suit,' continued Kate, outwardly unimpressed by Dave's brief history lesson, 'were the handcuffs and restraints that we found stashed away in a locked cupboard. There was also some women's clothing there, some of it quite kinky. And before you ask if Cooper was a cross-dresser, I doubt if it would have fitted him.'

'Any identifying marks on it that might give us a name?' I asked.

'None, Mr Brock, but—' began Linda.

'How long have we known each other, Linda?'

'Quite a few years now,' said Linda, clearly mystified that I had posed such a question at that precise moment.

'In that case, I think it's time you called me Harry, don't you? After all you're quite senior yourself now you've been appointed a crime-scene manager.'

'OK, Harry. I was about to say that I've saved the best bit until last. When I examined the built-in wardrobe in the bedroom, I found there was a wooden panel at the back, behind which was a safe.'

'I suppose it might be a standard installation,' suggested Dave. 'These apartments are obviously expensive and the residents are bound to have valuables.'

'Possibly,' I said. 'Have you been able to have it opened yet, Linda?' The finding of a safe interested me. If Cooper had had it installed after he'd moved in, rather than it having come with the package, so to speak, it meant that he wished to hide something that was either valuable or embarrassing. Although anything of real value would probably have been lodged in a safety deposit, though these days that's not as smart as you might think.

'No,' said Linda, 'I'm awaiting the arrival of a locksmith, but by the look of it – and I've seen a few safes over the years – this one is going to take some time to open.'

'Did you find a passport anywhere, Kate?'

'No, guv. What's more we didn't find a mobile phone.'

'That's strange, I thought everyone had a mobile these days. And judging by the luxury apartment in which he lived, I was certain that Cooper must have a passport. I'm sure he didn't buy that Belgian suit on the Internet.'

'There might be a passport in the safe, when we eventually get it open.'

'Well, I'll leave you to it,' I said. 'I'm going across the hall to speak to Mrs Maxwell again. She might be able to tell us something about this mystery man.'

'Hello, Mr Brock. Do come in.' Lydia Maxwell was wearing a cotton maxi summer dress, the halter neck of which left her suntanned shoulders bare. 'I was catching up on the housework, but it's so damned hot that I gave up and changed into this.' She waved a hand vaguely down her body. 'But your arrival is a good excuse to make a cup of tea. Do sit down.' She moved across to the kitchen area and put on the kettle.

'I was hoping that your husband might be here, Lydia. It's possible he might know something about Richard Cooper that would help us.'

'I'm a widow.' Lydia spoke in matter-of-fact tones without turning to face me.

'Oh, I'm so sorry.' I was furious with myself for jumping to the conclusion that a woman wouldn't be living alone in an apartment this expensive. Gail Sutton, my now ex-girlfriend, would have described my assumption as sexist and a typical example of male chauvinism, and I suppose she would have been right.

'Don't worry about it,' Lydia said.

'How long have you been widowed?' I asked, once she had seated herself and poured the tea.

'The accident was just over a year ago, so I'm just about getting used to the single life again.'

'Again?' I queried without thinking.

'Of course. I wasn't born married,' said Lydia with a twinkle in her eye as she smiled.

'I think I'd better give up.'

'Good idea. But as I was saying, I was always telling Geoff – my husband – that he drove his beloved Aston Martin too fast, and he came to grief on the A12 the other side of Colchester, on his way back from the marina near Lowestoft. That's where he kept the yacht which, incidentally, he'd called *Lydia*, in attempt to win me round I suppose.'

'Oh, I am sorry,' I said again, attempting to atone for my blunder.

'You needn't be, Mr Brock. We'd argued for most of the nineteen years of our married life. And to save you the trouble of working it out,' she said, shooting me another cheeky smile, 'I was married when I was eighteen and I'm now thirty-eight. And marrying that young was probably the mistake. Certainly the marriage was a mistake. Geoff was twelve years older than me, but it was his obsession with boats that really forced us apart because I had no real interest in them. In fact, I hated them.'

'I'm not very keen on them either,' I said, 'unless they have stabilizers and a crew of several hundred.'

Lydia laughed at my lame attempt to lighten the conversation. 'On one occasion we sailed all the way from Lowestoft to Erquy, in Brittany. Can you imagine it? I was sick practically all the way over, but when I'd recovered we went shopping and I saw the Breton sweater – the one I was wearing the other day – and told Geoff I liked it, so he bought it for me. In fact, he bought me two or three. Of course he thought it was an indication that I'd at last fallen in love with sailing.' She sighed, leaned forward and finished her tea. 'Another cup?'

'Please.'

Handing me my tea, she continued with her life story. 'He insisted on spending every spare moment on that wretched boat and we had some fearful arguments about it. It's ironic that he'd eventually seen sense, and was on his way back from the marina having at last sold the damned thing to a Russian millionaire.' She paused again. 'It wouldn't have been so bad if it had been moored nearer, somewhere on the south coast, say, but it was such an awful drive going to Suffolk and back every weekend. It's just as well I wasn't with him when he had his accident, but it had got to the point where I just refused to go any more. Even though I've heard that yachtsmen on their own very often make up their crew with shapely blonde bimbos, I'd reached the point where I no longer cared.'

'Did you have any children?'

'No. Geoff didn't want any, not again.'

'Not again?' I wondered if there was some hidden tragedy here.

'You would have thought that he'd learned his lesson after the first time. He'd been married before and had a daughter, but he crashed his car and they were both killed: wife and daughter. He told me later that it wasn't his fault. Whether it was or not, I don't know, but he always drove too fast. What's more, I didn't know that he was a widower until after we were married. Then as I said just now I was only eighteen, and I was very naive.'

'About Richard Cooper, Lydia,' I prompted, determined to steer her away from telling me any more of her marital and maritime history. 'What can you tell me about him?'

'Very little, actually. He moved in about a year ago, it must have been, but I rarely saw him. I did ask him in for a drink when he first arrived – a sort of welcoming gesture – but he declined. He was very polite about it and said he was extremely busy. To be honest, I hardly know any of the people here. They tend to keep themselves to themselves.'

'Did Mr Cooper say what he did for a living?'

'No, and I didn't ask. Well, one doesn't. He was always very civil whenever we met in the hall or in the pool. He'd pass the time of day, but he never started a conversation.'

'Are you talking about the pool down below, Lydia?'

'Yes, that one. As a matter of fact, I often saw him down there.'

'You're a keen swimmer, then?'

'I thought it would be a good idea to learn to swim well in case I ever fell overboard from Geoff's damned boat, so I took lessons from a professional. Then I found I really enjoyed it and I've kept it up ever since. That was one of the attractions of moving in here, the availability of a private pool.'

'Did you ever see Mr Cooper with the young man who knocked on your door yesterday after he'd found Mr Cooper's body?'

'No, but I often saw Mr Cooper with a young woman down at the pool.'

'Does this woman live in Cockcroft Lodge, d'you know?'

'I've no idea,' said Lydia. 'There are a lot of people living in these three blocks.'

'Have you any idea who she was?'

'No, no idea I'm afraid. But she was tall, about my height I should think. I'm five ten and she was more or less the same as me. She had a good figure, too, and was a strong swimmer. I wish I could do the crawl as fast as she does.'

'Can you think of any resident who it might be?' It was possible that Lydia was describing Chantal Flaubert, who the concierge had mentioned as being a holder of one of the non-residents passes to use the pool.

'It could be Mrs Webb, in Apartment A on the ground floor. She's always down there in her bikini making eyes at the men. But, of course, the young woman doesn't have to live here. The residents are allowed to give pool passes to two of their friends, so she could've been anyone.' Lydia paused. 'I suppose it could have been Mrs Webb wearing a wig. Women are very good at disguise when it comes to adultery.'

And that made me wonder if it was something that Lydia had practised herself. 'Yes, I know about the passes. The concierge told me.'

'I haven't used mine. I don't have any friends living near enough to make use of them. In fact, for some time now I've been thinking of moving, and this murder has finally made up my mind.'

'Where are you thinking of going, Lydia?'

'I'd like a house of my own rather than a flat, and ideally one with a pool. I've been considering Strand-on-the-Green or somewhere in that area, but I doubt that there's anything there that has what I want. I don't like this flat very much, but it was Geoff's choice and he was into this minimalist nonsense. Despite all my efforts, it still looks Spartan! It's no secret that Geoff left me well provided for, so I can afford what I like, more or less.'

'What was his profession?' I asked.

Lydia chuckled. 'He was what they call "something in the City". Actually, he was in the futures market and made a hell of a lot of money doing it. And he was insured up to the hilt when he died. All in all, I'm extremely well off. In fact, embarrassingly so considering that we hardly spoke to each other in the months before his death.' She sounded sad at having to admit it.

'You shouldn't really tell people that, Lydia, or you'll find yourself besieged by fortune hunters.'

'I haven't told anybody before, but you're a policeman, so I can trust you.' But she laughed as she said it. 'Can't I?'

'I wouldn't bank on it,' I said, thinking of a few coppers I wouldn't trust as far as I could throw a grand piano. 'Thanks for the tea.' I stood up and handed her one of my cards. 'If you think of anything else, I'd be grateful if you'd give me a ring.'

'I certainly will,' said Lydia, and smiled. I had the feeling that she'd ring me anyway, whether she had any information or not.

'By the way, was there a wall safe installed in this apartment when you moved in?'

'A wall safe?' Lydia raised her eyebrows. 'No, why should there be?'

I returned to Cooper's apartment in time to see the locksmith departing.

'Have you found anything interesting, Kate?' I asked hopefully.

'Our victim is a Belgian, guv, and his name is Dirk Cuyper.' Kate Ebdon put an open passport on the table. The photograph was quite clearly that of Richard Cooper.

I picked up the document and had a good look at it. 'So Cuyper, alias Cooper, was thirty-eight years of age,' I said, 'and was born in somewhere called Poperinge, wherever that is.'

'It's a small town a few miles from Ypres, otherwise known as Ieper, guv,' said Dave.

'Isn't that where that suit came from? The one in his wardrobe.'

'That's the one, Harry,' said Linda Mitchell, now quite at ease using my first name.

'Well, well! What is a Belgian doing in North Sheen

masquerading as Richard Cooper, who was in fear of his life and finished up being murdered?'

'Looks like a trip to Belgium, guv,' said Dave hopefully. 'Shall I give Colin Wilberforce a ring and ask him if he can locate someone in the Belgian police that we can talk to?'

'We may have to go to Belgium eventually, Dave, but we won't get in touch with the Belgian police just yet. Not until we have something more concrete to tell them. All we know so far is that we've got a dead man in an expensive apartment in North Sheen, and no explanation for any of it. No, we'll wait.'

'There was some sort of identity document in the safe, too, Harry,' said Linda. 'It was in an envelope together with a typed note.' She handed me the two items. 'But they're both in Dutch. Or now we know the victim is a Belgian, I suppose it's Flemish. I think the only difference is a dialectic one.'

I glanced at the words on the official-looking card that bore a photograph of Cuyper: *De drager Dirk Cuyper is een politieagent die aan de Federale Politie.*

'Good God!' I said. 'I wouldn't profess to understand this language, but two words jump out at me: *Federale Politie.*'

'Bloody hell!' exclaimed Dave. 'He's a copper.'

'It looks like it, Dave.' I scanned the note. 'I don't understand any of this, but there are some words here that do make sense, even though it's in Dutch or Flemish or whatever. It mentions a Commissaris Pim de Jonker, and there's a telephone number.'

Dave immediately pulled out his mobile. 'Shall I ring this Commissaris bloke, guv?'

'No, not yet. We'll get this note translated before we do any telephoning, otherwise we might be taking a leap in the dark.'

'There were some letters in the safe, too, Harry,' said Linda. 'They're written in Dutch or Flemish and are all signed Margreet – who I imagine is Cuyper's wife or girlfriend – and come from an address in Ieper. They're not written by the same women who wrote the other correspondence we found earlier.'

'It looks as though we've got some work to do on Monday,' I said. 'In the meantime, Dave, get that photograph of Cuyper, alias Cooper, copied and circulated to all the hotels in the vicinity. See if anyone recognizes him as someone who stayed there for a week or two. Assuming, of course, that what Dennis Jones told us is the truth. But I have to say that I've got doubts about him and his statement.'

'There was also a laptop computer in the safe, but it's password-protected and I can't get into it,' said Linda.

'I know just the lad to do that,' I said, thinking of Lee Jarvis, who had been of great help when we were investigating the murder of the actor Lancelot Foley. 'Dave, give Colin Wilberforce a bell and ask him to organize that, will you? And at the same time ask him to find out if there's anyone in the Interpol office who speaks Dutch or Flemish. Oh, and ask him to arrange the translation of the letters that were found in the safe.' I glanced at my watch. 'Once you've done that, I think it's time we spoke to Dennis Jones's ex-girlfriend.'

Judy Simmons was the name of Jones's ex and she lived in a flat not far from Richmond Park. Fortunately she was at home when we arrived.

'Miss Simmons?'

'That's me.' I guessed that she was about twenty-five, and she was painfully thin with lank blonde hair and glasses. She was shrewd enough to keep a firm hold on the edge of her front door.

'We're police officers from the Murder Investigation Team at Scotland Yard, Miss Simmons.'

'Oh yeah? Pull the other one.' She glanced suspiciously at Dave and me, and took in his stocky figure and the fact that he was black. The look was one of extreme scepticism. 'What are you selling?'

'I can assure you we are police officers,' I said, and we each showed her our warrant card.

'Oh! Sorry. What's it about, then?'

'I'm Detective Chief Inspector Brock and this is Detective Sergeant Poole. We'd like to talk to you about Dennis Jones.'

'Don't tell me the creep has been murdered.'

This did not bode well. 'No, Miss Simmons, but a so-called friend of his has been.'

'You'd better come in, then.'

We sat down in her cramped sitting-room-cum-kitchen, made

even smaller because an ironing board was standing in one corner with a pile of unironed clothes on it.

'What's this about Dennis and a murdered friend, then? I didn't think he had any friends.'

'When we were questioning him,' I began, 'he volunteered the information that you and he had just split up.' That wasn't strictly true, of course. Dave had insisted upon the information.

'Split up?' Judy Simmons laughed derisively. 'We were never together.'

'He assured us that he'd been in a relationship with you, Miss Simmons.'

'In his dreams,' she scoffed. 'I went out with him twice and that was once too often. Dennis Jones thinks he's God's gift to women, but not to put too fine a point on it, he's a pathetic wimp.'

'How long ago was this?' asked Dave.

Judy gazed thoughtfully at Dave. 'The last time I saw him must've been at least four months ago,' she said eventually. 'I met him at a health club – it's closed down now – and stupidly agreed to go out with him. It was more or less all right, but I should've knocked it on the head there and then. Unfortunately, I foolishly went on a second date a week later. It was dire. He took me for a meal in some cheap restaurant – well, café really – and expected me to go halves. So I told him what to do with the bill.' She chuckled at the recollection. 'He blinked. Then the cheeky sod asked me if I'd like to move in with him in some flat in Petersham!'

I laughed. 'I take it you refused, Miss Simmons.'

'Too bloody right I did. I told him what he could do with his proposition in no uncertain terms,' she said, and using both hands pushed her hair back and tucked it behind her ears.

'Did he ever mention a man called Richard Cooper?'

'Not that I recall.'

'Cooper apparently used the same health club where you met Jones, or more particularly the pool there.'

Judy shook her head. 'Doesn't mean a thing,' she said.

'Did he tell you what he did for a living?' Dave asked, knowing that Kate Ebdon had had reservations about his claim to have worked in an advertising agency.

'No, he never mentioned it. And I certainly wasn't interested enough in him to ask.'

'Thank you for your time, Miss Simmons. Sorry to have troubled you.'

'No problem. I'll tell you this, though. Dennis Jones is not a murderer. He wouldn't even have the guts to kill a fly.'

There are times when Dr Henry Mortlock can be extremely perverse, and today was one of those occasions. He had arranged to do the post-mortem examination of Richard Cooper at half past five that evening.

As was so often the case, Mortlock's perversity extended even further. I arrived at twenty-five past five to find that he had already completed the examination.

'That's what you're looking for, Harry.' Mortlock pointed to a couple of 9mm rounds in a kidney-shaped bowl. 'Straight into the heart. Either you're looking for a marksman or a bloody lucky shot. But that's your problem. I've done my bit.'

I took possession of the fatal bullets, and after Mortlock and I had signed all the necessary bits of paper I returned to Belgravia. There, I handed the rounds to Wilberforce. We signed more pieces of paper and I told him to get them to the ballistics laboratory as soon as possible.

I was in the office at nine o'clock on Sunday morning, but Wilberforce was there ahead of me. He seems to have an insatiable appetite for work once we have a murder enquiry up and running.

'I've spoken to the duty officer in the Interpol office this morning, sir, and he's been in touch with their Dutch speaker.' Wilberforce picked up a piece of paper. 'The note that was found with the ID document reads: *In the event of an emergency, Commissaris Pim de Jonker should be contacted on . . .* Then there's a Belgian telephone number for somewhere in Poperinge, sir, and the note goes on to say it is imperative that no other officer but Commissaris de Jonker should be spoken to. We've run a check on the number, sir, but details of the subscriber are withheld. In the circumstances, I thought it unwise to take the matter any further.'

'You were quite right, Colin. According to his passport, Poperinge is where Dirk Cuyper was born,' I said. 'See if you can get me that number.'

But there was a recorded message in Flemish on an answering machine.

'I'll try it again tomorrow. Perhaps the Belgian police are lucky enough not to have to work on Sundays.'

Having failed to make contact with Pim de Jonker, I located DS Tom Challis, to whom I'd assigned the job of examining the CCTV tapes obtained from the concierge. I'd intended to do it yesterday, but time had just run away from me.

'I'll have a look at the tapes now, Tom.'

'All set up, guv.' Challis led me over to a player in the corner of the incident room and put in the first of the tapes.

Nobody got into the lift carrying a firearm, or wearing a mask or behaving furtively. But that doesn't happen in real life, anyway. There were several shots of Lydia Maxwell in the lift in her swimsuit and a short towelling wrap. The indicator at the side of the recording showed her to have travelled between her floor and the basement pool area at three minutes past eight. There were shots of another woman similarly attired, and I wondered if this was the woman Lydia had seen in the pool. Other tapes showed the swimming pool itself, and one frame showed Dennis Jones making his way along the side of the pool towards the changing rooms.

'Mrs Maxwell claimed to have heard gunshots at a minute or so past one, Tom. Let me have another look at the tape that was running in the lift just before that time.'

Challis ran the tape again, and stopped it at fifteen minutes to one on the day of Cuyper's murder. 'There's just one woman in the lift, guv.' He pointed with his pen. 'The indicator at the side of the screen shows that she got in on the ground floor and exited on the first.'

'Are there any shots of the landing, Tom? Do we see where she went?'

Challis laughed. 'No. Mark Hodgson, the concierge, would have liked it that way, but it was vetoed by the management committee. They reckoned it would be too intrusive to see who had what visitors.'

It was either bad luck or the woman was conscious of the CCTV camera in the lift and deliberately avoided being recognized. Whatever the reason, at no time was there a clear shot of her face. All we could see was that she was about five foot ten tall, had shoulder-length brown or Titian hair and was wearing a black bomber jacket and jeans, with black knee boots.

'Meet Miss Everywoman, Tom,' I said. 'She could be Cuyper's killer or she could have been visiting any one of the other three apartments on that floor. Get one of the DCs to make enquiries of Apartments G and H, and I'll speak to Mrs Maxwell. I wonder if there was a car that came in that tallies with those times.'

'I've checked that with the concierge,' said Challis and referred to his pocketbook. 'The only car that entered between midday and five past two was a Volvo belonging to a resident.' He laughed and looked up. 'Apart from God knows how many Job cars coming through on blues and twos,' he added.

Apart from the outside chance that we had seen the murderess, I was forced to conclude that, like everything else in this enquiry so far, there was nothing that would immediately provide any further evidence of Cuyper's killer.

FIVE

'I've been doing a bit of research on the Belgian police, sir,' said Wilberforce, when I arrived in the incident room at nine o'clock on Monday morning. 'They've undergone a complete reorganization, and they've combined the judicial police, the gendarmerie and the town police into one huge force called the Federale Politie.'

'God help them!' I said. We in the Metropolitan Police are subjected to frequent upheavals as a result of the outpourings of the funny-names-and-total-confusion squad. This is a team of boy superintendents who sit in the ivory tower of Scotland Yard thinking up ways to interfere with us poor guys at the sharp end, secure in the knowledge that they won't get their own hands dirty. For example, Special Branch had been called that for well over a hundred years, but for some inexplicable reason the *wunderkind* decided to rename it the Anti-Terrorist Command. And they also decreed that Thames Division, the oldest part of the Met, should now be called the Marine Support Unit. Although it wasn't one of their masterpieces, I'm sure they claimed credit for the edict requiring road traffic accidents to be known as 'road traffic collisions'. But, as my pedantic sergeant once acidly enquired, 'How could an accident that involved a car overturning without leaving the road or hitting anything be called a collision?'

'I've been reading a report about the Belgian police, sir,' Wilberforce continued. 'It seems that Belgium, and Brussels in particular, has become the world capital of sex slavery. Apparently, the police over there were heavily criticized in a report that accused them of negligence, amateurism and incompetence in the handling of a number of paedophile murders. And that's why they got this drastic overhaul.'

'Thank you for that, Colin.' Although there are times when Wilberforce likes to air his knowledge, he often comes up with interesting background material, even though I think he probably culls it from the Internet.

I went into my office and called the number that had been found on the note that accompanied Dirk Cuyper's ID. This time there wasn't a recorded message, but the phone rang for quite a long time before it was answered.

'*Hallo, wie is dat?*'

I knew that Flemish is the language spoken in many parts of Belgium and that it is a dialect of Dutch. A Dutch police officer once told me that there are less than seventeen million Dutch people in the world and, because no one else can be bothered to learn Dutch 'just so that they can talk to us', the Dutch have to learn English. I was soon to find out that the same went for the Flemish-speaking Belgians.

'Is that Commissaris de Jonker?' I enquired.

There was a further pause and then, somewhat hesitantly, 'Yes, it is.' The voice spoke excellent English. 'Who is this?'

'Detective Chief Inspector Brock of New Scotland Yard, London, Commissaris.'

'Ah! How can I help you, Detective Chief Inspector?'

'For a start you can call me Harry, Commissaris. Otherwise half of our conversation will be taken up repeating my rank all the time.'

There was a muted chuckle from the other end of the line that sounded almost if it had been forced out. 'Good. I'm called Pim. Now, what can I do for you, Harry?'

It confirmed, yet again, that police officers the world over share a common bond that transcends any language difficulties that may arise, although in this case there weren't any. I explained about the murder I was investigating and that we'd discovered that the victim was a Belgian national whose name, according to his passport and the ID found in his apartment, was Dirk Cuyper.

For a moment there was absolute silence at the other end. And then, '*Mijn God, ik geloof het niet!*'

'I'm sorry, Pim,' I said, mystified by this sudden impassioned outburst of Flemish, 'but I don't understand.'

'My apologies, Harry. I said I don't believe it, but obviously I must. This has come as a terrible shock.'

'I understand that Dirk Cuyper was a police officer. Is that correct?'

There was another pause and then, 'Yes, he was one of the officers in my department.'

'What was he doing in London, then, Pim?' I doubted that he could have been on leave. Not for a year or more.

'I'm afraid it is too delicate to be discussed on the telephone, Harry.'

'Can you come to London then?'

'That is out of the question. It is much too risky.' De Jonker paused again, as if formulating a plan. 'Would it be possible for you to come over here? I will be able to tell you everything we know, and then perhaps that will lead you to Dirk's killer.'

'I'll call you back as soon as I know when I'll be arriving, Pim.'

'A trip to Belgium, guv?' asked Dave as I replaced the receiver. It was about the third time he'd asked that question since the murder had occurred.

'Looks like it, Dave.'

There was now little doubt in my mind that I was dealing with something extremely serious. If the commander was his customary indecisive self about granting me permission, I'd go over his head to the Deputy Assistant Commissioner, or even higher if necessary. But knowing that the DAC was a *real* detective, I knew that I wouldn't need to. However, protocol demanded that I started with our beloved commander. Now that it was just after ten o'clock, he would be in his office and would remain there until six o'clock, when he would go home. But I wasn't going to rush. I spent the rest of the morning going through all the statements we'd amassed. One might be forgiven for thinking that nothing had really happened since the murder – and it hadn't – but, believe me, that doesn't stop the paper piling up.

Having had lunch at my favourite Italian, I made my way back to the office at about half past two. I could no longer put off my interview with the commander and made my way to his office.

'Ah, Mr Brock.' Reluctantly pushing aside a bulky file, the commander stared at me with the sort of critical expression that implied I'd interrupted something important. 'What progress have you made with this suspicious death in North Sheen?' He leaned back in his chair and peered enquiringly at me over his half-moon spectacles, which I was certain had plain glass in them and were worn in the mistaken belief that they lent him gravitas.

'None, sir.'

'What d'you mean by that, Mr Brock?' The commander shot forward in his chair with an alacrity that I thought would be denied by his portly frame, his cheeks and double chin wobbling alarmingly. 'I must warn you that such a statement is tantamount to admitting neglect of duty.'

'It's gone beyond being suspicious, sir,' I said, ignoring his empty threat. 'There's no doubt it's a murder.'

The commander always described any death we were dealing with as a 'suspicious death', in case it subsequently turned out to be due to natural causes. He would never call it murder, manslaughter or even suicide until a jury had said it was. And only after the verdict had gone through every appeal process known to the legal system.

'Yes, yes. But what do we know about it?'

'Only that the victim was shot twice in the chest with two 9mm rounds, probably from an automatic handgun.'

'Well, who is this victim? And what is he? Why was he murdered? These are fundamental enquiries to which there should be an answer.'

'I couldn't agree more, sir,' I said, disarming the commander somewhat. 'He's a bit of a mystery man, but we have discovered that he's a Belgian citizen. And that brings me to my request, sir. I need to go to Belgium to follow up my enquiries.'

'I see no reason for that, Mr Brock. I suggest you speak to the Belgian Embassy.'

'I've already spoken to the police in Belgium, sir, and I can assure you that it is of paramount importance that I travel to Ieper without delay.'

'Where?'

'Ieper, sir. You may know it better as Ypres. Ieper is the Flemish name for the town.'

'Ah, yes!' The commander brushed a dismissive hand across the top of his desk. He hates being caught out, and I suspect he just had been. 'I can't give permission until I know more about it, Mr Brock.' He drew his abandoned file lovingly closer, signalling an end to our brief exchange.

I had no intention of telling the commander that Richard Cooper was actually Dirk Cuyper, a Belgian police officer. The mere whiff of some secret operation going on in the Metropolitan Police District – because that is what I think it was – would send him spiralling into his bogus detective mode.

'There's no point in appealing to the DAC, either, Mr Brock.' The commander looked up sharply and smiled owlishly as he delivered his parting shot. 'You'll fare no better with him,' he added coldly. 'The DAC is a stickler for the correct procedure.'

'Thank you, sir.' I knew that the moment I left his office the commander would be on the phone to the DAC, peddling his version of our conversation, just in case I did go up the chain of command.

Not that the commander's intervention would make any difference. The DAC, as I've said before, is a real detective, and he and I go back a long way to when I was a DC on the Flying Squad and he was my DCI. The commander, on the other hand, is the beneficiary of what is known in the Job as a sideways promotion. To be thoroughly bloody-minded about it, when the Uniform Branch got fed up with his meddling in the control of football crowds and his frequent and unsuccessful attempts to solve London's traffic problems by unilaterally imposing his own hare-brained schemes, he was duck-shovelled off to the CID, where it was thought that he could do no harm. Unfortunately he now believes that he really is a detective and frequently offers advice on crime investigation, a subject for which he is totally unqualified.

I returned to my office, closed the door and made a phone call to Fiona, the DAC's secretary, to arrange an urgent meeting.

Unfortunately, the DAC's office is at New Scotland Yard, over a mile away, and I had no intention of walking there in today's blistering heat.

I put my head round the door to the incident room. 'I'm going to the Belgian Embassy if anyone asks, Colin.'

'D'you want a car, sir?' asked Wilberforce. He knew exactly who I was talking about when I said 'anyone'.

'No, I'll take a cab.' I could have asked Dave to drive me, but I did not wish to put him in the invidious position of having to lie about where he'd taken me. I know that he would have done so unhesitatingly, but no senior officer has the right to put a subordinate in such an awkward situation.

'Go in, Mr Brock,' said Fiona. 'He's expecting you.' The DAC's secretary shot me a conspiratorial smile.

'I've just had your commander on the phone bending my ear, Harry. What's the SP?' The DAC waved a hand at one of the armchairs in his office and sat down in the one opposite me.

I gave the DAC chapter and verse on the murder of Dirk Cuyper, alias Richard Cooper, and recounted the somewhat mysterious telephone conversation I had had with Pim de Jonker, the Commissaris at the Federal Police office in Ieper. I also suggested that the fewer people who knew about it the better, at least until we knew what it was all about.

'So what's a Belgian police officer doing living in an expensive drum in North Sheen?' Having posed that rhetorical question, the DAC stared into the middle distance for a moment or two before returning his gaze to me. 'We've had no official notification that the Belgian police sent anyone over here to work under cover. You'd better get across there and find out what it's all about, Harry. It sounds very much as though this Cuyper was on to something and was topped because of what he found out. Incidentally, don't worry about the commander: I'll square your trip with him.'

'Thank you, sir. I'll get over there as soon as I can.'

'And when you get back from Belgium, report to me direct. Not a whisper to anyone else, Harry, and that includes the commander. At least not until we know what it's all about.'

When I left Scotland Yard, I walked out to Victoria Street and found a coffee shop. If, following our discussion, the commander had made enquiries as to my whereabouts, which I was certain he would've done, I wanted to make it seem that I actually had been to the Belgian Embassy in Grosvenor Crescent. I deliberately timed my return to the incident room for ten minutes to six. The commander had an inflexible rule: he always left for home at six o'clock on the dot. Thus he now had only ten minutes in which to grill me about where I'd been before hurrying off home. It was widely known that he was terrified of Mrs Commander.

'The commander would like to see you urgently, sir,' said Wilberforce, the moment I stepped through the door.

'What's that all about, I wonder?' I asked of no one in particular, and made my way to the commander's office. 'You wished to see me, sir?' I said, having been granted permission to enter the great one's office.

'Ah, Mr Brock. Close the door, and tell me how you got on at the Belgian Embassy.'

'I regret to say I drew a blank there, sir.'

'Mmm!' The commander always managed to make that short and oft-used utterance of his sound thoughtful and at once critical. 'I've just been speaking to the DAC, Mr Brock.'

'Really, sir?'

'He informed me that a short while ago he engaged in a telephone conversation with the head of the Federal Police in Brussels.'

'Anything to do with my job, sir?' I asked innocently.

'It would seem so. The DAC told me that the Belgian Police are quite exercised about the murder of Richard Cooper. He has therefore directed that you proceed to Belgium with all despatch to liaise with the appropriate authority.'

'I shall make the arrangements immediately, sir,' I said, astounded, as ever, that the commander managed to sound his pompous best when passing on a direction from the DAC. But then I knew that the DAC scared the pants off him. Probably as much as Mrs Commander did.

Grateful that the DAC had covered up my visit with an entirely spurious tale about speaking to the head of the Belgian police, I returned to my office and telephoned Commissaris Pim de Jonker.

'I'm coming to see you tomorrow, Pim.'

'That's good, Harry. Are you coming alone?'

'I was intending to bring my Detective Sergeant Dave Poole with me.'

There was a pause before de Jonker answered. 'Could I ask

you to be as a discreet as possible, Harry? If you appear obviously to be two police officers, it may alert parties that I would prefer did not know you were here. I'll explain everything when you arrive.'

'In that case, Pim, I'll bring a woman officer with me, and then it'll look as if we're a couple on holiday.'

'That's a good idea, Harry. The less people who know you're coming, the better. I'm sorry it's all so secretive, but I'll explain everything when you arrive. It would be best if you flew to Calais, that's the nearest airport to us for direct flights from London.'

'Will you be there to meet us?'

'Not me, Harry, but my Inspecteur Piet Janssen will be,' said de Jonker, speaking so mysteriously that I was beginning to wonder what the hell this was all about. 'Let me know your arrival time as soon as you can.'

When I'd finished speaking to de Jonker, I sent for Kate, Dave and Colin Wilberforce.

'Kate, you'll be coming with me to Ieper. I can't explain why at present, Dave, but you're going to have to stay here. If and when I ring in, Colin, I'll use the special number in the incident room, which only you or Dave will answer.' I paused for a moment. 'This time we'll call it the Daventry Club.' We were always extremely cautious on occasions such as this to use the specially installed phone with an unlisted number. If anyone did call it to test where it was, they would think they'd got a wrong number. I then turned to Dave again. 'It's probably as well to leave you here anyway, Dave, because if there are further enquiries to be made while Miss Ebdon and I are in Belgium, you're more conversant with what's going on than anyone else.'

'What *is* going on, guv?'

'I haven't a clue, Dave, but I'm assured by Commissaris de Jonker that all will be made clear when Miss Ebdon and I get there.'

After Dave and Colin had left the office, Kate remained. 'Do you *really* not know what this is all about?' she asked.

'No, Kate. You know as much as I do now.'

'How long are we likely to be in Belgium? D'you at least know that?'

'Probably just the one night, but be prepared for two or three. And for God's sake don't call me "guv" once we're on our way.'

'I'd better get my Old Bailey outfit ready, then.'

Kate's Old Bailey outfit, as she termed it, consisted of a black suit, black tights, heels and discreet gold earrings, in addition to which her hair was always immaculately coiffed. If it was done for effect it certainly succeeded at the Central Criminal Court, where she beguiled the judge and barristers alike and caused the female ones to spit chips when she entered the witness box.

'No, come as you are, Kate. Pim de Jonker suggested that we try to look like tourists.'

'That makes life much easier, but I still don't know what to take.'

'I've got news for you in your moment of crisis, Kate,' I said. 'They do have shops in Belgium.'

'Really?' said Kate. 'I asked for that, I suppose.'

On Tuesday morning, Dave collected me from my flat in Surbiton and then went on to New Malden to pick up Kate before delivering us to Heathrow Airport.

Kate had dressed as I'd suggested and was wearing her usual jeans and white shirt. For the trip, she'd added a denim bomber jacket and a baseball cap with her ponytail poked through the gap at the back. That and an expensive pair of trainers completed the outfit. She assured me that her large brown-leather shoulder bag contained all she would need for 'our holiday'.

For my part, I was wearing a blazer and chinos, but had decided against wearing a tie. At the last minute I'd grabbed my old panama hat, which these days I hardly ever wore, but just as quickly decided to abandon it. I too had a shoulder bag with a few basic necessaries in it.

After a forty-minute flight we arrived at Louis Blériot Airport at Marck, just outside Calais, at ten o'clock. It was now four days since Dirk Cuyper's murder and so far we had got nothing. But that I hoped was about to change.

We presented our passports to an officer of the Police aux Frontières, who gave them no more than a cursory glance before returning them.

As we moved away, I spotted a vaguely piratical figure wearing jeans and a leather jacket standing near a door at the side of the concourse. His hair was long enough to touch his collar and he had a beard and square rimless spectacles. He was holding up a piece of cardboard upon which was written 'TAXI – MR BROCK'.

'I'm Brock,' I said, as Kate and I approached the man with the sign.

'Inspecteur Piet Janssen, sir, Belgian Federal Police.' The piratical one mouthed my name without actually looking at me. 'Please to follow me.' And without waiting for an acknowledgment, he strode out of the terminal building and across to a BMW saloon with a taxi sign on the roof. There were several superficial dents in the bodywork and it was apparent from its filthy state that it hadn't been washed in months.

Janssen ushered us into the taxi. 'Don't worry, sir,' he said, once we'd settled in the back seat. 'It's actually a police car that we normally use for undercover work, and it's maintained to a very high standard.' That claim was confirmed once we were on the motorway and he accelerated to a steady 130 kilometres an hour, which was the speed limit. I noticed that he was careful to drop to 120 when we crossed the border into Belgium.

Just under an hour later, we drove into a market square and then took several turnings before stopping outside a hotel.

Although I'd ventured one or two questions during the course of the journey, Janssen had chosen to remain silent, concentrating on his driving. However, once we'd stopped he turned in his seat.

'My apologies for all the cloak-and-dagger stuff, sir, but the Commissaris will explain everything. He'll be in the bar when you're ready. He appreciates that you'll probably want to unpack and have a shower, and he asked me to tell you not to hurry on his account.'

'Where are we, Inspecteur?' I'd tried reading signposts, but by the time I'd converted kilometres into miles I'd missed the next two or three.

'It's better if you call me Piet, sir. For security,' Janssen added mysteriously. 'We are in Poperinge, which is about twelve kilometres from the local office of the Federal Police in Ieper.' He escorted us through the door of the hotel, pointed out the reception desk and left us to register.

'Do you speak English?' I asked the pretty young girl behind the desk.

'Of course, sir,' said the young woman and smiled.

'Good. My name is Harry Brock, and this is Miss Kate Ebdon. I understand that bookings have been made for us.'

The receptionist keyed this information into her computer and glanced up. 'You are in room two-one-seven, Mr Brock; and your room is two-one-eight, Miss Ebdon.' She glanced enquiringly at us, possibly wondering why we weren't to share a room.

'We're not married. Yet,' said Kate, smiling at the receptionist. 'The rooms do include en suite facilities, I hope.'

'Of course, Miss Ebdon,' said the receptionist and gave Kate another smile. 'Every room in the hotel has an en suite shower. Welcome to Belgium. I hope you enjoy your stay here.'

SIX

I had a quick wash and ran my electric shaver across the stubble that had grown since this morning. I was about to knock on Kate's door when it opened and she emerged. She was dressed in a denim skirt, loose sweater and what my mother would have described as sensible shoes. And she was wafting enticingly of Miss Dior perfume. I was amazed that she had managed to pack all that into a shoulder bag.

'Time to go downstairs and meet Commissaris de Jonker, Kate,' I said, and ushered her towards the lift.

'Hello, Mr Brock, Miss Ebdon.' The receptionist waved as we walked through the reception area.

'Hi!' said Kate, and waved in return. 'Where's the bar?'

'Through there, madam,' said the receptionist, and smiled as she pointed to a set of double doors over which was a large sign that read 'BAR'.

I wasn't sure whether Kate was playing the part of the dumb tourist or whether she hadn't seen the sign. With Kate you never can tell.

The bar was a large room, and I wondered how we would recognize Pim de Jonker or, for that matter, how he would know us, given that there were other casually dressed couples at different tables and one or two seated at stools in front of the copper-topped bar. But I needn't have worried. A man stood up from a table in the far corner and walked towards us.

'Harry, I'm Pim.' De Jonker was tall and slender, somewhere between forty and fifty years of age – it was difficult to tell – and immaculately dressed in a light-grey suit that was clearly of a continental cut. I like to think I know a thing or two about suits. His face bore a woebegone expression that implied he was carrying the troubles of the world on his shoulders. It was an expression that was rarely to change during our brief acquaintanceship. His hair was greying slightly at the sides and his old-fashioned wire-framed spectacles, set beneath bushy eyebrows, were perched on the bridge of a hooked nose: a combination that gave him a slightly evil, almost Faginesque appearance. Although he didn't look like a typical policeman, I could imagine that his sudden arrival among the unrighteous would scare the life out of the average Belgian criminal or, come to that, a villain of any nationality.

'How did you know what I looked like, Pim?' I asked, as we shook hands. I hoped that the casual wear into which both Kate and I had changed would have made us appear less like police officers.

'It was not too difficult.' De Jonker produced a photograph taken of Kate and me crossing the car park at Calais Airport, walking behind Inspecteur Piet Janssen towards our 'police "taxi".'

'Good on yer, Pim!' exclaimed Kate enthusiastically. She was always impressed by efficient police work. 'I'm Kate Ebdon,' she added, seizing de Jonker's hand and shaking it firmly.

'It is good to meet you, Kate.' De Jonker inclined his head very slightly, but I noticed that he did not hold on to Kate's hand any longer than was necessary. Unlike my friend Henri Deshayes of the Police Judiciaire in Paris, who had unashamedly flattered Kate with Gallic charm, it seemed that de Jonker intended treating her as a fellow police officer and nothing more. 'And now let's have a drink before we go in for lunch. Incidentally, Harry, the Federal Police are paying all your expenses. It's the very least we could do.'

We crossed to the table where de Jonker had been sitting, and at his suggestion each of us settled for a glass of Stella Artois. Given the heat of the day, it was a sensible suggestion that was thoroughly approved of by Kate, who muttered something that sounded like, 'I'm good for a tinny.'

'This hotel is one we use for confidential meetings,' de Jonker began in little above a whisper, 'and we trust the staff here completely. Even so, it would be as well not to mention that you are police officers. Or that I am. The fewer people who know of our meeting the better.' He paused to take a sip of his beer. 'You are probably wondering about the secrecy I've insisted on, and why we are meeting here, twelve kilometres away from the office in Ieper.'

'I must admit that it is a bit unusual, Pim, but it's something we have to do in Britain from time to time.'

'I'm glad you understand.' The grave expression on de Jonker's face became even graver. 'It was a shock to hear that Dirk Cuyper had been murdered, Harry. Have you any leads yet?' He moved his head a little closer as though fearful that he might miss something of vital importance, the expression on his face becoming graver still. 'What I am trying to ask is if you have any names of suspects, people he might have associated with and who might have intended to do him some harm? Any names of people associated with the sex-slavery racket he was investigating would be a great help to us.'

'Nothing so far, Pim. From our enquiries it would seem that he was very much a lone operator, at least as far as the residents in the apartment block where he was living were concerned.'

'I'm pleased to hear that; it was in line with his orders.' De Jonker moved even closer and was still speaking in a whisper. 'Dirk Cuyper was working under cover, and that is why the Chief Constable at Scotland Yard was not told of Dirk's presence, if you wondered why you did not know about this plan. But, as I think I said on the telephone, the fewer people who knew about him the safer he was.' He paused to spread his hands in a gesture of despair. 'But it was not enough. Ironically, that was one of the reasons that our chief decided to select one of my officers, rather than send an officer from Brussels who might have been known in London.' He sighed and looked out of the window. It was unfortunate that at that very moment a funeral cortège consisting of a white Mercedes hearse and three identical white Mercedes saloons passed the window. 'It seems to have gone horribly wrong,' he said, shaking his head.

'Am I to understand that Dirk Cuyper was not your choice for the assignment?'

'No, he wasn't. Personally, I didn't think he had sufficient experience. He was an inspector, you see, Harry. But he was well educated and he'd been to university – Ghent, I think – and the chief was adamant that he should be the one to go. I'm afraid they are a little remote in Brussels, and all they have to go on are the personnel records.'

'I know exactly what you mean, Pim.' I'd encountered similar decisions in London. 'Would it help you at all if I spoke to your people in Brussels and explained what we know?'

'Certainly not, Harry,' said de Jonker hurriedly, and looked extremely nervous at the prospect. 'Protocol demands that I inform them. I could be in trouble if they knew I had asked you to come here. Visiting officers should go first to Brussels, you see.'

'If that's the case, how are you explaining the expenses of this hotel?' I asked.

'I shall hide it in the accounts somehow,' said de Jonker after a moment or two of thought.

'What was Dirk Cuyper's precise mission in London, then, Pim?' asked Kate, as usual getting straight to the point.

De Jonker sighed and launched into a brief lecture that I suspected he had given many times before, and which was along the same lines as the briefing Wilberforce had given me about the reconstruction of the Belgian police, although not as detailed. In fact, it was so similar that I wondered if de Jonker had obtained it from the same source. But I didn't comment on it.

The waiter appeared at de Jonker's elbow and leaning forward deferentially, whispered in his ear.

De Jonker turned to Kate and me. 'Our table is ready. Shall we go in? We can continue our discussion while we're eating.'

We were shown to a table in an alcove in the far corner of the restaurant that had clearly been selected for its distance from other diners, most of whom appeared to be German or British tourists.

Before either de Jonker or I could do so, the solicitous waiter had pulled Kate's chair back, waited for her to sit down and flicked a crisp linen napkin across her lap. He then promptly gave each of us a menu, but as it was in Flemish Kate and I had to wait for de Jonker's advice.

'I would recommend the dish of the day,' said de Jonker and, glancing up from the menu, added, 'Today it is a plate of cold Belgian meats and cheeses, and I usually follow that with some ice cream made with Belgian chocolate.' He paused and patted his stomach. 'But don't tell Mrs de Jonker,' he said, with a slight softening of his features that could almost have passed for a smile. 'If you would prefer something more substantial, I can make recommendations.'

'No, Pim, that will suit me fine.'

'Sounds ripper,' said Kate.

Seeing de Jonker's bemused expression, I said, 'Kate is Australian, Pim, and she sometimes lapses into her own language. Roughly translated, it means that it all sounds perfect.' It was a comment that caused Kate to smack me on the back of my hand, followed by a laugh in which I joined.

'Ah! Ripper! That's a good word. I must remember it.' For the first time since our meeting de Jonker's face broke into a smile. I think we were at last softening his reserve.

The waiter was there in an instant, and de Jonker ordered the meal and three more glasses of Stella Artois, confiding to Kate and me that it was the only thing to drink with meats and cheeses.

'I take it that Dirk Cuyper was actively pursuing something to do with sex slavery, then, Pim,' suggested Kate.

'That was his mission, yes. Usually, the women are enticed from Eastern Europe with promises of employment on the domestic staff of some European Union bigwig in Brussels. On other occasions they are even offered a part in a film.' De Jonker shook his head, as though finding it hard to believe that anyone could be hoodwinked that easily. 'Believe it or not, the Belgian film industry is beginning to get more adventurous with their productions,' he added, as though defending it. 'However, to suggest that a part awaits these girls is merely a lure because these poor women – usually young girls – finish up in brothels, where they virtually remain prisoners.'

'If these women come from Eastern Europe, Pim, what was Dirk Cuyper doing in London?' I asked.

'You have a large number of migrants from other parts of the European Union, Harry, as well as illegal immigrants who have somehow made their way to Calais from the Middle East – from Libya and Syria, for example – and then are smuggled into Britain.' He stopped to give a scornful laugh. 'Or just walk through the Channel Tunnel, I believe. But I don't have to tell you that people smuggling is a big operation.'

'And it's almost impossible to prevent,' said Kate. 'Over five thousand lorries pass through Dover every day, Pim, and even accepting that half that number are inbound it's still impossible to search every one of them.'

'As many as that, Kate? I don't think you will ever stop it,' continued de Jonker. 'The trouble is that many of these migrants – even the legitimate ones – find that when they get to your country, or ours for that matter, it's not the paradise they thought it would be. And that gives the sex slavers easy pickings. You say you don't have the resources to prevent people being smuggled into England, let alone *out* of it, and they finish up here.' He paused to wipe his mouth with his table napkin. 'I was wondering, Harry,' he began tentatively, 'what information you are able to tell me about the situation in London?' He took out a notebook and looked up expectantly, his pen hovering over a blank page.

'I can't help you at all, Pim,' I said. 'You see, Kate and I are in the department that deals with murder and other related serious crimes. I'm afraid we know nothing about sex slavery.'

'Oh, that's a shame.' De Jonker was clearly disappointed at my answer, almost crestfallen.

'Did Dirk Cuyper get any information at all before he was murdered, Pim?' I asked.

De Jonker took a document from his pocket and handed it to me. 'This is a copy of the only information he sent me. It is not on official police paper for obvious reasons. It is just four names, one of whom is a woman. Dirk identified them as being heavily involved, but I don't know why he wasn't able to tell me more.'

'Is there any chance that Dirk's other reports were intercepted or hacked into in any way?' asked Kate.

'We know how vulnerable emails and communications of that sort can be, Kate.' De Jonker afforded her one of his rare smiles and tapped the side of his nose. 'Dirk always addressed his reports to me using my *nom de guerre*, and sent them by post to the secure private address here in Poperinge that we keep for such matters. The ordinary post stands much less chance of interception than electronic mail, but just to be absolutely safe he signed them with the codename Mercury.'

'The messenger,' observed Kate.

'Will another officer be sent to London, Pim?' I asked.

'Not now, Harry. Dirk's murder has made the people in Brussels realize just how dangerous it is, and with hindsight it was an unwise thing to do. My chief in Brussels accepted that Dirk was probably out of his depth, even though he did a good job to the best of his ability. It would be just as difficult for you to try looking for sex slavers in Brussels. We have an expression in our language: each to his own.'

'We have that expression too,' I said, remembering how sometimes Metropolitan officers were sent abroad, or even to other parts of the UK, only to find themselves floundering.

'The murder of Dirk Cuyper is a great loss to us,' de Jonker continued. 'As I mentioned earlier, he was well educated. He spoke faultless English, and it looked as though he was getting somewhere. But there are dark forces at work and it seems they will stop at nothing.' He paused to give a shrug of despair. 'He had a pretty wife, too, Renata, but they did not have any children, so that's a blessing of sorts. And Renata is young enough to marry again.'

I'd put Cuyper's list of names in my pocket without reading it. Time enough for that when we returned to London. 'I'll check these names with our records when I get back to the Yard, Dirk,' I said, tapping my pocket. 'It may be that they are well known to us.'

'I would be most grateful if you could pass on any information you have, Harry, particularly about the sex slavery that you learn. I'll give you details of the accommodation address here in Poperinge and the name I use. You can either write to me or call me on the telephone, but only on the number you called me on yesterday. Whatever you do, don't telephone the Federal Police office in Ieper.' De Jonker tore a page out of his notebook and scribbled something on it. 'That is the name and address you should write to, Harry. In the meantime, you may care to have a wander round the town. It won't take long, because it's not very large. Normally I'd give you a conducted history tour of Ieper, but too many people there know who I am.'

'And we'd be condemned by association, I suppose.'

For the first time de Jonker laughed outright. 'Exactly so, Harry. But we will meet here again this evening for dinner, yes? I'll telephone your room when I arrive. In the meantime, I must get back to Ieper and brief my boss on what has happened. You know how it is, Harry: a policeman never stops work.'

I did know, no matter the nationality of the detective involved. But I had never been in the position that Pim de Jonker now found himself. He had been forced by higher authority to send his friend Dirk Cuyper to do a job that he probably thought wouldn't be too dangerous, but Cuyper had been murdered. I couldn't begin to think what that must be like, and I hope I never find out.

We stood up, but as we were about to say goodbye to de Jonker, he paused, a pensive look on his face.

'What is it, Pim?'

'Renata Cuyper lives here in Poperinge, Harry. I wonder if you would be prepared to call on her and perhaps explain what happened to Dirk?' De Jonker spoke hesitantly and the expression on his face managed to combine pleading and sympathy. 'Right now I'm not exactly the most popular man she knows. And it might help having Kate with you,' he added.

'Of course, Pim. Just give me the address and tell me how to get there.' The prospect actually appalled me, but I couldn't refuse a fellow police officer, albeit of another nationality. Now it was my turn to pause. 'Is Mrs Cuyper likely to be at home?'

'Almost certainly. She's a schoolteacher, and now that the schools are on holiday you're sure to find her there.'

'Does she speak English, Pim?'

'Of course. Anyway she teaches the language.' De Jonker shot me one of his rare smiles, then gave us Renata Cuyper's address and directions to a street only a hundred yards away.

'This looks like the place, Kate.' The Cuypers' neat terrace house and those adjacent to it were square in every particular. In fact, nowhere was there anything curved that would soften the severity of the architect's rigidly austere lines. Even the short driveway, upon which stood a small Renault saloon car, was paved in square slabs that had been laid with painstaking symmetry. The surrounds to the front door and the integral garage were highlighted with white stone so that they presented a stark contrast to the warmth of the distinctive Flemish bricks with which the houses were built.

'Mrs Cuyper?'

'Yes.' Renata Cuyper was no older than twenty-five, if that, and her attire – short denim skirt and a white tee shirt – and the fact that she was barefooted emphasized her youthfulness. She wore heavy black-rimmed spectacles that reminded me she was a schoolteacher. She had a superb figure, good legs, long black hair, beautiful skin and the right sort of make-up. But for a reason I couldn't fathom, despite this overt perfection, she was completely devoid of sexual attraction.

'My name is Harry Brock, Mrs Cuyper,' I said, 'and this is Kate Ebdon. We're with the police in London.'

Renata Cuyper nodded. 'You'd better come in,' she said nervously, before turning and mounting the stairs. The impression was immediate: she wasn't pleased to see us.

The sitting room, which was on the first floor, at the front of the house, was simply furnished. There was a settee against the wall in front of the wide window and two matching armchairs on either side; the space between them was filled with a large, squarely placed coffee table. It was as though the furniture had been placed with a symmetry that deliberately matched the exterior of the house.

'Please sit down,' said Renata Cuyper, glancing at her wristwatch. It was something, I noticed, that she did frequently during our brief interview and she also turned her head from time to time and glanced out of the window behind her. 'May I get you some tea or coffee?'

'No, thank you. As a matter of fact we've only just had lunch.'

Cuyper's wife sat in the centre of the settee, immediately drawing her legs up to her chest and locking her arms around them. She stayed in this tightly bunched, stressful pose all the time we were talking to her. Kate and I sat opposite each other in the armchairs.

'I suppose you've come to tell me what happened to Dirk.' It was a bald statement, spoken without emotion of any sort: no obvious regrets and no tears.

'Yes,' I said. This was going to be difficult. 'I believe that Pim de Jonker has told you that your husband was shot.'

'Who?'

'Pim de Jonker, the Commissaris who was Dirk's boss.'

'Oh yes, of course. I was told he was shot.' Still Renata

Cuyper did not express any emotion.

'Our enquiries are still at a very early stage, Mrs Cuyper.'
Renata Cuyper nodded. 'Yes, I imagine so.' There was just
a trace of bitterness in the comment. 'It must be very difficult
for you. But do you have no idea why it happened?'

'Not at this stage, I'm afraid, Mrs Cuyper,' said Kate. 'It was
only yesterday that we found out that Dirk was a police officer
and was in London on official business, and that might compli-
cate matters.'

'Where did this shooting take place?' Renata Cuyper's blue
eyes fixed me with an uncompromising stare, and she fired the
question in much the same way as I imagined she would pose
a question to her pupils before suggesting that they had not
read the set book.

'He was living in a flat in North Sheen, near Richmond in
south-west London.'

'With a woman?' She glanced out of the window again, as
though uninterested in the answer.

That question took me aback somewhat. 'Our information is
that Mr Cuyper was living alone, and nothing we've discovered
leads me to think otherwise.' I had no intention of mentioning
the kinky women's wear and the handcuffs and restraints we'd
found in Dirk Cuyper's wardrobe at Cockcroft Lodge. In view
of what we'd learned since arriving in Belgium about his
mission, it may well have been that he'd collected them as part
of his investigation. But the copper in me said otherwise.

Mrs Cuyper gave me a frosty smile. 'You policemen will
always defend each other,' she said.

'But women police officers won't,' snapped Kate. I got the
impression that she was getting a little tired of Renata Cuyper's
apparent indifference to her husband's death. 'I can assure you
that what Mr Brock says is correct.'

Renata Cuyper shrugged. 'Maybe. But I can tell you that
Dirk's head would always be turned by a pretty woman, and
in our short marriage he had several affairs. In fact, I was told
by a friend that she'd seen him in a restaurant in Ieper with
some tart just before he went to London.'

Renata Cuyper spoke as though she had learned the lines she
had just delivered, and that added to the suspicion that was

beginning to grow on me about this whole affair. I also noticed that at some stage she had removed her spectacles and seemed to be managing quite well without them.

Suddenly a telephone rang somewhere in the house and Renata Cuyper tensed.

'Do you want to get that, Mrs Cuyper?' I asked.

'No, it's all right.' Renata still seemed apprehensive almost to the point of being terrified, but then the answering machine kicked in and she relaxed. All we could hear was a muffled message in Flemish.

'To return to what we were talking about, Mrs Cuyper, do you think your husband was having an affair in London?' Looking at Renata Cuyper, I wouldn't have blamed him. The woman seemed as cold as charity.

'How on earth would I know that?' responded Renata tartly. 'I doubt that he would have written and told me,' she added sarcastically.

'Did he write at all while he was away? Do you have any of his letters?'

'No. He said he had been forbidden to communicate with me in case it gave him away. Frankly, I don't believe him.' Renata paused and coloured slightly. 'I mean, I didn't believe him. To me it sounded like one of his typical cover stories, designed to put me off the scent of what he was getting up to.'

'I have been assured that he was in London on official business, Mrs Cuyper,' I said.

'That's what Piet Janker told me.'

'I think you mean Pim de Jonker,' I said.

'Oh yes, of course,' said Renata hurriedly, and blushed again.

'Do you know the names of any of the women he was seeing, Mrs Cuyper?' Kate asked.

'Haven't you heard that the wife is the last to know?' Renata Cuyper stood up, obviously tiring of the interview. 'Thank you for coming to see me, Mr Brock,' she said, merely affording Kate a dismissive toss of the head. 'I'll show you out.'

SEVEN

Kate and I had spent the afternoon wandering around the small town of Poperinge, but it didn't appear that there was a great deal to see. Presumably because we were from England, Pim de Jonker had suggested we should visit Talbot House, the home of the Christian Toc H movement founded by an army padre during the Great War. But neither of us was in the mood for sightseeing, and instead we decided to waste a pleasant hour or two over coffee and waffles sitting outside a café in the market square. Having nothing better to do but watch the world go by made a relaxing change from the hurly-burly of London.

'What d'you make of it all, Harry?' asked Kate, as our second cups of coffee arrived together with two more waffles.

'It all strikes me as a bit iffy, Kate. What was your take on Renata Cuyper?'

'Apart from the fact that I disliked the cold bitch the minute I set eyes on her, I think she was bogus. And the phone ringing really put her on edge. After that she just couldn't wait to get rid of us.'

'I'm beginning to think the whole set-up's bogus.'

'Do we even know if this de Jonker guy is a copper?' Kate sliced a corner off her waffle and coated it with a generous amount of Chantilly cream. 'We could ask him for his ID.'

'Not a good idea, Kate. Anyway, d'you know what a Federal Police warrant card looks like?'

'We saw the one that was in Dirk Cuyper's safe and I suppose de Jonker's would be the same.'

'If Cuyper's ID was the real thing. We can do some checks when we get back to the Smoke. If it is a genuine covert operation, then de Jonker's wise to act the way he's been acting. But I get the impression that he's trying to get as much information out of us as he can, while giving us very little in return.'

'Yeah, I sussed him for a sticky-beak the moment he started jabbering. So, what's the order of the day, Harry? Stay shtum?'

'Sounds right, so long as we don't alert him to our suspicions.'

'There was another thing,' Kate said. 'Renata, or whatever her name really is, got de Jonker's name wrong. She called him Piet Janker.'

'I noticed that, Kate, but she may only have met him the once. I wouldn't set too much store by it.'

'Maybe, although de Jonker did say he was not Renata Cuyper's most popular man, from which I assumed that she might've remembered him. And there's another thing, Harry,' Kate continued. 'Janssen's so-called "police" taxi that brought us here didn't have a police radio in it. That's the first police vehicle I've ever come across without a force radio.'

'Yes, I wondered about that, Kate. But the sensible thing is to play along with de Jonker and get the hell out of here ASAP. We might pick up something useful if de Jonker and company are actually part of this sex-slavery gang. But if they think we've rumbled them, we could be in danger. I don't think these guys take prisoners.'

'We could do a runner, Harry.'

'No, we'll stick it out, Kate.'

We returned to our hotel at about six and had a drink before going back to our respective rooms to wash and change for dinner. At seven thirty exactly I received a call from Pim de Jonker to say that he was waiting for us in the bar. I tapped on Kate's door and we went downstairs.

'How did you get on with Renata Cuyper, Harry?' de Jonker asked, anxiously I thought, once we each had a beer in front of us.

I felt far happier dealing with de Jonker now that I'd more or less made up my mind that he was bogus. I wasn't quite sure what sort of answer he was hoping for or what he hoped to hear, but I decided it would do no harm to give him my own interpretation of the woman's mood as if I had actually been talking to a recently bereaved copper's wife. 'She wasn't what I'd expected the grieving widow to be like, Pim. As a matter of fact, she seemed to be rather indifferent. I got the impression that the marriage had been an acrimonious one and she wasn't all that sorry he'd been killed. She certainly didn't waste any time before telling us that Dirk was a serial womanizer.'

'I'm afraid that was true, Harry.' De Jonker looked at me over his spectacles and nodded gravely, leaving me with the impression that he was pleased to hear it. 'He was a good policeman, though.' He took a pipe with a bent stem from his pocket and caressed the bowl for a moment or two, but realizing he wasn't allowed to smoke here, returned it to his pocket with a sigh of regret.

'Is that the reason you sent him to London, Pim? Because he was a womanizer?' Kate put her glass carefully in the centre of a beer mat and looked straight at de Jonker, once again going to the heart of the matter. 'Was the idea that he would try to discover what these people were doing by engaging some of their prostitutes?'

'That may have been the reason my chief in Brussels picked him,' said de Jonker. 'Sometimes I think he knows more than I give him credit for.' It sounded a reluctant and vague admission, and reinforced the belief that de Jonker might be a sex slaver himself and was attempting, in a rather clumsy way, to tap us for information.

'Had Dirk Cuyper ever undertaken any similar sort of enquiry before, Pim?'

'No.' De Jonker answered without hesitation.

'I was interested to know whether he had any experience in this particular field, that's all.'

'Unfortunately no, Harry.' De Jonker relaxed slightly. 'But when the boss in Brussels tells you to do something, you get on and do it.' He shrugged, implying that it was useless to argue with the system.

'We'll do what we can to find his murderer, Pim, but any information we dig up about the sex-slave trade will have to be passed to the department at Scotland Yard that deals with it. However, at the same time I'll let you have anything we find out,' I said, hoping that would satisfy him if he was bogus and we'd been unwittingly involved in an elaborate charade.

If, on the other hand, my suspicions were ill-founded and he really was a Belgian policeman, the whole plan struck me as having been poorly conceived. But I wasn't about to say so.

My personal opinion of this particular operation was irrelevant, and it may well be that the names on the piece of paper de Jonker had given me over lunch would eventually lead us to Cuyper's murderer. Yet somehow I didn't think so. The longer I spoke to de Jonker, the less I was inclined to share any information with him. Don't ask me why; just call it copper's nose.

'Yes, I quite understand, but you will send it to the secret address I gave you, won't you?'

'Certainly, Pim.' Over the course of our two meetings with de Jonker, I'd come to realize that he was out of his depth with this whole business. And that applied whether he really was the policeman he claimed to be or just playing a part.

All of which prompted a question. One of the statistics on Colin Wilberforce's 'fact paper' about Ieper stated that it had a population of about 35,000 people. And from what I'd seen of Poperinge, the population there was probably even less.

'What's the crime rate like in Ieper, Pim?' It was the sort of question that one policeman often asks another from a different area or a different country.

De Jonker waggled his hand from side to side. 'Up and down, Harry, up and down.' His answer was so non-committal that it clinched it as far as I was concerned. Any real copper would have had the facts at his fingertips and would have followed up with the usual gripe about lack of resources. 'Shall we go in for dinner?'

Dinner was a relatively quiet meal and I got the impression that Pim de Jonker would be pleased to see the back of us. If he was playing a part, the strain of trying to delude real police officers must have been severe. Certainly, the whole business of coded messages, secret addresses and covert hotel meetings smacked of the fantasy world of spy fiction, and seemed like a massive scam with Kate and me the flies enmeshed in de Jonker's web.

It was gone half past ten when we finished dinner and Kate and I retired to our rooms.

Kate paused at her door. 'I don't know about you, Harry, but I'll be glad to get the hell out of here. That de Jonker guy is beginning to annoy me.'

*   *   *

After a leisurely breakfast on the Wednesday morning, we found Inspecteur Piet Janssen waiting in the lobby of the hotel. Once we were in the BMW police 'taxi' that had collected us at Calais, we set off for the airport, arriving less than an hour later.

'Good bye, sir. Good bye, madam.' Apart from that brief stilted farewell, Janssen had not uttered a single word since picking us up. Perhaps he was disappointed that we hadn't told him and de Jonker the identity of Cuyper's killer.

But then again, perhaps de Jonker had told him to keep his mouth shut.

Dave Poole met us at Heathrow and drove us straight to Belgravia.

'Good morning, sir. I trust you and Miss Ebdon had an enjoyable time in Belgium.' Colin Wilberforce was his usual bright and efficient self, but the greeting was spoken with a suggestive smile. 'The commander said he wanted to see you the moment you returned,' he added, before I could respond to what was clearly a loaded comment. But as it was the second time that Kate and I had been abroad recently and stayed overnight, albeit on police business, I suppose the rumour mill had been working overtime. After all, Kate was an attractive woman and the troops could be forgiven for putting two and two together. And if they were envious, who could blame them?

'By the way, sir,' continued Wilberforce, reading an entry on his computer screen, 'Appleby checked Jones's story about an advertising conference at Heathrow, but it seems no one's heard of Jones or the company he was supposed to have been visiting. Of course, Jones is a common name, but in your absence Mr Driscoll told Appleby to knock it on the head because it was evident he was wasting his time.'

'Good decision,' I said. 'I've got a feeling that Jones wasn't anywhere near the airport the day Cuyper was murdered.'

'One other thing, sir. Tom Challis found a member of staff at a hotel who recognized the photograph of Cuyper.' Wilberforce handed me a slip of paper. 'I thought you'd want to follow that up yourself.'

'Thanks, Colin, I'll do that. Who was the member of staff? D'you have a name?'

'Not a name, sir, but Tom said it was the hall porter he spoke to. Oh, and Tom got our surveillance people to take a photograph of Jones. He thought you might want to ask the hotel people if they'd seen him with Cuyper. In fact, Mr Driscoll directed that photographs of everyone who's come to notice be displayed here in the incident room.'

Once again I was impressed by the efficiency and initiative of the guys I was lucky enough to have working with me. Some senior officers don't realize it, but an investigating officer is only as good as his team. And if you upset them, they can sink you without trace just by acting dumb. Believe me, I've seen it happen.

Anticipating that the interview with the commander was unlikely to be a fun-packed event, I thought it advisable to take time to have a cup of coffee before making my way to the great man's office.

'Ah, Mr Brock. You've returned. I take it you have prepared a written report about what you discovered in Belgium.' Pushing a file aside, the commander leaned forward, linked his hands on the desk and gazed at me over his half-moon spectacles as though inspecting an interesting example of marine life. 'I hope your visit will prove to have been worth the expense.' It was strange how money and paperwork seemed always to dominate conversations with the commander.

'I'm afraid I have nothing to report, sir.'

The commander moved sharply back as though he had received an electric shock. 'What d'you mean: nothing to report? Are you telling me that your visit to Belgium has been a complete waste of time and money? That won't please the DAC, you know.'

'The Belgian police paid all the expenses, sir.' I hoped that that would soften the fact that I wasn't going to tell him anything. However, if de Jonker and company proved not to be police officers it meant our expenses had been paid for by a criminal gang, and that would most certainly send the commander spiralling out of control. That apart, I realized that I was in the ticklish situation of trying to placate one senior officer as a result of a more senior officer's order. 'The DAC directed me to report the details of my visit to Belgium to him and to no one else, sir.'

'I'm sure the DAC didn't intend that you should keep that information from me, Mr Brock.' The commander afforded me the sort of patronizing smile that seemed to question my ability to understand a simple statement.

This is where you jump in the deep end, Brock, old son, I thought, *and you haven't got a lifebelt.* 'The DAC particularly directed me not to report details of my enquiry to anyone but him, sir.' I paused deliberately. 'And he made a point of including you specifically in that prohibition.'

'Good grief, Mr Brock, that is absolutely—' The commander spluttered and went red in the face, but managed to stop just short of criticizing the DAC, something which in his view would have been tantamount to a form of Metropolitan Police treason. Quickly recovering, he said, 'I'll have a word with the DAC. I'm sure you misunderstood his direction, Mr Brock. In the meantime, you'd better lose no time in getting across to Commissioner's Office to see him.'

I returned to the incident room and gave Wilberforce the four names that Pim de Jonker claimed to have got from Cuyper. 'Do the usual searches on those, Colin, and let me know the result ASAP.'

As Kate had accompanied me to Belgium, I decided to take her with me to see the DAC. But not until we'd had lunch at a nearby trattoria.

When we left the restaurant, the sun was high in the sky and it was blazing hot. I couldn't be bothered to take a Job car, and I didn't intend to walk. I wasn't going to risk the Underground, either, having no desire to be plagued by itinerant musicians and beggars, apart from the very real possibility of being mugged. I hailed a cab, and to hell with the expense, even if the commander disallowed the claim which, in his present mood, he was very likely to do.

Since 1967 New Scotland Yard has been housed in a charmless glass and concrete pile in Victoria, and now more than ever it looked like a run-down fortified third-world airport. Rumours have been abounding for some time that a new home would be found for the force headquarters. After all, the Metropolitan Police is staffed by people who are great movers and shakers, even though they often move in the wrong direction and shake for no apparent reason.

I always get the impression that gaining access to Commissioner's Office would be much easier if I were a member of the civil staff. However, having eventually persuaded a doubting security guard that Kate and I actually were police officers, we finally reached the DAC's office.

'He's on the phone at the moment, Mr Brock, if you'd care to take a seat.' Fiona, the DAC's secretary, gestured towards a bank of easy chairs, but no sooner had Kate and I settled than the secretary glanced at her telephone console and spoke again. 'You can go in now,' she said.

'Harry, Kate, come in and take a pew.' The DAC's jacket was hanging over the back of his chair, his shirtsleeves were rolled up and his tie slackened off. He possessed none of the starchy pomposity of my revered commander and he certainly didn't worry about his image. 'What's the spiel, then, Harry?' He moved from behind his desk and sat down alongside us.

I told him, as succinctly as possible, what we had learned during our short stay in Belgium, adding that de Jonker had promised to pay all our expenses.

'I should hope so, Harry.' The DAC laughed. 'How did you rate this de Jonker guy?'

'Out of his depth,' I said, 'and I suspect Dirk Cuyper was floundering even more so. But the hierarchy over there wanted him specifically for the job, and so he went.' It was no good beating about the bush with the DAC, he'd been a detective for too long and wanted straight answers. I took a deep breath. 'That said, guv'nor,' I continued, 'I think the whole set-up is bogus.' I went on to explain the cloak-and-dagger antics of de Jonker and his sidekick Janssen, the so-called trustworthy hotel, and de Jonker's instructions about how we should get in touch with him. 'I think the point of the whole exercise was to get as much information as possible from us without giving anything away.'

'Spit it out, Harry,' said the DAC.

'Frankly, I don't think de Jonker is a police officer, sir. When I suggested we should smooth the waters by having a word with his chief in Brussels, he nearly had kittens. They of all people would know about such an operation, despite what de Jonker said. Furthermore, he didn't seem to know the first thing about law enforcement in the way you'd expect a copper to know, no matter what nationality, and when I asked him about the crime rate in Ieper he hadn't got a clue. All this business of coded messages, secret addresses and covert hotel meetings just didn't ring true. In short, I reckon that de Jonker isn't a copper at all and that he set up this meet solely for the purpose of finding out what had happened to Cuyper. Having thought about it, I think Cuyper was in this country to set up a sex-slavery operation, not to investigate it. But once we got out there I decided to see it out.'

'I would have done the same, Harry,' said the DAC. 'You never know, you might've come back with some useful information, even though you haven't found out who killed Cuyper. What's your view, Kate?'

'I agree completely with Mr Brock, sir,' Kate said promptly. 'From what Cuyper's so-called widow, Renata, told us, Cuyper was frequently over the side; and de Jonker said that was why he was picked for the job. That said, I don't think she was Cuyper's widow; I think she was a plant.' She paused. 'Her behaviour would certainly fit in with what Mr Brock said about the whole shebang being bogus, sir.'

'Well, there's one way of finding out,' said the DAC. 'I'll speak to my oppo in Brussels.' He flicked down a switch on his intercom. 'Linda, see if you can get that guy in Brussels I met at an Interpol conference about six months ago. Yeah, that's him.' He picked up the list of names de Jonker had given us. 'I don't suppose you've had time to check these names, have you, Harry?' he asked.

'They're being put through the system as we speak, guv, but I don't hold out much hope that it'll get us any nearer finding out who topped Cuyper. If this set-up is as big as I think it is, they'll have covered their tracks.'

'I'm surprised they didn't cement his body into a motorway bridge somewhere,' commented Kate drily.

The DAC laughed. 'They aren't building any at the moment, Kate. I checked.' The phone buzzed. 'Hello? Ah, Maurice, how are you?' The niceties having been exchanged, the DAC went on to tell his contact, as succinctly as possible, what Kate and I had experienced in Poperinge. After a lengthy conversation during which he gave his contact all the details we had gleaned, he replaced the receiver and looked up, a thoughtful expression on his face. 'De Jonker and Janssen aren't police officers, Harry. Any minute now I imagine a large number of Belgian police officers will descend on that pair from a great height. He'll ring back with the result. In the meantime, Harry, follow up all the leads you've got and keep me posted. I'll tell your commander that if there's anything you need in connection with this enquiry, you're to have it without question.'

And that reminded me of a rather pressing problem. 'There's just one other thing, guv'nor,' I said, as Kate and I stood up. 'The commander wants me to brief him—'

'He's been on the dog already, Harry,' said the DAC. 'I've told him all he needs to know.' And with that enigmatic statement he returned to his desk.

On our way back to Belgravia, Kate asked, 'What did the DAC mean when he said the commander had been on the dog, Harry?'

'It's rhyming slang, Kate. Dog-and-bone: phone. I'm surprised you didn't know that,' I said, delighted that for once my Australian DI, who often fooled we Pommies with her indiscriminate use of Strine, had for once been fooled herself.

As the DAC had more or less told me to get a move on, Kate and I went straight the offices of the building company that was developing the site of the former health club. Fortunately, the company was halfway between the Yard and Belgravia police station.

'You'll need to see the project manager dealing with it,' said the helpful receptionist once we'd told her who we were and what we wanted. 'If you'd like to take a seat, Chief Inspector, he's just dealing with a client.'

'I'm beginning to think the world's full of project managers,' said Kate as we sat down. 'That's what Dennis Jones was supposed to be doing in an advertising agency.'

'Appleby made enquiries at Heathrow and came up with nothing, Kate.'

'Yes, Len Driscoll told me.'

A man came out of a door behind the receptionist's desk, nodded briefly to the receptionist and made for the lift.

The man who followed his visitor out of the office was stocky, maybe five foot eight in height, with a shock of wiry grey hair. He was wearing a suit and a collar and tie, but looked as though he'd be more comfortable in work clothes and a hard hat. The hand that grasped mine was firm and rough. 'Sorry to have kept you waiting, Chief Inspector. I'm Bob Maynard, the project manager for the site you're interested in. Come through.'

'I'm Detective Chief Inspector Harry Brock and this is Detective Inspector Kate Ebdon, Mr Maynard,' I said as we took seats in the project manager's cramped office. There were blueprints pinned to two of the walls, and rolls of what I took to be plans standing up in a box beside his cluttered desk. On a table near the window was a model of a group of buildings, presumably of some project under construction.

'How can I help the police then, Chief?'

'We're investigating a murder at Cockcroft Lodge in North Sheen—'

'Cockcroft Lodge?' queried Maynard, thoughtfully savouring the name. 'I'm pretty sure that's not one of ours.'

'It's not the ownership of the building that matters, Mr Maynard. The murder's got nothing to do with your company, but it's the site you're developing in Richmond that we're interested in. I understand it was a health club with a swimming pool and gymnasium.'

'Ah, got it! I'm with you now. What d'you want to know about it, then?'

'So far we've been unable to discover very much about the victim, but we've been told that he visited this club on a regular basis. It's a long shot, I know, but we often have to clutch at any passing straw.'

'I'm afraid I don't know anything about the management of the place before we acquired it, Chief Inspector. As far as I'm concerned, it's just another parcel of land that we're building on.'

'We didn't think you would be able to help much, Mr Maynard,' said Kate, 'but we were wondering if you can give us the names of anyone you've had contact with. I'm talking about the previous owners or staff. Anyone at all who we can talk to, because it's imperative that we find out more about our murder victim. Then we might get a lead on who killed him.'

'I'll see what we've got in the paperwork.' Maynard crossed to a filing cabinet and pulled out a thick dossier. 'I didn't realize how much mundane stuff you had to do in your job,' he said, elbowing the drawer shut and turning back to his desk. 'Now, let me see. Ah, here we are. It was owned by a Mr Victor Downs, or owned by his company. I've got an address for him, but that's all I can do for you, I'm afraid.' He looked up and grinned. 'Unless either of you wants to buy a new-build town house on the site of an old health club.'

I laughed. 'No thanks. I don't know what you're asking for them, but as it's in Richmond, I couldn't afford it.'

Maynard laughed too. 'Neither could I. Ah, I remember this. God knows why, but when one of our staff did the initial survey after the purchase, they took possession of all the staff photographs that were hanging in the entrance hall. I told my secretary to bin them, but they're still here.' He took the photographs out of the file and handed them to me. 'Any good to you, Chief?'

'They might come in useful, Mr Maynard,' I said, taking the prints and handing them to Kate. 'Thanks for your help.'

'I'm sorry I wasn't able to be more helpful,' said Maynard as we shook hands.

EIGHT

Kate and I returned to our offices in Belgravia, and I told her to wait in case the DAC rang back with more details about the bogus police officers in Poperinge.

Dave picked up a car and we drove to Victor Downs's address in Hampstead. It proved to be an elegant house that was undoubtedly worth a small fortune, and caused me to think that Downs wasn't a run-of-the-mill owner of a health club. I suspected that it had been but one entry among many in a substantial property portfolio.

'Yes, sirs?' The Thai butler who opened the door was immaculate in black jacket and striped trousers. He gazed at us with a face devoid of expression.

'We're police officers,' I said, an announcement that elicited no change of expression. 'We would like to have a word with Mr Downs, if he's available.'

'Please come in, sirs.' The butler spoke excellent, but stilted and slightly accented, English. 'I will inform the master of your presence. Wait here, please.' He pointed peremptorily to a spot in the centre of the tiled hall and disappeared through a door leading off at one side. Moments later he returned. 'Please to step this way, sirs.'

I have found over the years that when people are unexpectedly visited by the police, they are either apprehensive that they are about to receive bad news or even more apprehensive that some crime in their past has at last been detected. Victor Downs's face was, however, as devoid of expression as was that of his butler.

'My man tells me you're from the Old Bill, squire.' Downs possessed a well-built, muscular body, a bald pate, a discreet gold earring in his left ear and bushy sideburns that joined up with an abundant unkempt moustache. I suspected that somewhere beneath the expensive suit he was wearing there lurked a number of tattoos. It was evident from his tanned complexion that he spent a lot of time in the sun, and I assumed that he passed much of the winter in warmer climes than this country could offer.

'That's correct, Mr Downs,' I said, and introduced Dave and myself.

'Local nick, are you?'

'No, Scotland Yard. Murder Investigation Team.'

This news had no impact on Downs's facial expression. 'What can I do for you, then?' He selected a Montecristo cigar from a cedarwood box on the mantelshelf and waved it nonchalantly at a couple of easy chairs. 'Take the weight off of your plates o' meat, gents.' He remained standing in front of the fireplace, which had a rather fine Georgian stripped pine surround. It seemed a little out of place and I suspected that it had been installed after the house had been built. Above it was an abstract painting that jarred badly with the various pieces of antique furniture in the room, themselves seemingly incompatible one with another. Dave subsequently dismissed Downs as 'a man with too much money and too little taste'.

I explained briefly about the health club that Downs had once owned and why I wished to speak to anyone who had been involved in its management.

'I never went near the place, squire, and I ain't got a clue who was running it.' Downs spoke dismissively and spent a moment or two expertly examining his cigar. He held it to his ear and rolled it between his fingers before cutting off the end with a six-inch-high model of a guillotine and applying a flame from a table lighter that was a miniature version of the Blackpool Tower, both of which were on the mantelshelf. Despite this apparently professional way of attending to his expensive cigar, he then left the band on it. 'It was just somewhere to put some of me moolah, temporary like,' he continued. 'It was one of many and when this building company come up with the right amount of noughts behind the number, I flogged it. Know what I mean?' It was obvious from his idiomatic English and rhyming slang, delivered in a rich cockney accent, that Downs was the archetypal self-made man.

'So you don't know who was in charge of the place, Mr Downs,' said Dave.

'Not a clue, squire, but I'll have a word with my accountant, if you like. He's the main man. He's got an eagle eye and he knows everything, so long as it has something to do with money. Hold on.' Downs walked to the door. 'Ram, get the bookkeeper on the trombone, will you?' he shouted. A minute or so later a 'candlestick' telephone rang. 'Real antique, that phone,' volunteered Downs as he crossed the room to a rosewood davenport that must have been worth a couple of grand at the very least. To Dave's horror, Downs placed his lighted cigar on the edge of this priceless piece of furniture before picking up the receiver. After a brief conversation, he turned to me and said, 'Apparently it was some bird called Katherine Thompson. The bookkeeper reckoned she managed the whole caboodle. According to him he settled a pretty big redundancy package on her. With my money! I'll have to speak to him about that.' Rooting about in the davenport until he found an old envelope, he wrote Katherine Thompson's details on the back of it. 'There you go, squire,' he said as he handed it over.

'Thank you, Mr Downs,' I said, taking the proffered envelope. Downs walked to the door. 'Ram!' he shouted.

A few seconds later, the Thai butler appeared. 'Yes, sir?'

'Show these gents out, Ram.'

'Please to come this way, sirs.'

I decided to push on to Katherine Thompson's flat, and it was close to five thirty by the time we pulled up at the block where she lived. It was in a narrow street near the River Thames at Ham – referred to as a village by its inhabitants – that was situated between Richmond and Kingston. Thanks to a bit more of Dave's positive driving, we arrived there from Hampstead in record time. Outside the block, a removal van was parked behind an ageing Ford Escort, which must have been at least twenty years old.

The flat we were looking for was on the first floor and we were obliged to stand aside as two removal men inched their way down the stairs struggling with a large television set.

'If you're from the removal company—' began a woman standing in the doorway of the flat where we had been told Katherine Thompson lived.

'We're police officers,' I said, cutting across what I was sure was going to be a complaint.

'Oh, sorry. D'you want me?'

'If you're Katherine Thompson.' I recognized her as being one of the staff members whose photographs the project manager of the building company had given us, but it's always as well to make sure.

'I am, and if you're here about that car parked outside—'

'We're not interested in your car, miss.'

'Oh, it's not my car, but the wretched thing's been there for weeks now. It's an eyesore. I keep complaining to the council, but nothing's been done about it. Anyway, it doesn't matter now I'm moving.'

Katherine Thompson was no beauty, but she was a strikingly good-looking woman in a coarse sort of way. She had a good figure and noticeably sensuous lips, but what could have been an attractive face was slightly marred by rather spiteful penetrating brown eyes. She had long black hair that was pinned up untidily, as though she couldn't be bothered to do anything else with it but which I suspected would be attractive when cared for and worn long. She was attired in a pair of denim shorts that showed off her legs to advantage, a paint-stained shirt and a pair of flip-flops. But to counter this overall appearance of scruffiness, her toenails had been carefully varnished a bright red.

'How can I help you, then? Has there been a burglary or something?'

I was about to tell her why we were there when we were interrupted by one of the removal men reappearing halfway up the stairs. 'We're off to grab a bite to eat now, love.' He glanced at his watch. 'Back about half six. All right?' Without waiting for an answer, he scurried back down the stairs. I suspected that Katherine Thompson had probably told him what she thought of him and he wanted to avoid a further confrontation.

'Isn't it marvellous?' she exclaimed in frustration. 'No one seems to be able to get anything right these days. Anyway, sorry to loose off like that. Do come in. I don't know about you, but I could do with a cup of tea. If they haven't taken all the necessities, that is.'

We followed her into the sitting-room-cum-kitchen and introduced ourselves.

'Detectives, eh? Oh dear, that sounds serious.' She paused in the act of filling the kettle and frowned as though trying to work out why she had been visited by a couple of detectives. 'I'm sorry there's nothing to sit on, but as you can see I'm in the middle of moving.'

'I don't envy you the turmoil,' I said.

Katherine Thompson laughed. 'Thanks, but it actually looks tidier without furniture than it has done for ages. Anyway, I please myself when and how I clean it or tidy it. I live alone, you see . . . at the moment.' She shot me a flirtatious smile, but then as quickly changed back to the critical. 'I've only got a few sticks of furniture, but the speed those removal men are working they're going to take half the night before they've got it all in the van. They didn't get here until three this afternoon, and I'd just phoned the company and asked why there were only two of them. They said they'd send two more and that's who I thought you were. Sorry! Are mugs all right for the tea?'

'Yes, fine,' I said, hoping she would soon run out of things to complain about.

'Just as well, because all the cups and saucers seem to have gone,' she said and put a teabag in each of the three mugs on the worktop. 'What's this all about?' she asked, as she poured in boiling water. 'Are you sure it's me you want to speak to?'

'We understand that you were the manageress of a health club in Richmond,' began Dave.

'That's right, although I was usually known as the manager,' said Katherine.

'But I understand it's now closed, Miss Thompson,' said Dave, well knowing it was.

'It's Kat, Sergeant,' she said, handing us mugs of tea.

'What is?' asked Dave, looking round the room as if seeking a feline of some description.

'Kat is short for Katherine. Everyone calls me Kat. Anyway, why does managing a health club interest the police, particularly now it's closed? It's being pulled down so they can build flats or houses or something. The trouble is, some people have got no soul.'

'We're investigating the death of a man named Richard Cooper,' I said. 'He was a regular user of your swimming pool, or so we've been told.' This was no time to explain that Cooper was actually Dirk Cuyper, who had passed himself off as a Belgian police officer. Anyway, that was nothing to do with Kat Thompson and any attempt to explain it would only have complicated matters.

'I'm sorry, but the name doesn't ring any bells.'

'As he was a frequent visitor at this health club in Richmond, we thought you might have known him,' said Dave.

'No, I didn't know him. Did someone suggest I did?' She raised an eyebrow and took a sip of her tea.

'It was just one of many possibilities that we have to follow up,' said Dave, skilfully avoiding identifying his source of information.

'It was quite a big set-up, and I didn't know every member of the club just because I was the manager,' said Kat. 'I had a staff that dealt with membership, and others who checked passes when members arrived; and there were poolside attendants and personal trainers. Without wishing to sound conceited, a lot of the men who used the pool at the club seemed to fancy me, but there were always men like that among the membership. I used to wander around all day in my Speedo, and when these guys see a girl with all her bumps in the right place wearing a wet figure-hugging swimsuit their testosterone runs riot. You'd be surprised how many times I got chatted up.'

'You're a keen swimmer, then?' I said, thinking that could be the only reason she spent all day in a swimsuit.

'Yes, I love it. I'd spend as long as I could in the water, and at one time I even thought about trying to get into the Olympic team.'

'What happened?' I asked.

'Oh, I eventually gave it up. It gets to the point where training takes over your life and doesn't leave time for anything else. Well, that wasn't my scene. Anyway, as a matter of interest what happened? I mean, how did this guy die?'

'He was murdered at about midday last Friday at his apartment in Cockcroft Court, North Sheen.'

'Murdered?' Kat Thompson sounded shocked. 'How was he killed?'

'We don't know at this stage,' I said. 'We're awaiting the results of the post-mortem.' I knew exactly how he'd died, of course, but I wasn't going to tell anyone who didn't need to know. 'I don't think there's anything else, but perhaps you'd give Sergeant Poole your new address in case we need to speak to you again.'

'Sure, and I hope you catch whoever did it.' Kat gave Dave details of an address in Thames Ditton, and her mobile phone number.

'Thames Ditton isn't far from Kingston,' I said. 'There's a good swimming pool there. It's called the Kingfisher.'

'Yes, I know where it is. I've sometimes used it in the past.' Kat gave me a quizzical smile. 'But as a matter of interest, do you policeman always walk around armed with obscure bits of information on the off-chance that someone will ask for them?'

'No, I live in Surbiton.'

'I might see you in the pool one day, then.'

'There's no chance of that, Kat,' I said. 'Exercise is bad for your health.'

It was gone eight o'clock by the time we got back to the incident room and Dave had put the photograph we'd now identified as Kat Thompson on the board with everyone else who'd so far come to our notice.

'You've done enough for one day, Dave,' I said and sent him home to his wife, Madeleine. Tonight was one of those rare nights when his ballet-dancer wife had the evening off, and he deserved to spend a few hours with her when the opportunity arose. It didn't often happen during the course of a murder enquiry.

Detective Sergeant Gavin Creasey, the night-duty incident-room manager, stood up and waved a piece of paper in my direction.

'The DAC rang, sir. He asked if you would ring him the minute you got back.'

'Is he at home or in his office, Gavin?'

'In his office, guv.' Creasey smiled, and I knew what he was smiling at. The commander was always out of the office on the dot of six o'clock, with all the alacrity of a rat going up a drainpipe, but the DAC had been known to work through the night on the rare occasions that demanded it.

'Is Miss Ebdon still here?'

'Yes, guv. In her office.'

I paused outside Kate's open door on the way to my own office. 'D'you want to come in, Kate? I'm about to ring the DAC. I suspect he has some news.'

'I hope so,' said Kate as she followed me into my office. 'This enquiry's beginning to get whiskers on it.'

I tapped out the DAC's direct number and he picked up on the first ring. The conversation was brief, but the DAC was never one to waste words.

'Our Belgian friends haven't let the grass grow under their feet, Kate,' I said once I'd finished my conversation with the DAC. I poured a couple of glasses of Scotch and handed one to Kate. 'They've nicked de Jonker and Janssen, as well as the woman who was posing as Cuyper's wife.'

'So she wasn't his wife, despite all that spiel she gave us about Cuyper being a womanizer and de Jonker confirming it.'

'She didn't even live in the house where we spoke to her, Kate.'

'I thought she was a bit like a cat on hot bricks, Harry. As I said at the time, she was in one hell of a rush to get us out of the place. On reflection, she seemed pleased that we refused a cup of tea. Perhaps she thought the owner would be back at any minute, particularly after that phone rang.'

'Apparently the couple who live there were away on holiday on the French Riviera. The upshot is the Belgian police have nicked her for housebreaking as well as anything else they can turn up. Anyway, the three prisoners are now being interrogated at some length and anything they get they'll pass on to us. They've already learned that years ago de Jonker was an actor, and that Renata's real name is Anna Veeltkamp, a convicted prostitute.'

'Perhaps she did know Dirk Cuyper after all,' said Kate sarcastically. 'I reckon she must be an actress too. She certainly did her best to appear completely without sex appeal, and that takes some doing for a tom.'

'More to the point, it tends to prove that Cuyper, de Jonker, Janssen and now this Veeltkamp woman are all part of the same little team.'

I glanced at my watch. It was now half past eight of what had been a very long day. It seemed ages ago that Kate and I had left Belgium, but it was only this morning.

'Go home, Kate. See you tomorrow.'

NINE

The following day, a Thursday, was the first of August and it was still as hot as ever. There is no doubt that when we finally get an English summer, it takes some beating. Even so, the great British public was now complaining that it was too hot, but it seems to be a feature of our national psyche that we're not happy unless we've got something to moan about.

'I've finished doing the searches on the four names you gave me, sir.' Colin Wilberforce handed me a sheet of paper the moment I walked into the incident room.

'Thanks, Colin. Where's Dave?'

'Gone out for a haircut, sir.'

'About time, too,' I said. 'Ask him to see me when he gets back.'

Kate and I had only just seated ourselves in my office when Dave returned.

'I'm just having a look at what Colin Wilberforce has turned up on the four names that Pim de Jonker reckoned Cuyper had given him, Dave,' I began. 'I must admit that when I first saw them, I thought Cuyper or de Jonker had made them up, particularly now we know that our two Belgians weren't coppers at all. But it seems the owners of these names really exist.'

'Even so,' said Dave, 'he could've got them from anywhere. Frankly, guv, I doubt if they're worth the paper they're written on. If dishonest detectives can pick names out of the phone book to pad out a report, there's no telling what a bogus dishonest detective would've got up to.'

'Now that we're fairly certain that Cuyper was actually part of the sex slavery ring operating in this country,' I said, 'I think it's fair to conclude that these names are nothing to do with it or they're competitors in the same racket.'

'I don't think there's any doubt about it, guv,' said Kate. 'Pim de Jonker was obviously hoping we'd tell him, but he didn't think we'd sussed him out so that he got his collar felt by the real Belgian Feds. As you mentioned to the DAC, de Jonker was very keen to extract any information from us without giving anything away.'

I read off the names. 'Bernie Stamper, Sid "the Caretaker" Ellis, Charlie Mukherjee and Renée "the Duchess" Hollande,' I said. 'Mean anything to either of you?'

'They sound as though they're escapees from a cheap American crime novel,' said Dave.

'The names don't ring any bells with me,' added Kate, who knew a lot of villains. Or to be more accurate, a lot of villains knew Kate and probably had plenty of time in prison to regret the day they'd ever met her.

'All four have got form,' I continued. 'Give Linda Mitchell a bell, Dave, and tell her about this little quartet. It might help her to narrow the fingerprint search, and it'd be nice to know if any of them left their dabs in Cuyper's flat. But now I think it's time to start all over again.'

'Doing what particularly, guv?' asked Dave.

'Like having another look at Cuyper's flat, for a start. Have we heard anything about his laptop?' I asked. 'Someone was going to organize Lee Jarvis, our self-confessed computer geek, to break into it for us.'

'He's at Cuyper's flat now,' said Dave, 'and Charlie Flynn is with him in case he turns up something a bit tasty. Mr Driscoll thought it best to keep the laptop *in situ* so to speak.'

I didn't know why Len Driscoll had decided that, but I didn't question it.

'Hello, Mr Brock.' Lee Jarvis looked up as Dave and I walked into Cuyper's apartment. Jarvis was still as thin as ever and looked as though a stiff breeze would blow him away altogether. And his acne was just as bad as the last time I saw him.

'Any luck, Lee?' I asked. It proved to be an unwise question.

'There's no luck attached to this business, Mr Brock.' Jarvis leaned back in his chair and stretched his arms above his head. 'It's all skill and cunning know-how.' He lowered one arm and tapped his temple with a forefinger.

'I'll take your word for that, Lee. Let me put it another way. Is there anything on there that you've found so far that I should know about?'

'Dunno. I haven't had any luck yet.' And with that enigmatic statement, Jarvis dedicated himself once again to caressing the computer's pad and studying the screen intensely.

It must have been something to do with my arrival, not that I ever considered computers to be anything other than my implacable enemies, but Lee Jarvis suddenly cried, 'Gotcha, mate!' This, I presumed, was the geek equivalent of 'Eureka!'.

'Is this good news?' I asked cautiously.

'Yeah, we're in.'

'Good. In the meantime, Dave, I'll have another look round the apartment, just in case anything fresh springs to notice. If our friend here comes up with anything of value, give me a shout.'

But I didn't get the chance. I was about to go into the bedroom when the door chimes rang.

'All right, Dave, I'll get it,' I said, wondering if we were about to get lucky and that the caller would be the person who had terrified Dirk Cuyper into moving to a hotel, according to Dennis Jones at least. But I was surprised to see that it was Lydia Maxwell from the apartment opposite.

'Oh, Mr Brock. I was hoping you'd be here. I've remembered something that might be useful and I thought this might be a good moment.'

'You were lucky to find me here, Lydia, but I'm afraid I can't let you in. This is still a crime scene.' It wasn't, of course, not any more, but I preferred not to have anyone in the apartment who didn't need to be there. Especially someone who might be a suspect, and at this stage of the enquiry no one was yet ruled out.

'I quite understand, Mr Brock, but if you do have a moment to spare, you could come across to my place. I promise I won't keep you long because I know you must be busy.'

It is a foolish detective who overlooks anything, even the seemingly trivial, that might help him to solve a case. As I had definitely reached an impasse in the murder of Dirk Cuyper, I had to find out what it was that Lydia Maxwell had remembered that might help me.

'Do take a seat, Mr Brock,' she said, once we were in her apartment. 'I've just made some coffee. Would you like a cup?'

'Thanks, Lydia, a cup of coffee would be most welcome.' I sat down on one of the white leather settees. The last time I was in her apartment I'd noticed that they were rather ugly pieces of furniture, but they were very comfortable even so.

'It is real coffee, Mr Brock, not that instant stuff.' Lydia crossed to the kitchen area, took down bone-china cups and saucers and poured the coffee. 'Black or white?'

'Black, please.'

Lydia was wearing a white all-in-one suit with flared legs, and heels that added at least two inches to her height. She wore a chain-link belt upon which was a medallion on its own six inches of chain, and a discreet wristwatch, all of which I was certain were gold. I noticed that the diamond engagement ring and the wedding band she'd been wearing the last time I saw her, no longer adorned her left hand, and I wondered briefly whether she had met another man or just forgotten to put them on again after she'd showered.

'You said that you remembered something that might be useful, Lydia,' I said, once she had placed the cups of coffee on the small table between us.

'I don't know if it's of any use, and I hope I'm not wasting your time, but I remembered that I saw a woman calling at Mr Cooper's apartment on a couple of occasions.'

'When was this?' I took out my pocketbook and got ready to make a few notes. I hoped that what Lydia Maxwell was about to tell me would be of some value, rather than a story made up by a lonely woman seeking attention or desperate for company. It wouldn't be the first time that had happened to me in the course of a murder investigation.

'It must've been about five or six months ago, I suppose.' Lydia gave a sigh of frustration. 'If only I'd known what was going to happen,' she suggested with a shy smile, 'I'd have made a note in my diary. All I can tell you is that she turned up twice in the same week. Actually, I should say I only saw her twice. She may have come more often.'

'Was this one of the women you'd seen with Mr Cooper in the swimming pool downstairs?'

'It's possible that I saw her there, but I can't be absolutely certain. Women look so different when they're wearing a swimsuit, goggles and a swimming cap.'

'Can you describe her?'

Lydia adopted a pensive expression. 'She was about my height, I suppose, and I'm five foot ten. She had shoulder-length Titian hair, and she was French.'

'How do you know that? Did you speak to her?'

'No, but it was the way she was dressed. She had a camel-coloured coat with very wide lapels and collar, black knee boots and a brown-, cream-and-black scarf tied loosely. There was no doubt she was French: there was that certain *je ne sais quoi* that's an absolute giveaway.'

'That's very detailed, Lydia.'

'It was based purely on envy, Mr Brock.'

I suspected that Lydia was fishing for a compliment, and she got one. 'I don't think an elegant woman like you need to be envious on that score,' I said.

Lydia put a hand to her mouth and coloured slightly. 'Oh, Mr Brock, I wasn't . . .' she began and, obviously embarrassed, lapsed into silence. But then she recovered. 'And I forgot to mention that she was carrying a tan leather Longchamps clutch bag.'

'Did you see this woman's face?' I was thinking in terms of a computer-generated likeness, not that I had a great deal of faith in the system. The operators are first-class, but the witnesses tend to be unreliable. And if you have more than one witness, you're likely to finish up with descriptions that could be of two entirely different people. On one occasion, three witnesses managed to produce a composite image of a suspect who was a dead ringer of our esteemed commander, something that created widespread mirth in the incident room. Until the commander saw it and ordered that it be removed.

'No. I really only saw her sideways on, but I did notice that she was wearing sunglasses.'

'Five or six months ago it would have been March or February, Lydia. Are you sure she was wearing dark glasses at the tail end of winter?'

'I'm certain. A lot of women wear them as a fashion statement.

Not that I've ever done so unless it's very sunny. I'm too afraid of walking into something,' she added, and giggled at the thought.

'As a matter of interest, how was it that you happened to see this woman, Lydia?' I was beginning to grow rather suspicious of her account. In the first place, it was very detailed; on the other hand, my ex-girlfriend Gail once told me that women are always bitchy enough to notice in great detail what other women are wearing, although that may just have been Gail's view. I also wondered how Lydia Maxwell had happened to observe this woman on *two* occasions, particularly as the front doors of the apartments at Cockcroft Lodge were solid rather than having an inset glass panel. And Lydia's did not have a spy-hole. Finally, I wasn't prepared to accept Lydia's rather flimsy assumption that the woman was French based merely on what she'd been wearing. But then I don't know about these things.

Although it had only been a passing thought at the outset of this case, it occurred to me that Lydia Maxwell could have been the very person who had scared Cuyper enough to force him to flee his flat. Living opposite, she was in the perfect position to have killed him. She could calmly have shot him and made up the story about hearing gunshots; and then, by a stroke of good luck, panicky Dennis Jones arrived and helped her to play the innocent. What's more, she had now had ample time to dispose of the firearm, but no one had thought of her as a suspect at the time and she wasn't searched, neither was her apartment. There would be little point in doing so now.

If that were true, we would have been wasting our time looking at all those CCTV tapes. That said, of course, the woman we'd seen on those tapes who was in the lift at roughly the time of Cuyper's murder could match the woman that Lydia had just described.

Nevertheless, I determined that I would have one of my officers look into Lydia Maxwell's background, particularly the road accident that killed her husband. It would also be interesting to verify the story she'd told of her inherited wealth. She'd said that her late husband had made a lot of money from the futures market, and no doubt she'd received a handsome payout from

the life-insurance policy. And in all probability now received
a handsome pension.

'I was on my way to take the lift down to the pool for a
swim. I was wearing a towelling wrap over my swimsuit, as
the residents here tend to do, and a pair of flip-flops. Not
exactly the thing to inspire one's self-confidence when
confronted by a walking fashion plate. I'm sure you've heard
your wife say that,' she added archly.

'And the second time?' I didn't rise to the comment about
a wife.

'The same.'

'What time of day were these visits, Lydia?'

'Just after eight in the morning. It's my usual time for swimming. I usually listen to the eight o'clock news headlines on
the radio before I go down. Then I come back up, take a shower
and have a plate of muesli. Actually, having thought about it,
the second time I saw her was probably a little later because
I was on my way back from the pool. About a quarter to nine.
Yes, that was definitely the case, because I felt even less
composed on that occasion. My hair was dripping wet, I was
carrying my flip-flops in one hand and my wrap in the other,
and of course I wasn't wearing any make-up. I must've looked
like a drowned rat, and I always hope I won't meet anyone on
those occasions. But on that occasion I met her.'

'Did you speak to her?'

'Yes, I said good morning the second time. But she ignored
me completely. Of course, to be charitable, she may not have
spoken any English.'

'Did you happen to see if she was admitted to the apartment
by Mr Cooper, Lydia?'

'I know she wasn't, she had her own key.'

'And you haven't seen this woman again since?'

'No, I haven't, but that doesn't mean she hasn't been here.
It was just luck, I suppose, that I saw her on those two occasions. Would you like another cup of coffee?'

'No thanks, Lydia,' I said. 'In fact, I must get back, but thank
you for that information. I think it may prove to be very useful.'

'Well, I wasn't sure,' she said, standing up at the same time
as I did. 'I expect you get plagued with people who imagine

themselves to be armchair detectives, but I thought I'd better mention it.'

'You did the right thing,' I said, and paused. 'I know you said that you didn't see this woman's face, but d'you think you'd recognize her again?'

'I very much doubt it, not unless she's wearing the same clothes. Why? Do you know who she is?'

'Possibly.' Of course, if Lydia Maxwell was the murderess she could have made up this whole story about seeing a woman enter Cuyper's flat. What better way to allay suspicion? But setting aside that thought for a moment, I was thinking of Renée Hollande, aka the Duchess, whose name had been one of the four on Dirk Cuyper's list, although we didn't know much about her. Not that we could any longer place credence on what de Jonker had told us. 'We might be lucky enough to obtain a photograph of her at some stage.'

'If you do, Harry—' Lydia blushed. 'Oh, I'm so sorry, Mr Brock, that was rather rude of me, but it just slipped out.'

'That's all right, Lydia. Harry will do fine. After all, I'm calling you by your first name.'

'If you do get a photograph, just knock on the door. I'm here most of the time, except when I'm swimming. Or house-hunting.'

'Have you had any luck with finding somewhere?'

'Not yet. I think I told you that I've been looking mostly in the Strand-on-the-Green area, but I've not seen anything I like. I may have to look further afield, or even out of London altogether. I might try Surrey. Goodbye . . . Harry.' Lydia shook hands, and closed the front door as I crossed the hallway to Dirk Cuyper's apartment.

It was an interesting snippet of information that Lydia Maxwell had provided, mainly because, whoever this woman was, she possessed a key to Cuyper's flat. But this was based on the assumption that Lydia Maxwell's story was true. On the other hand, Lydia might have been laying a false trail. Perhaps she'd had an affair with Cuyper and he'd eventually tired of her. A woman spurned can react in an unpredictable way: ranging from just walking away, through cutting the legs off all his suits, to murder.

She had a confident personality, and I wondered if the

tempestuous marriage that she'd told me about had been
her fault rather than her late husband's. There again, she might
have made up that story to gain some sympathy and allay
suspicion.

But there were other things that were making me think. I
wasn't at all sure that Lydia's use of my first name had 'just
slipped out' and I didn't think the throwaway line about my
wife was accidental, either.

TEN

I t was getting on for midday when I returned to Cuyper's apartment. I repeated to Dave what Lydia had told me about the mysterious Frenchwoman she had seen letting herself into Cuyper's flat.

'Could be Renée Hollande, I suppose, guv.'

'Maybe, but I was told by Renata Cuyper – or Anna Veeltkamp, as we now know her to be – that Cuyper had a string of girlfriends. And Pim de Jonker confirmed it, for what that's worth. Of course, all that is meaningless now we know that he wasn't a copper at all.'

'It was probably deliberate disinformation anyway,' said Dave. 'This mystery caller could be anyone.'

'Renée Hollande was one of the names de Jonker gave us, but that was probably fiction as well,' I continued. 'I reckon the woman Mrs Maxwell claimed to have seen was one of Cuyper's fancy birds and he'd given her a key to his flat. It looks to me as though there are two strands running in parallel here, Dave, and somehow we've got to separate his love life from his villainy. I think this woman was someone else entirely.'

'I don't think there are two strands,' said Dave. 'If he's part of this sex slavery racket, these women are very likely potential prostitutes, or are on the game already.'

'It's anybody's guess, Dave,' I said, and then shared my theory with him that Lydia Maxwell might have been the murderess.

'It's possible, I suppose, guv. In fact, I've come to the conclusion that anything could be going on in this investigation. But you might have a point with Lydia Maxwell. She was a bit too helpful,' Dave said thoughtfully. 'But if Cuyper was into the sex slavery business, I doubt we'd get anything from this mystery woman, even if we find her. Or, as you suggested, she could just be one of his bits on the side and he'd given her a key because she was flavour of the month.'

'I've at last managed to go through his laptop, Mr Brock,' said Lee Jarvis. 'I was listening to what you were saying, and it looks as though you might be right. There are folders with the names of four women on here.'

I crossed the room and looked over Jarvis's shoulder at the screen of the laptop. As Jarvis had said, there were the names of four women. 'What did you mean when you said folders, Lee?'

'Well,' began Jarvis, leaning back with the air of a professor about to begin a lecture to a rather unreceptive class.

'Keep it simple,' I said, recognizing the signs of an expert given free rein.

'They're really separate files, Mr Brock, and each one will contain information.' Jarvis pressed a key and opened one of the folders.

'It looks like a CV,' I said, peering more closely at the screen.

'All four are similar,' said Jarvis.

'What else have you found on that infernal machine, Lee?' I asked.

'Nothing.' Jarvis leaned back and folded his arms. 'I've been right through it and there's not a scrap of information except for these four folders. I can't believe that's all he had on there. I reckon someone must've hacked into it and cleaned the hard drive, but I don't know why they left these.' He laughed. 'Anyway, that's your problem, Mr Brock. I shouldn't think it was your victim, though.'

'Why d'you say that, Lee?'

'Well, Mr Brock, what's the point of cleaning off your hard drive and then locking the laptop in a safe that Mrs Mitchell told me was very difficult to get into? Whoever it was had to have been a master locksmith and be as good at computer technology as me,' he added, and laughed again.

'Well, where the hell did he keep all the stuff about his enquiries and the names he sent de Jonker?' I was actually thinking aloud.

'Now we know what we know about Cuyper and de Jonker, there won't have been any piles of information, anyway. It was all make-believe,' said Dave. 'I don't think there was ever anything more than those four names on that computer.'

'You could be right at that, Dave,' I said, and turned back to Jarvis. 'Can you print off those four folders or files, or whatever you called them, Lee?'

'Haven't got a printer,' said Jarvis, 'but I can send them through to your incident-room desktop as attachments and they'll be there in a second. D'you want to send any message with it?'

'Yes, Lee, ask DS Wilberforce to do a search of records on those names,' said Dave, knowing that anything to do with computers finished up making me downright bad-tempered.

'Well, that's all I can do for you, Mr Brock,' said Jarvis, having tapped a few keys, which I presumed was all that was involved in the esoteric art of message-sending. 'What d'you want done with the laptop?'

'I'll take it back to Belgravia and put it in the property store,' said Dave.

I rang Colin Wilberforce at the incident room and passed on Lydia Maxwell's description of Cuyper's visitor. I told him to arrange for further house-to-house enquiries to be made of the residents of Cuyper's block at Cockcroft Lodge as a matter of urgency. It was an outside hope that someone else may have seen the unknown woman, or even have spoken to her or perhaps made a note of her car number. But I knew from experience that was the least likely piece of information we'd receive, although we might get really lucky and find her arrival was recorded on the gate CCTV.

'On second thoughts, Colin, cancel that. Dave and I are here, so we'll do it ourselves. It shouldn't take too long unless we strike gold. What did the house-to-house reports say about the other residents in Cuyper's block?'

'One moment, sir.' Wilberforce spent a few moments reading the summary of those enquiries that were entered on his computer under H2H. 'Negative, sir. No one heard anything or saw anything, and none of them received any visitors at about that time. Do you want the names of the residents, sir?'

I noted the names as Wilberforce read them out, thanked him, and turned to Dave. 'I think it's time we had a talk with the people in this block, Dave.' I told him what Wilberforce had said about the initial house-to-house enquiries.

'There's always the possibility that it was one of them who topped Cuyper, I suppose, guv.' It was Dave's way of saying that he didn't think the house-to-house team hadn't done their job properly and, by implication, that I hadn't either. But as I've said before, Dave is my right hand and thinks of the things I haven't thought of.

We started on the ground floor.

The woman who answered the door of Apartment A was, I guessed, pushing fifty. Barefooted, she was wearing a very short leopard-print satin bath wrap and had untidy blonde hair that almost reached her waist. She looked very embarrassed to find two men on her doorstep, one of whom was very large and menacing.

'Can I help you?' she asked, at the same time giving the impression that she didn't really want to.

I glanced briefly at the list Dave had in his hand. 'Mrs Webb? Mrs Fiona Webb?'

'Er, yes. What is it?' The woman glanced apprehensively over her shoulder.

'I'm Detective Chief Inspector Brock, Mrs Webb, and this is Detective Sergeant Poole. We're investigating the murder of your upstairs neighbour Richard Cooper. May we come in?'

'It's not really convenient right now.' Even though Fiona Webb spoke in the sort of cultured tones that hinted at a private education, she lacked the confidence that usually goes with it.

'It really is very important, Mrs Webb,' said Dave.

'Oh, all right, then.' Fiona Webb was clearly reluctant to admit us, and in what I took to be a fit of irritability shut the front door more firmly than I imagined she would normally have done. 'Please sit down,' she said as we followed her into the living area of her apartment. She sat in an armchair opposite, and tugged at the hem of her short bath wrap in a vain attempt to cover her thighs. 'I don't know how I can possibly help you. I told the policewoman who came here the other day that we hadn't heard anything.'

'Who was that, Fi? I 'eard the bleedin' door slam. Oh bloody 'ell!' The man who had entered was wearing a short towelling wrap and he too was barefooted. A good ten years younger than

Fiona Webb, he was shaven-headed and spoke with a cockney accent. From our knowledge of the layout of Cuyper's flat, Dave and I knew that he had come from the bedroom.

'Are you by any chance *Mister* Webb?' Dave's impish sense of humour always seemed to take control of him on occasions such as this.

'Er, yeah, that's right mate. Andy, er, Webb.' The man spoke hesitantly and glanced at Fiona.

'Yes, he's my husband.' Fiona Webb was beginning to sound more confident. 'Don't either of you ever have a bit of fun with your wife in the middle of the day?'

'We're police officers, Mr Webb,' said Dave, a statement that brought about a noticeable intake of breath from the man. 'It looks as though the officer who came here before got the names wrong.' He glanced down at the list. 'I understood that your husband's name was Dudley, Mrs Webb.' He managed to look wide-eyed and innocent, but I knew he was just playing this couple along.

'Oh God! Look, we're—'

'Can I save you a bit of time, Mrs Webb?' I said. 'If you and this young man are having an affair, it's no concern of ours. Our concern is to learn how the man in the apartment above this one happened to get himself murdered last Friday.'

'I said when you arrived that I—'

'Let me finish,' I said. 'One of the residents in this block claims to have heard gunshots at about one o'clock last Friday, the day of the murder. Did you hear anything?'

'No, I didn't.'

'What about you?' I turned to Fiona's paramour. 'What is your name, by the way? Your real name.'

'Andy Curtis.'

'Were you here last Friday, Mr Curtis?'

'No, I wasn't,' said Curtis. 'I was at work all day.'

'Was anyone here with you last Friday, Mrs Webb?'

'I don't see that that's anything to do with you,' said Fiona crossly.

'I'm afraid it is, Mrs Webb. This is a serious matter and I would advise you not to prevaricate.'

'Oh hell!' Fiona Webb chewed her lip and glanced across

the room, as if trying to think how she could excuse what would undoubtedly prove to be her immoral behaviour.

'It don't worry me 'ow many other guys you've been screwing, Fi,' said Curtis and leered at her exposed thighs.

'D'you have to be so bloody coarse, Andy?' Fiona's use of swear words sounded out of place, spoken in her cultured tones. 'And I don't like being called Fi.' She turned angrily on her lover. 'Why don't you put some clothes on and get the hell out of here?'

'That makes a bleedin' change,' replied Curtis. 'Thirty minutes ago you almost tore me kit off. Now you want me to put it back on.' He gave an exaggerated sigh as if to emphasize the unpredictable whims of women.

'Well, I've changed my mind,' said Fiona. 'Make sure you shut the bloody door on your way out and don't bother coming back.'

Curtis returned to the bedroom to reappear a couple of minutes later attired in jeans, a tee shirt and a denim bomber jacket. He didn't acknowledge Fiona as he crossed the sitting room, and he ignored us. Seconds later we heard the front door slam.

'Oh well, I suppose that's goodbye to takeaway pizzas,' said Fiona.

'I take it he was the delivery man,' said Dave.

'That's how I met him. Good in bed, brain dead.' Fiona sighed. 'Does my husband have to know anything about this, Inspector?'

'It's Chief Inspector, Mrs Webb. And as I said before, it's no concern of ours what you do as long as it's legal. However, I take it that you had a visitor on the day of the murder.'

'You don't have to beat about the bush,' said Fiona. 'OK, I was in bed with a man who wasn't my husband.'

Dave handed her his pocketbook. 'If you'd be so good as to write down his name and address, Mrs Webb, we shall be discretion itself.'

Fiona scribbled the details in the book and returned it, her glance lingering on Dave longer than was necessary. I firmly believe he would have been in serious danger had he been here alone.

Dave handed it to me without comment. The name Fiona Webb had written down was Dennis Jones and a Petersham address.

'How did you meet this Mr Jones, Mrs Webb?' I asked.

'In the pool downstairs.'

'You're a keen swimmer, then?'

'Not really, but I like the atmosphere.'

I think the 'atmosphere' that really attracted her was the availability of men.

'How long did the affair with Mr Jones last?'

'It was a one-off, and I do mean off. When it came to it, he couldn't perform.' For a moment or two, Fiona Webb looked pensively at the floor. Eventually she looked up, a worried expression on her face. 'I suppose I ought to tell you, Mr Brock, before you hear it from someone else, that I had an affair with Dick Cooper.'

'Did you also meet him in the pool?' I wondered if Fiona Webb was the woman Lydia Maxwell said she saw letting herself into Cuyper's apartment.

'Yes, I did.'

'And how long did that last?'

'We got together approximately five or six times over a period of about two weeks.'

'Did one of you end it, or did it end because he was murdered?' I asked.

'I ended it about a month ago.' A solitary tear rolled down Fiona's cheek.

'Amicably?'

'Hardly. It was when I discovered that he was a sadist. I don't have to elaborate, do I?'

'No, I think I get the picture, Mrs Webb.' However, it made me consider the possibility that if Lydia Maxwell had had an affair with Cuyper and ended it for the same reason, she might've taken more drastic action than just walking away. 'Have you ever seen a woman visitor in this block who's been described to us as wearing a camel-coloured coat with wide lapels and collar, black knee boots, and a loosely tied brown-, cream-and-black scarf?'

'No, I haven't.'

'While your affair with Richard Cooper was going on, did he come down here or did you go up to his apartment?'

'It depended. Sometimes he came here and sometimes I went up there. I had to be careful, though. It was all right for Dick because he wasn't married, but I didn't want anyone to see me going into his flat. I'd told him to ring my mobile three times in quick succession if the coast was clear, but not to leave a message. And he always made sure the door was open.'

It was evident that Mrs Webb was a practised serial adulteress. 'When you were in his apartment, did you ever meet another woman there?'

Fiona Webb laughed scornfully. 'If you mean did he arrange a threesome, the answer's no. I'm not into that sort of thing.'

'I'll get an officer to call to take your fingerprints, Mrs Webb,' I said, having decided that I'd got all that I could get out of her.

'Whatever for?' Fiona started in alarm at this statement.

'For elimination purposes. As you've admitted being in Mr Cooper's apartment, we need to eliminate your prints from all the others.'

'But suppose my husband's here when you come to do it?' Fiona's alarm had not abated.

'We'll take his as well, Mrs Webb,' said Dave, waving a nonchalant hand. 'And we'll say we found a number of prints on the main door and are eliminating all the residents, then any that are left could belong to the murderer.' He paused. 'Or the pizza-delivery man.'

'I'm sorry we intruded,' I said as Dave and I rose to leave.

'Actually you did me a good turn getting rid of the pizza man, Mr Brock. He was beginning to get boring.' She laid a hand on my arm as I turned to leave. 'You promise you won't say anything to my husband about my, er, visitors, will you?' she implored. I assumed that a divorce would put paid to her current lifestyle, and that would certainly not suit this lady.

'That woman didn't have to wear an animal print bath robe to prove she was a cougar,' observed Dave drily as we knocked at Apartment B. However, neither there nor at any of the other apartments in the block did we learn anything that would push our hunt for Cuyper's killer any further forward, and no one had seen the woman thought by Lydia Maxwell to be quintessentially French.

'All we've achieved is to add another suspect to our list, Dave.'

'But we still haven't got enough evidence to nick any of them.'

'Back to the factory, then,' I said. Detectives always call their offices 'the factory'. Don't ask me why, although years ago an old and somewhat jaundiced detective sergeant told me it's where CID officers manufacture evidence. That may have been true in days gone past, but the Department has undergone a thorough cleansing since then. A former Commissioner once said that a good police force is one that catches more criminals than it employs.

ELEVEN

'Regarding the women whose details were found on Cuyper's laptop, sir,' said Wilberforce, the moment I stepped through the door of the incident room. 'There is no trace of any of them in Met Police records nor on the Police National Computer.' He handed me a printout of the names. 'It looks as though one of them is either French or Walloon.' He paused and looked up. 'A Walloon is a French-speaking Belgian, sir.'

'I do know what a Walloon is, Colin.' Sometimes Wilberforce was guilty of providing too much information.

'Yes, of course, sir. Her name is Chantal Flaubert. Then there are three with Flemish or Dutch names: Margreet Kloet, Roos Groenink and Lotte Skyper.'

'What else does it say about these four women?'

'The three Flemish women,' said Wilberforce, glancing up from the computer screen, 'are recorded as being prostitutes who originally operated in Brussels, where they were in great demand among EU personnel, but are now brothel keepers in various parts of London. There's a brief life story of each, but regrettably no addresses and no photographs. Cuyper, if he made the entries, has marked all four of them as "Opposition". I presume they're people on the other side in this turf war. It doesn't say whether Flaubert is a prostitute, but he's put a note in her folder to say that she's particularly dangerous.'

'Perhaps you'd go further afield with your searches, Colin, starting with the DVLA. If those women are resident here, they're bound to have a driver's licence.'

'Already in hand, sir,' said a rather smug Wilberforce and tugged at his cauliflower ear, 'but the DVLA takes a long time to come back. By the way, sir, I've located the whereabouts of the four people whose names were given to you by de Jonker.'

Grabbing the printout, I went along the corridor to Kate

Ebdon's office and sank into her armchair. In view of what we'd learned about Cuyper, I didn't attach too much importance to the four suspects named by him. The question of their whereabouts could wait until later. Instead, I brought Kate up to date with the latest developments, such as they were. 'It would be useful to find this woman who was seen calling twice at Dirk Cuyper's place, Kate, if in fact she exists.' And I repeated my suspicion that Lydia Maxwell might be more devious than at first she seemed.

'I think it's more likely that Mrs Maxwell's mystery woman, if she exists, was one of Cuyper's sleeping partners,' commented Kate. 'In which case, as Dave suggested, he might've given her a key.'

'Yes, maybe, Kate. We seem to do nothing but speculate in this job. But first, we'll see Dennis Jones. I know you interviewed him immediately after his discovery of Cuyper's body, but it may be that he's remembered something else since then.' I told her what Dave and I had learned that morning from Fiona Webb. Kate shrugged and expressed the view that Fiona Webb wasn't very choosy if she picked someone like Jones. Nor was she surprised that Jones had failed to please the promiscuous Mrs Webb.

She glanced at her watch. 'Half past five. Knowing what I do about advertising agencies, there's a good chance Jones will be at home by now, guv.'

'I don't think he does work in advertising, Kate. According to Appleby, Jones didn't visit anyone at Heathrow as he claimed to have done.'

The Munstable Street address in Petersham that Dave Poole had copied from Dennis Jones's driving licence was a three-storey Victorian house overlooking the River Thames. The house had been converted into flats and Jones's flat was on the top floor. Needless to say, there was no lift.

I was surprised that a young woman answered the door. In view of Judy Simmons's condemnation of Dennis Jones as a tight-fisted wimp, I wondered what attraction he possessed that enabled him to have installed a live-in lover. If that's what she was.

'Hi!' The girl appeared to be no more than seventeen or eighteen, if that, or it may have been the little-girl effect of being bare-legged and wearing a very short denim skirt, the sort Dave called a pelmet. But Kate needed only a glance at the girl's inexpertly applied and excessive make-up to decide that she was not all that she hoped we would think she was. And that immediately raised questions in my mind, and doubtless in Kate's too.

'We're police officers,' I said. 'Detective Chief Inspector Brock and Detective Inspector Ebdon.'

'Gosh!' The girl pulled open the door and stepped back to allow us to cross the threshold.

'Always ask for this,' said Kate, producing her warrant card, 'and don't be afraid to examine it closely.'

'Oh, sorry,' said the girl, 'but you looked like the police.'

'That's what they all say,' said Kate, emitting a sigh of exasperation. 'May we come in?'

We followed the young woman into the sitting room and I was pleasantly surprised to find it was remarkably clean and tidy. I've visited so many places that aren't that I've come to expect untidiness, unwashed crockery, piles of dirty clothing and an overriding odour of boiled cabbage or curry.

'What's your name?' I asked, as the girl showed no sign of offering it.

'Oh, sorry! I'm Sally Grey.'

'May we sit down?' asked Kate pointedly as no invitation to do so was forthcoming.

'Oh, sorry! Yes, of course.' Sally Grey seemed to be full of apologies.

'We were hoping to speak to Dennis Jones, Miss Grey,' I said, as the three of us sat down.

'I haven't seen him since last Thursday. Er, he didn't come home on Friday and he didn't come home all weekend. It's, um, I mean, what's more he didn't show up at the agency the day before yesterday. I don't know what's happened to him.' The girl's delivery sounded stilted enough to be a script she had learned, but not very well.

'Am I to understand that you work together at the advertising agency that employs Dennis Jones, Miss Grey?' In view of

Kate's knowledge of advertising agencies, this was a dangerous question for Sally Grey. Not that she knew that. Yet.

'Yes, we do. I only started there last week. I come from Devizes and this is my first time in London.' The young woman was doing her best to appear bright and knowledgeable, but the ordeal of Kate's intensive probing was betrayed by beads of perspiration on the girl's forehead.

'Where is this agency?' Kate asked casually.

'Er, I'm not sure. I think it might be in Shepherd's Bush, but I don't know London very well and Dennis takes me to work in his car. I've never paid any attention to how we get there.' Sally glanced at me, lowered her eyes and crossed her legs. It was a rather amateurish attempt to be beguiling, I suppose.

'What do you do there?' Kate enquired innocently, giving the impression that she was really interested. 'Layout, design, graphics, customer relations? What exactly is your role there?'

'Oh, I, er, well, as a matter of fact I'm still learning,' said Sally, avoiding eye contact with either of us. 'I'm sort of being shown round everything at the moment so that I can decide what I want to do.'

'They're going to let you decide what to do, are they? That's interesting,' said Kate. 'And you're living here with Dennis Jones?' Her raised eyebrow implied 'already'.

'Yes, of course, I'm his sister. I was lucky to get this job in advertising, but having got a degree in graphic arts helped, I suppose.'

'Splendid. How long ago did you graduate?' Kate managed to make her relentless questions sound as though they were asked out of interest in the girl's new career.

'Oh, the beginning of this year,' said the girl airily.

'Odd time of the year to graduate,' commented Kate, but let it pass. 'So, how old are you, Miss Grey?'

'I'm twenty.' Sally Grey didn't ask why Kate wanted to know her age, and I put that down to naiveté.

'If you're Dennis Jones's sister, Miss Grey, why isn't your name Jones as well?'

There was a distinct pause. 'Oh, I, um, changed it,' said the girl eventually. 'I want to be a model, you see,' she added, gazing at me once again with what she undoubtedly thought was a sexy smile. 'And I thought Sally Grey would be a better name than, um, Kelly Jones. But Dennis got me this job in advertising, so I've settled for that while I'm waiting to get a chance on the catwalk. I've had a couple of offers already,' she added brightly.

'Have you got your A level results yet?'

'No, not yet, but I'm expecting them any—' Sally Grey suddenly stopped, her face going red as she realized she'd been trapped by a seemingly innocent question.

'When you've stopped giving my chief inspector that stupid come-hither look, young lady,' said Kate sharply, 'you can tell me the truth. You obviously haven't learned the script that Dennis gave you, so I want to know your real name and how old you are. And when you've done that, you can tell me what you're doing in this flat. Otherwise we'll adjourn this interview to the nearest police station.'

Sally Grey burst into tears. Suddenly her clumsy attempt at sophistication vanished.

'I'm waiting,' said Kate, after a few moments had elapsed.

'My name really is Sally Grey, and I'm sixteen.' The girl mumbled the reply through her tears.

'And what are you doing here?'

'I'm Dennis's girlfriend.'

'And do your parents know you're here?'

'No.'

'Right, Miss Grey,' I said. 'Let's begin again, because if you waste any more of our time my Inspector certainly will remove you to a police station. Where is Dennis Jones?'

'Staying with a friend.'

'Why is he staying with a friend?' I asked.

There was another long pause before the girl answered. 'He said it was something to do with being questioned by the police last Friday. When he got home that evening he was in a terrible state and told me that he was sure he was going to be arrested.'

'But you said that he hasn't been home since last Thursday. Now you're saying that he came home on Friday.'

'I'm sorry. You're confusing me.'

'Did he say why he thought he was going to be arrested?' I asked.

'When are you due to leave school, Miss Grey?' asked Kate, before the girl had a chance to answer my question.

Tears welled up in Sally Grey's eyes again. 'Next year,' she mumbled.

'So this is all nonsense about working at an advertising agency.'

'Yes.'

'I thought so.' Then Kate came across with one of the cripplers for which she was well known in the Job. 'How long has Dennis Jones been your schoolteacher, Sally?'

I haven't the faintest idea how Kate had worked that out, but it proved yet again that a good woman interrogator is a very good interrogator indeed.

'Ever since I went into Lower Sixth,' said Sally, hardly able to get the words out. The tears were now running down her face unchecked, and pulling up the bottom of her tee shirt, so her suntanned midriff was revealed, she buried her face in it as the sobs took over and her whole body was shaking.

'And of course he's had sexual intercourse with you.' Again Kate made a statement, rather than asking a question.

'I don't see—'

'Yes or no?' snapped Kate.

'Yes,' mumbled Sally.

'How long has this been going on?'

'Two months.'

'And that's how long you've lived here with him, is it?'

'Yes.'

'You said you came from Devizes. And the school you were at is a girls' boarding school?'

'Yes.'

'And the name of the school?'

Sally mumbled a name, but Kate couldn't understand what she said.

'Here, write it down.' Kate handed over her pocketbook. 'And while you're at it, write down your parents' address.'

Kate took back her pocketbook and glanced at the name of the school. 'I doubt that they'll be too pleased at you having it off with one of the masters.'

'Are you going to tell my parents and the school?'

'Is there any reason why we shouldn't?'

'I'd rather you didn't.'

'In that case we won't, but we will tell them that you're safe and we'll tell your school as well.' Once again, Kate regretted the instruction that did not allow police to inform parents of the whereabouts of their daughter when she was the age of this young woman. 'Nevertheless, young lady, I strongly advise you to go home, because your parents must be worried sick. But I can tell you now that it's most unlikely that you'll ever see Dennis Jones again.'

'And now, Sally,' I said, 'you can tell us where we can find him.'

'I can't.' The girl looked up at me with a tear-stained face. 'He said I mustn't tell anyone, otherwise it would get him into terrible trouble.'

'Let me explain the situation to you, Sally,' said Kate patiently. 'As your teacher, Dennis Jones was a person in a position of trust and has therefore committed an offence for which he will be arrested. If you don't tell me where he is, or if you phone him to tell him we're looking for him, you will be guilty of assisting an offender. Do I make myself clear?'

Sally Grey nodded her head and, realizing that she had no alternative, leaned over the side of her chair and picked up her handbag. Opening it, she found a slip of paper which she handed to Kate.

'And he's still at this Feltham address, is he?'

'Yes,' admitted Sally.

'Good. And now I'll take a brief written statement from you setting out what you've just told us.' Realizing that they would have to go to court and knowing that witnesses and victims sometimes renege on their verbal statements, Kate was making sure she got the allegations against Dennis Jones in writing.

'Why on earth did Jones have this address on his driving licence? And more to the point, why did he show it to Dave Poole?' I asked, once we were back in our car.

'Two reasons, Harry,' said Kate. 'Dave is very insistent and Jones is a galah.'

*   *   *

I decided we must go straight to the address in Feltham that
Sally Grey had given us. Contraventions of the Sexual Offences
Act were something which Homicide and Major Crime
Command did not usually deal with, and I was annoyed that
we had become unwittingly embroiled in an illicit liaison
between a teacher and his pupil. I said as much to Kate.

'No worries, Harry. We'll soon get shot of it,' said Kate, as
we pulled up outside the address. 'Once we nick Dennis Jones
for having it off with Sally Grey, we can question him further
about the Cuyper murder, and then hand him over to the locals
for the abuse of trust job.'

A rather plain woman answered the door of the neat semi-
detached house in a street fairly close to Hounslow Heath. She
appeared to be in her late twenties or early thirties, but her grey
mid-calf skirt and grey blouse together with the fact that her
face was devoid of any make-up, made her look older. Her hair,
parted in the centre, stopped just below her ears and was quite
straight as though a sexually attractive coiffure was something
that she deliberately avoided.

'Can I help you?'

'We're police officers,' I announced.

'Whatever's wrong?'

'I'm Detective Chief Inspector Brock of New Scotland Yard
and this is Detective Inspector Ebdon. We'd like a word with
Mr Dennis Jones. I've reason to believe he's staying here.'

'Is this a joke?' The woman laughed, but it was without
humour. 'He lives here,' she said. 'I'm Ann Jones, Dennis's
wife. You'd better come in.'

'Surprise, surprise,' whispered Kate, as we followed Ann
Jones into the sitting room. Dennis Jones was sitting in an
armchair watching television as we entered the room, but leaped
to his feet as he recognized us.

'We've just been to Munstable Street, Mr Jones,' I said, 'and
we've spoken to Miss Sally Grey. She's told us everything.'

'What do they mean, Dennis?' Ann Jones glared at her
husband with her hands on her hips. It was undoubtedly an
aggressive pose and she appeared ready to start a fight. I
decided that she had all the signs of someone who'd gradu-
ated from the London School of Economics and would rather

be known for her brains than her looks. She struck me as the sort of person who probably knew a bit of law, but thought she knew it all. That made up my mind for me: discretion was out.

'I don't know what you're talking about,' said Jones.

'Miss Grey has stated in writing that you and she have had a sexual relationship spanning a period of two months and that you accommodated her in the flat at Munstable Street, Petersham, where she is still residing. Therefore, Dennis Jones, I'm arresting you for abusing your position of trust as a schoolteacher by having a sexual relationship with one of the female pupils at the school where you work. You do not have to say anything, but it may harm your defence if you do not mention when questioned something which you later rely on in court. Anything you do say will be given in evidence.' I didn't ask him if he'd understood the caution, because nowhere did it say I had to. Frankly I couldn't have cared less whether he understood it or not. I'd cautioned him and that was that.

'Oh God!' exclaimed Jones, clearly in shock at this unexpected twist of fate.

'Tell me it's not true, Dennis,' Ann Jones demanded, adopting an even more intimidating stance as she turned to face her husband. 'What's this about the flat in Munstable Street? D'you mean to say that you held on to it after we moved here last year? I don't wonder we were short of money. And that explains why you spent so many evenings away from home. Working in a supermarket, were you?' She scoffed derisively. 'Anyway, how did the police know you were there?'

'It's the address on his driver's licence,' said Kate, who had obviously taken an instant dislike to Ann Jones and wasn't worried about fuelling the woman's annoyance even farther.

I'd wondered why that address was on his driver's licence, but it now became clear. He'd omitted to change it when he and his wife moved from Munstable Street.

'Goodbye, Ann,' said Jones in a resigned voice, as Kate escorted him towards the front door.

'Well, you needn't think I'll be waiting for you when you come out of prison, Dennis Jones. And if you get bail don't expect to find me here, because I shall be long gone,' shouted

Ann Jones as she suddenly darted between her husband and the door and began delivering punches to his chest and face.

Kate moved in quickly and seized Ann Jones in a bear hug from behind, lifting her effortlessly clear of the floor. 'You can cut that out, sport,' she said, 'unless you want me to nick you as well as your husband.'

Once order was restored, we took Jones to Hounslow police station, in Montague Road, and told the custody sergeant to put him in an interview room while I made a phone call to the CID at Richmond. I was assuming that the Petersham flat where Dennis Jones had installed Sally Grey was the venue of the offence he'd committed; but if it wasn't, the local law could sort it out.

That settled, Kate and I went to the interview room where Jones was being guarded by a uniformed officer.

'It's not what you think,' said Jones, the moment Kate and I walked through the door.

'You sound like a character in a badly written soap opera, Den,' said Kate, as she settled herself at the table, beside me and opposite Jones. 'And what did you think we were thinking?'

'Sally and I are serious, and we're going to get married.'

'We're not here to discuss that,' I said, cutting off any attempt by Jones to discuss the matter for which he'd been arrested. 'The purpose of this interview is to talk to you further about the murder of Richard Cooper.'

'When you arrested me, you told me that I needn't say anything—' Jones began.

'That was in connection for your alleged breach of trust arising from your sexual relations with a pupil,' I said. For a schoolteacher, this man did not seem very bright. 'But if you think that you've committed an offence with regard to the murder of Richard Cooper, I'll happily caution you.'

'Of course I had nothing to with it,' Jones protested. 'So why d'you want to talk to me about it again?'

'Because, sport, we don't believe you,' said Kate, now at her aggressive best. It was at times like this that her Australian accent, hardly noticeable most of the time, became deliberately more marked and menacing. 'After all, you lied to us when you said you worked in advertising and claimed you were at some sort of conference at Heathrow Airport on the day of Cooper's murder. And that caused Mr Brock to send one of his officers to the airport, where he wasted his valuable time checking that fairytale you came up with, only to discover that you'd been lying all along. That little exercise took nearly a whole day because the airport is a bloody big place and you'd made up the name of the company you said you'd been to see. Furthermore, there was no accident on the M4 that could've held you up on the day of Cooper's murder. And that,' she added, finally, 'is called wasting police time.'

'I didn't want you to find out about Sally,' whined Jones.

'We're not amateurs at this police business, Den. If you thought for one moment that we wouldn't find out, then you were sadly mistaken.' Kate laughed at the man's stupidity. 'You should have changed the address on your driving licence, but we won't bother to charge you with that because you'll have another address very soon. And if that wasn't enough, there's the lie you told us about Judy Simmons.'

'Who?'

'I thought so.' Kate shook her head slowly, implying both doubt and impatience. 'She's the woman you said was your ex-girlfriend. And you told us you'd just split up from her. Well, Den, we interviewed her and she told us that the last time she saw you was at least four months ago and that she'd only ever been out with you twice. Hardly what I'd call a live-in lover. I won't tell you what else Miss Simmons said, but it wasn't very complimentary.'

'Is that how long ago it was?' said Jones lamely. 'Time goes so quickly.'

'Except when you're in prison,' said Kate crushingly, 'and it goes very slowly in there. Mind you, the hardened lags who'll be your cellmates will just love you.'

'What else can I tell you?' Judging by the tremulous tone of his voice and the expression on his face, Kate's last comment had unnerved Jones a great deal.

'The truth, Dennis,' I said, taking over the questioning from Kate. 'For a start, where were you on the day of Cooper's murder? Until you arrived at Cockcroft Lodge, that is.'

'I was with Sally.'

'Where did your wife think you were?'

'I told her I'd got a job in a supermarket during the school holidays.'

'And she believed you?'

'I think so.'

'Did Richard Cooper ever mention a woman who was seen letting herself into his apartment on several occasions? A witness has described this woman as being possibly French, some five foot ten tall, and stylishly dressed with shoulder-length Titian hair.'

The sudden change in questioning threw Jones for a moment or two. 'Er, no, he never mentioned anyone like that,' he said eventually.

'When you were using the swimming pool at Cockcroft Lodge, did you ever see a woman like that in his company?'

'No,' said Jones.

'Are you sure you've no idea who this person was who you said scared the pants off Richard Cooper, Den?' Kate posed the question in a tone that was almost conversational.

'No. I keep telling you, I don't know.' The desperation in Jones's voice was becoming even more marked.

'If I find out that you're lying to us, Den,' Kate continued, 'I'll come after you in whichever prison you happen to be banged up.'

Jones went white and gripped the edge of the table.

'You didn't mention that you'd met a Mrs Fiona Webb in the pool at Cockcroft Lodge, Dennis,' I said.

'Oh, that.' Jones sounded dismissive. 'I couldn't be bothered with her, she wasn't my type.'

'That's not the story Mrs Webb told us, Den,' said Kate. 'She reckoned you couldn't get it up.'

Jones flushed, but said nothing.

'You'll be kept at this police station until officers come to escort you back to Richmond police station, where you'll be interviewed by the CID, Jones,' I said.

By the time Kate and I left the interview room at Hounslow, Jones was near to tears.

'What d'you think, Kate?' I asked, once we were in the car and on our way back to Belgravia.

'He's a bloody weasel, Harry. What baffles me is why Cuyper

should've befriended him in the first place. Seems to indicate very poor judgment on his part if that's the best he could do for a minder. On the other hand, Jones might not have been the great friend that he claimed he was. Perhaps Cuyper just picked him as a one-off for the day when he had to come back to Cockcroft Lodge. He wasn't to know that the bloke was a drongo if he'd only met him in the pool a few times, I suppose. But whichever way you look at it, I think he's in over his head.'

'I think you're right, Kate. It's most unlikely that Jones had anything to do with Cuyper's death, but I'm not dismissing him entirely. He might be cleverer than we've given him credit for. Anyway, he's bound to go down for having it off with one of his pupils, so we'll know where to find him if we turn up anything that implicates him.'

Kate smiled. 'I don't really blame Jones for shacking up with young Sally Gray,' she said thoughtfully. 'At least that young girl's got a bit of sex appeal about her, which is more than you can say for that wowser Jones is married to.'

'That's one I've not heard you use before, Kate.'

'What is?'

'Wowser.'

'Oh, that. It's a prude or a killjoy, Harry, and I reckon Ann Jones qualifies on both counts.'

It was well past nine o'clock by the time Kate and I got back to the office. DI Len Driscoll had dismissed the team, and after I'd bought Kate a beer in a pub in Pimlico Road we went home. To our separate homes, that is.

TWELVE

On Friday morning I decided it was time to visit the hotel where Tom Challis said Cuyper had stayed immediately prior to his murder.

Dave and I arrived there at ten o'clock. It was a well-known hotel in central London and boasted five stars. From what little we knew of Cuyper, he wouldn't have stayed anywhere cheaper. The more we found out about his lifestyle, the less we seemed to know about him.

We were ignored by the doorman, whose antennae told him that we were not bona fide guests, and we entered the vast sterile foyer, where well-dressed foreigners wandered about aimlessly. There were four or five weird-looking youngsters wearing what are known as distressed jeans, and were obviously a pop group of some sort that in the present economic climate even this hotel could ill afford to turn away. Some instinct told me that there was bound to be tuneless music in the lifts to appease those foreign tourists who are terrified of being anywhere that is completely silent lest they should think they've died.

We approached the desk of the hall porter, the man Challis said had recognized Cuyper's photograph. In any event I would have consulted him first. In my experience, the hall porter is the one person in establishments like this who knows everything. And if he doesn't know it, it's either not worth knowing or it hasn't happened. But things change, and according to the brass plate on the hall porter's desk he was now called 'the concierge'. Immaculate in a green tailcoat, he was probably in his fifties, balding and heavily built.

'Good morning, sir.' The concierge carefully donned a pair of horn-rimmed spectacles that hung from a gilt chain around his neck, and quickly assessed the value of the suits Dave and I were wearing. 'How can I help you?' He knew damned well we weren't about to book a penthouse suite for a fortnight.

I discreetly displayed my warrant card. After all, one does not enter a hotel of this calibre cavorting across the foyer loudly trumpeting to all and sundry that the Old Bill has come among them.

'Thought so,' said the concierge, and gave me a knowing nod. 'Perhaps you'd care to come into my office?' Without waiting for an answer, he turned to his assistant. 'You've got the desk, Charlie,' he added, in a manner that reminded me of those war films where the captain says, 'You have the con, Number One.'

'Very good, sir,' said Charlie.

The concierge lifted the flap of his counter and ushered us through to his office. There was a wide curtained window in the middle of the partition separating the room from the counter, but the curtains were open. 'It's a one-way mirror, guv'nor,' he explained, once I'd introduced Dave and me. 'I like to keep an eye on young Charlie until he's got a proper handle on the job.'

Maybe that was the reason, but I suspected that the concierge would want to monitor everything happening in the foyer regardless of who was manning the desk.

'I suppose it's about Richard Cooper,' he continued. 'I had your Sergeant Challis round here a day or two back. He said you'd be likely drop in at some time.' He picked up the phone, tapped out a number and said, 'Tray of tea for three in my office, please, Rodica. No, my dear, it's the concierge speaking. Now concentrate, there's a good girl. I want a tray of tea for three in my office.' He repeated the order very slowly, enunciating every word, before turning back to me with a sigh. 'Romanian,' he muttered and shot a quick glance at the ceiling. 'So, what d'you want to know, guv'nor?'

'The dates that Cooper booked in and when he booked out would be a start.'

The concierge opened a notebook. 'I got those details from reception after your sergeant came in. I thought you'd want to know. Mr Cooper arrived here on Wednesday the tenth of July.'

'And when did he book out?' asked Dave.

'He didn't. He left here just before midday on the twenty-sixth and we haven't seen him since. He reserved the room until the end of August, and of course the receptionist swiped his credit card. So he'll pay for it, whether he's here or not.'

'That means you're still holding his room for him, then?'

'Indeed we are. Ah, that'll be the tea,' said the concierge as a knock at the door was followed by a middle-aged woman in waitress's uniform entering the office. 'Put it down there, love.' He pointed at his desk. 'Where are the biscuits, Rodica?'

'You never asked for no biscuits,' said the waitress churlishly and flounced out of the office.

'You can't get the staff these days.' The concierge shook his head, and closed the door after the departing waitress.

'Am I right in presuming that all Cooper's belongings are still in his room?' I asked.

'Yes, they are. Is there a problem?'

'You could say that,' put in Dave. 'Shortly after he left here on that Friday, he was killed. I reckon the management might have a job getting the credit card company to part with money.'

'Oh dear, oh dear!' The concierge chuckled at the thought. 'What happened? Get run over, did he?' He poured three cups of tea.

'No,' said Dave. 'He was murdered.'

'Murdered, eh?' The concierge nodded, handed round the tea and took a slurp from his own cup. 'These things happen,' he said, with the air of a man to whom nothing was new or shocking any more. 'So what happens about the stuff in his room?'

'That's not really our concern,' I said, 'but we'll get in touch with his next of kin and get them to arrange collection of his stuff.' I didn't mention that right now we didn't have a clue who his next of kin were. 'In the meantime, I'd be grateful if you didn't mention this to anyone. So far, we've managed to keep it from the media.'

'You can stand on me, guv'nor,' said the concierge, tapping the side of his nose with a forefinger. 'But I suppose the general manager will have to be told.'

'I wanted to have a word with him anyway, just to put him in the picture. And we'd like to see what there is in Mr Cooper's room and possibly take some of the items with us.'

'Don't worry about the general manager. He'll do as he's told,' said the concierge. 'He's foreign, you know. That's why I'm called a concierge now: it was his idea to change it. Frankly I couldn't see anything wrong with being called a hall porter. It was good enough for my old man, and it was good enough for his father before him.' He tapped out a number on the desk telephone. 'It's the concierge, sir. I have the police with me. They'd like to have a word with you about a serious matter. Very good, sir. Thank you, sir.'

'Is he there now?' asked Dave.

'Yes, he said to go up. I'll get one of the bellboys to show you the way. You won't have any trouble from the GM, he's a pussycat, and I think he comes from a country where they're scared stiff of the police.' With that dismissive condemnation of the general manager, the concierge led us out to the foyer and shouted for a boy.

A youth in page's uniform skidded to a halt in front of the concierge. 'Sir?'

The concierge inspected the boy critically, as though assessing his ability to conduct us to the top man's office. 'When you've got your breath back, lad, take these two officers up to the general manager.'

The page delivered us to an oaken door on the first floor, knocked and scurried away.

The general manager, a small man with a neat goatee beard, a pencil moustache and pince-nez, stood up as we entered. I was surprised to see that he was wearing morning dress, a mode of attire that I thought had long been abandoned even in hotels with a global reputation.

'I'm Detective Chief Inspector Brock of the Murder Investigation Team, and this is Detective Sergeant Poole.'

'Please take a seat, gentlemen.' The general manager had a slight accent that could have been German or Swiss or even Dutch, it was difficult to tell. He indicated two chairs with a wave of the hand.

'We'll not keep you long,' I began, declining to sit down. 'We're investigating the murder of Richard Cooper, one of your guests, and wish to search his room if you've no objection.'

'Do you have a search warrant, Chief Inspector?' It was the standard knee-jerk reaction from someone who probably watched too much television.

'We can get one,' said Dave, 'but we would have to seal Mr Cooper's room with tape and put up a large notice indicating that it was the subject of a police investigation. In several languages, of course.'

I don't know how Dave dreams up these fictitious little threats, but they inevitably have the desired effect.

'Oh, good heavens! That's the last thing we want in a respectable hotel,' the general manager said hurriedly, his hands waving about and twitching alarmingly as they searched for somewhere to park.

'We may need to seize certain objects from the room,' said Dave.

'Of course, of course.' The general manager was suddenly at pains to get rid of us as quickly as possible. Perhaps he thought that Dave might put a uniformed policeman outside the door to Cuyper's hotel room. 'I'll get someone to show you the way.' He tapped out a number on his telephone and summoned whoever had answered. Moments later a woman of severe countenance arrived. 'This is the housekeeper,' he said.

The housekeeper, an unsmiling middle-aged woman in a black dress, took us to Cuyper's room and used her pass card to unlock the door before standing back to allow us to enter.

'There you are, sir.' She too spoke with a foreign accent. Her duty completed, she immediately took off, almost running towards the lifts.

'Do you get the impression we're contagious, guv?' said Dave. 'The pageboy ran away, the manager couldn't get us out of his office fast enough, and the housekeeper nearly broke a leg escaping.'

'It's a natural fear of the police,' I said loftily. 'I doubt they've got anything to hide.'

'Except their price list, sir,' muttered Dave.

The search took less than ten minutes. I wasn't really disappointed at the lack of contents in the room because I'd not expected to find anything that might point to Cuyper's killer. The little we'd learned of the victim's behaviour since arriving in this country had shown us that he had always been very careful to cover his tracks.

'The only thing in the wardrobe, guv,' said Dave, 'is a spare suit with an English label, but there's nothing in the pockets. There are some clean pants and a few pairs of socks in the drawers of the dressing table and a Gideon Bible, but nothing else. Plus the usual toiletries in the bathroom, and that's about it.'

'There aren't any papers or letters of any sort either, Dave, but I'd not anticipated finding any. And no mobile phone,' I said. 'I thought everyone had one these days.' Once again we'd drawn a blank. We returned to the ground floor.

'Any joy, guv'nor?' asked the concierge, having emerged from behind his counter. An American approached him and asked him to call a 'yellow cab'. 'My assistant will do that for you, sir. Charlie, call a black cab for the gentleman.' He raised his eyebrows and turned back to me.

'No,' I said, 'but I didn't really expect to find anything. Tell me, did anyone call at the hotel asking for Mr Cooper?'

'Like this man for example,' said Dave, producing the surveillance photograph of Dennis Jones.

The concierge glanced at the photograph and shook his head. 'No. In any case, Mr Cooper specifically asked that if anyone called for him, we were to tell them that there was no guest of that name in the hotel. That was passed on to the telephone operators as well. And I asked to be told if anyone did call, and to get the name.'

'Did he mention that a woman might turn up asking for him?'

'No, guv'nor, he didn't mention any names at all. Mind you, it wouldn't have surprised me to learn he had a bit of woman trouble. You can tell, you know. I noticed that quite a few of the lady guests couldn't take their eyes off him when he crossed the foyer. And it was reciprocated. But I don't think it went any further than flirting with the eyes.' The concierge smiled at the recollection. 'I'll say this, though: Mr Cooper was a very generous man, if you get my drift.' He gave me an exaggerated wink before adding, 'So we took great care of his interests.'

'Well, thanks for your help,' I said.

'No problem, guv'nor. If there's anything else I can help you with, just give me a bell.'

Back at the factory, I sat down in my office with a cup of coffee and gave some thought to the mysterious woman, possibly French, who had a key to Cuyper's apartment. I was still considering the possibility that she was the Titian-haired woman glimpsed on the CCTV tapes riding up in the lift at twelve forty-five on the day of the murder. DC Sheila Armitage had established that the woman had not visited Apartments G or H on the first floor. We knew she hadn't called at Apartment F: that was occupied by Lydia Maxwell. The only logical conclusion, therefore, was that she had called at Apartment E: Cuyper's apartment. Now we had to find her and either eliminate her from our enquiries or charge her with Cuyper's murder. If we had supporting proof, that is. But that wasn't going to be easy. I wish I could remember the name of the instructor at the Crime Academy who told us that murder was one of the easiest crimes to solve. I'd invite him to come and solve this one for me.

Then a disturbing thought occurred to me: she might not have been the only one of Cuyper's friends or acquaintances who had a key. Or she was a plant who'd somehow put the black on Cuyper, obtained the key and then passed it, or copies of it, to someone of evil intent. We had so far managed to keep the news of Cuyper's murder from the media. Consequently, some of his previous callers – apart from the killer – might not know he was dead and might call again. But what if there was something in the apartment that the killer had wanted but couldn't find at the time, and returned later to recover it?

I rushed out to the general office. The only two officers there were Detective Sergeant Liz Carpenter and DC John Appleby.

'Are either of you authorized to carry firearms?' I asked.

'I am, guv,' said Liz.

'So am I, sir,' said Appleby.

'Good. I want you both to draw weapons and get up to Cuyper's apartment ASAP.'

'There are two of our people there already, guv'nor,' said Carpenter.

'I know, but they're not armed. There's a chance that someone, unaware of Cuyper's murder, might call. We know already of a woman, thought to be French, who has a key to the apartment and has been seen by Mrs Maxwell letting herself in. She might also be the woman who travelled up in the lift at about the time of the murder. We're clutching at straws, but anyone who knew

Cuyper well enough to have been given a key might be able to tell us more about him than we know already. And right now we know precious little. There is also the possibility that the murderer might return, looking for something, so be on your guard. I'll arrange for a night-duty team to relieve you, and I'll ask the concierge to give you a call if anyone enquires for Cuyper and to send them up. Keep in touch.'

From there, I went to the commander's office with an authorization form.

'Ah, Mr Brock.'

'I'd like your authority for four officers to be issued with firearms, sir. They will be—'

'Granted,' said the commander and almost snatched the form, without waiting to hear the reason. The DAC had told him to give me anything I needed and, like I've said before, the commander is terrified of the DAC.

After Dave and I had taken a break for lunch, we got back to the office at about two. DS Wilberforce was waiting for us.

'I've located one of the four names that were in the Belgian report, sir. Bernie Stamper is in Stone Mill prison doing five for burglary. It was his seventeenth offence.'

'You mean it was the seventeenth time he'd been caught, Colin. How long's he been inside?'

'Two years, sir. Due for release in six months' time. Provided he's been of good behaviour.'

'Should be very cooperative then,' I said. 'Give the prison governor a bell and see if we can see Stamper this afternoon.'

I didn't even have time to drink a cup of coffee before Wilberforce was knocking on my door again.

'I've spoke to the governor at Stone Mill, sir, and she said you can go up as soon as you like.' Wilberforce laughed. 'She said that Stamper is quite willing to be interviewed.'

'Decent of him to grant us an audience,' said Dave. 'I'll get the car up, guv.'

I'd met Kelly Johnson, the governor of Stone Mill prison, once before, but at a different prison. Aged in her mid-forties, she was attractively dressed in a grey trouser suit, with an open-necked white shirt, and her long black hair was fashioned into a ponytail.

'Long time no see, Mr Brock.' She levered herself off the desk upon which she'd been perching and shook hands firmly. The last time we'd met, I'd concluded that she was of the old school, more of a governor than a social worker. These days, many of the graduate-entry recruits come from outside the prison service, are fast-tracked straight into assistant-governor posts, and believe they are there to reform their charges. Believe me, the number of reoffenders I've dealt with over the years undermines the theory that they can be reformed.

'What sort of guy is Stamper, Mrs Johnson?'

'He's a bloody villain, of course, Mr Brock, otherwise he wouldn't be here. Curiously enough, he's one of the few who doesn't claim he was wrongly convicted or "I never never done it". And he's been as good as gold while he's been in stir. Doesn't mix much with the other inmates, and talks about trying for a Classics degree.' Kelly Johnson laughed at the thought. 'To be honest though, I think that's just chat. But at least it's one step up from finding God, which is what a lot of them do when they're nearing parole.' She laughed at her own cynicism. 'Maybe I've been in this job too long. Anyway, he's in an interview room ready to talk. I'll get one of the officers to show you along there.' She walked round the desk and flicked down a switch on her intercom. 'Ask Mr Willison to see me, Janet.'

'The governor said you wanted to have a chat, Mr Brock, and you an' all Mr Poole.' Bernie Stamper was a wizened, balding little man with the foxy features of the career criminal. According to his file, he was a month away from his sixtieth birthday and had spent a large portion of his adult life behind bars, mostly for burglary, theft and taking motor vehicles without the owner's consent. Anyone less likely to be on the brink of acquiring an academic degree was difficult to envisage. 'Mrs Johnson said you was from the Murder Squad. I dunno as how I can help you with no murders. Murdering ain't my game, not since my old man got topped.'

'What's that got to do with it, Bernie?' I asked, as Dave and I sat down opposite Stamper.

'I'd have thought you'd have known about that, Mr Brock, what with all them files you've got up the bladder-o'-lard.'

'Perhaps you'd better tell me about it, Bernie.' It was ages since I'd heard the phrase 'bladder of lard'. Cockney rhyming slang for Scotland Yard, it was very much a term used by villains of Stamper's generation.

'It was like this, Mr Brock,' Stamper began, adopting a conversational tone. 'My old man – he was called Charlie Stamper – got caught up in an armed blagging on a warehouse down London docks, when I was about two, I s'pose. But the nightwatchman turned out to be a have-a-go hero, so my old man give him a bit of a tap on the head with a sash weight, just to keep him quiet like. Trouble was, this old geezer's skull was thinner than usual, see, and he snuffed it. I mean to say, Mr Brock, they shouldn't go about employing geezers with thin skulls as nightwatchmen on account of everyone expecting 'em to get hit on the head from time to time. It's all part of the job; an occupational hazard, you might say. That's what life's all about. Know what I mean?'

'Can we get on with it, Bernie?'

'Yeah, sorry, Mr Brock. Well, while all this was going on, your lot had got the warehouse surrounded. My old man tried to leg it by jumping in the river, but the river coppers dragged him out and nicked him. Course, next thing he's up the Bailey and nine months later he gets topped in Wandsworth nick. Mind you he did have Pierrepoint, him what was the official hangman, to do the job. But it quite put me off doing armed blaggings when I grew up, Mr Brock.' Stamper's face remained expressionless as he delivered that humourless understatement.

'That's all very interesting, Bernie,' I said, 'but I'm not here to talk about your long form for burglary, or how your old man finished up taking the drop. How well did you know Richard Cooper?'

'Who?' Stamper looked genuinely puzzled. 'Villain is he?'

'You might know him better as Dirk Cuyper, a Belgian.'

'Sorry, Mr Brock, don't ring no bells with me. Never heard of him.'

I'd had a feeling all along that the name wouldn't register with Stamper, and I was more inclined to my original thought that Cuyper had found Stamper's name and probably the other three, from reading back-copy newspaper reports of trials. Nevertheless, I got Dave to read the other three names to Stamper.

Bernie Stamper listened intently, but after some consideration shook his head. 'Don't mean nothing to me, Mr Poole. They sounds like characters in one of them Damon Runyon books.'

'How do you know about Damon Runyon, Bernie?' asked Dave.

'Well, I'm studying the classics, ain't I, Mr Poole? When I gets me degree, I'm going after one of them jobs lecturing English up one of them universities. Better than doing porridge. Know what I mean?'

'I'm sure that would be a very good career change, Bernie,' said Dave.

THIRTEEN

On Saturday morning, I was sitting in my office shuffling through the meagre pile of statements that had been taken, wondering what the hell to do next. One after another, my enquiries and those of my team had finished up in an investigative cul-de-sac.

The interview with Bernie Stamper had turned out to be a complete waste of time and tended to confirm my original thought that Cuyper – or even de Jonker – had culled these names from newspaper reports. Even so, I decided I'd better pursue the other three names, because if I didn't bother it's a racing certainty that one of them would have fast-tracked me to the Belgian's killer. On the other hand, if I went to the trouble of interviewing them – wherever they were – I knew, deep down, that I'd get nowhere. I describe this unenviable and in my case seemingly recurrent situation, where everything goes pear-shaped, as Brock's law of criminal investigation. But putting speculation aside, there was an overriding problem: I didn't know where the three were, even though Wilberforce's best efforts were being concentrated in that direction.

However, all that was to change in the next few minutes. I had wandered out to the incident room to see if Wilberforce had anything new to report, and to get myself a cup of coffee from the illegal coffee machine. I say 'illegal' because the Commissioner's electricity police are ever alert to the misuse of the Commissioner's power supply and carry out daring raids on the offices of poor innocent police officers. And not only is the Commissioner concerned: our beloved commander worries about this malpractice and the effect it has on the police budget, as if his own money was under threat. Consequently, the illegal coffee machine is well hidden and only a few chosen detectives know where to find it. And they're all in my team.

'I was just on my way to see you, sir.' Colin Wilberforce stood up and waved a piece of paper in my direction.

'What about, Colin?'

'We've a report, from the HAT DI at the scene in Hampstead, that Victor Downs has been murdered, sir. As you interviewed him in connection with the Cuyper murder, Superintendent Dean has assigned you the investigation.'

It seemed a pretty slender reason for lumbering me with a second murder, but Patrick Dean was right to make that call because there might, just might, be a link to Cuyper's murder, although right now it appeared to be no more than coincidence. When Dave and I had interviewed Downs, I'd immediately come to the conclusion that he was up to no good, even though Wilberforce assured me that Downs had no criminal record. To undertake such searches of records was routine for anyone coming to our notice in the course of an enquiry. Therefore Downs was ostensibly as clean as a whistle, and his activities were probably limited to shady property deals. Maybe. 'Where is everyone, Colin?'

'Dave Poole is on his way to the scene, sir. Miss Ebdon is in her office, and Mr Driscoll is directing those members of the team who aren't here already to go straight to Hampstead.'

I poured a cup of coffee for Kate and took her cup and mine along the corridor to her office. 'Victor Downs has been murdered, Kate,' I said, placing the coffee on her desk. 'The owner of the health club where Kat Thompson worked.'

'I'd better get things rolling, then, Harry.' Kate stood up, but I waved her down.

'There's no rush,' I said. 'He's dead, so drink your coffee.'

Outside Downs's Hampstead house a uniformed sergeant clutching a clipboard was talking to an inspector.

'DCI Brock, HMCC,' I said to the sergeant, 'and this is DI Ebdon.'

'The HAT DI's inside, sir,' said the inspector.

'Who is it?'

'Jane Mansfield, sir. Your DS Poole arrived a few minutes ago and is with her, and Doctor Mortlock is here already.'

'Good grief!' It was not often that Henry Mortlock, the pathologist, got to the scene of a Saturday murder before I did.

Kate and I entered Downs's elegant house and met the HAT DI in the hall.

Detective Inspector Jane Mansfield had the appearance of being too young for her rank, and looked more like the head girl of a public school. But she was obviously on top of her job, otherwise she wouldn't have been on the Homicide Assessment Team. She was petite, with short brown hair and a cheerful smile. I had a feeling she'd be a frighteningly good hockey player.

'We've not met before, have we? DCI Harry Brock, HMCC, and this is DI Kate Ebdon.'

'Pleased to meet you, sir.' Mansfield's handshake was firm and her eye contact didn't waver. She ignored Kate. 'I don't know if you got my latest message, but you have a double homicide here.'

'That's all I need,' I said. 'Who discovered the bodies?'

'Police were alerted by a private firm of carriers. Their driver tried to deliver a parcel yesterday afternoon at about four o'clock, but got no answer. He thought it a bit strange because he's made several deliveries here before and he noticed that Downs's car was outside. Downs has a resident's parking permit. The driver tried again this morning, but there was still no reply. He called the local police and they effected an entry at nine twenty-four.'

'So these two could have been topped any time yesterday,' I said.

'Possibly, sir. The body of the manservant, name of Ram Mookjai, was found halfway up there.' Mansfield pointed at the manservant's slumped body, lying face down on the curve in the flight of stairs. 'Downs's body is in the bedroom on the first floor and that, presumably, was why Mookjai was on his way upstairs. Both had been shot at close quarters, Mookjai in the back. Downs was stark naked, and it doesn't look as though he'd made any attempt to defend himself.'

'Looks as though he didn't see it coming, mate,' said Kate, stating the obvious conclusion. Her Australian accent was a little more noticeable, and I thought I detected an element of hostility between these two women DIs. Perhaps they'd met before.

'That was the view I came to, Miss Ebdon, that the murderer was known to the victim.' Mansfield's response was cold, and tended to confirm my original impression of a mutual enmity. There was definitely a remoteness between these two, as though they were separated by a thin sheet of ice.

'Judging from the position of the body, it looks as though the manservant was shot first, Jane,' I suggested.

'I would think so, sir.' Mansfield glanced at Ram Mookjai's body as though making a fresh assessment. 'He probably admitted the visitor and was shot as he went to inform his master of the visitor's arrival. Which is more or less what I said just now.'

'Thanks for the rundown, Jane. We'll take it from here.'

'Right, sir. If you think of anything else I might know, give me a call. That's my mobile number.' I noticed that it was Dave to whom Mansfield handed her card. Perhaps my dislike of mobile phones and computers had now spread forcewide. 'Doctor Mortlock's in the bedroom on the first floor, and Linda Mitchell is here somewhere, along with her team.'

Kate, Dave and I went upstairs to the master bedroom in time to see Henry Mortlock packing his ghoulish instruments into his bag. Linda Mitchell was nearby waiting for the signal to start.

'These two killings are not unlike the murder of Cooper or Cuyper, or whatever the damned man's name was, Harry. Two shots to the chest in the region of the heart for Downs. Two in the back for the manservant. Mind you, I might be completely wrong in making that comparison,' Mortlock added, making an uncharacteristic admission of fallibility. 'Further and better particulars when I've got them on the slab.'

'Anything else? The fact that he was naked might indicate sexual intercourse.'

'Very likely, Harry. I've taken swabs and handed them to Mrs Mitchell for analysis.' Mortlock nodded in Linda's direction. 'I don't know if you want to send the bedclothes to the lab as well, but I'd advise it.'

'When are you likely to do the post-mortem, Henry?'

'It'll have to be tomorrow morning, I suppose, as you chaps are always in such a tearing hurry for results.'

'On a Sunday, Doctor?' queried Dave sarcastically. 'Won't it interfere with you going to church?'

Mortlock gave Dave a withering glance that seemed to despair of his reason. 'No, it won't, Sergeant Poole. It'll interfere with an important golf match.'

Kate Ebdon organized a house-to-house enquiry team, not that either of us thought that much would be learned from talking to the neighbours, and we waited while Linda Mitchell's merry band went about their business. Her murder technicians began videoing and photographing every aspect of the crime scene, as well as dusting for fingerprints and collecting the slightest pieces of scientific evidence that might help me find the creator of my latest problem.

By the time Linda had declared herself reasonably satisfied – she was only ever reasonably satisfied – that she had gathered all the trace evidence it was almost nine o'clock. We gathered in the tiled hall to determine how to proceed next.

'All right to shift the bodies, Harry?' asked Linda.

'Yes, go ahead.'

'Nothing from the house-to-house, guv,' said Kate, having just received the reports from her enquiry team. 'Nobody heard anything or saw anything. More than a few of the drums they called at had a distinct waft of cannabis, but this is Hampstead after all.'

'I didn't expect the locals to be falling over themselves to offer valuable information that would lead us immediately to the culprit, Kate. And as far as cannabis is concerned, it's not worth the cost of a phone call to the local nick. But now that Linda's finished, we can get going on a thorough search of the property.' I paused until Dave was out of earshot. 'Kate, have you met Jane Mansfield before?'

'No. Why d'you ask?'

'I got the impression that you hated the sight of each other.'

'She's a bloody wowser, Harry. A stuck-up cow. Some graduate entrants are all right, but some – like her – get right up my nose.'

'How d'you know she's a graduate entrant, Kate?'

'You can tell.'

There was no point in arguing with that definitive statement, but fortunately any further discussion on the matter was interrupted by the return of Linda Mitchell.

'There's a very upmarket safe in the study, Harry,' Linda announced.

'I presume Downs left it open.' I suggested whimsically.

Linda just laughed. 'There wouldn't be much point in shelling out five or six grand for a state-of-the-art safe and then leaving it unlocked.'

'Locksmith, then?'

'I doubt if the bloke we usually employ could open it. You'd probably need someone from the makers.' Linda chuckled. 'Or a good peterman. But they're probably all doing time, and they'd only blow it up anyway.'

'Did you come across any computers in your examination of the scene, Linda?' asked Kate.

'No, I didn't. If Downs had a laptop, it's probably in the aforementioned safe. Incidentally, Harry, there aren't too many fingerprints about the house, so the results shouldn't take too long. Either Downs was careful who he invited in or he had a fastidious cleaner.'

'I've a feeling that might have been Ram Mookjai, the manservant,' I said. 'He struck me as being a highly efficient sort of general factotum.'

'Except when it came to access control,' said Dave cynically. 'But as you said earlier, guv, it looks very much as though Downs knew his killer. If the scenario of our visit here on Wednesday was repeated, Ram would've told the visitor to wait in the hall while he went and alerted the boss.'

'But he only made it to the point halfway up the stairs where his body is,' said Kate.

'And that tells me something else,' said Dave. 'The killer must've used a weapon fitted with a suppressor. Otherwise Downs would've heard it.'

'Unless he was as deaf as a post,' volunteered Kate.

'He wasn't, ma'am.' Dave called Kate 'ma'am' in much the same way as he occasionally called me 'sir': when either of us had made a stupid comment. 'His hearing was normal when we saw him, and he wasn't wearing a hearing aid. What's next, guv?' he asked, turning to me.

'We'll start with the master bedroom,' I said. 'Kate, perhaps you'd make a start on the rooms down here.'

Victor Downs's body had been removed to Henry Mortlock's carvery, along with that of the manservant Ram Mookjai. The evidence recovery team had removed Downs's bedclothes for scientific examination, just in case they revealed a DNA sample that wasn't Downs's and we were lucky enough to be able to match it in the database.

'It looks as though he was expecting female company, guv,' said Dave, 'though whether it was a female who killed him remains to be seen. But he'd obviously got his kit off in antici-pation, and put it all on that chair.' He pointed to a neat pile of clothing that consisted of a white shirt and a pair of slacks. Nearby, on the floor, was a pair of sneakers with socks carefully rolled and placed inside. 'He had a liking for the fancy gear, I'll say that for him,' he added, pointing at a pair of men's mauve briefs that had been tossed across the room.

'You can be very old-fashioned at times, Dave,' I said. 'He could as easily have been expecting a man.'

'Yeah, I suppose so.' Dave went through the pockets of the trousers and took out a leather key case. 'Well, well, well,' he said, 'I do believe our Victor Downs has left us with the wherewithal to open his safe.' He held up two keys that were similar in pattern but not identical.

The study was on the ground floor, at the back of the house. Richly carpeted and wood-panelled, it was dominated by a desk old enough and large enough to have belonged to someone historically important. The distinctive aroma of cigars pervaded the air, and there were two cigar butts in a pewter ashtray on the desk.

Dave inserted the two keys in their respective locks, twisted the lever and the door of the safe silently swung open. 'Thank you, Uncle Victor,' he said. 'And lo and behold, here is a laptop. We can't be lucky this often, can we, guv?' he asked, as he removed the computer.

'What d'you reckon that is, Dave?' I pointed at a piece of tape stuck to the inside of the safe door.

Dave glanced at it and read it aloud. 'Tristram 1713.'

'Any idea what it means?' I asked.

'Laurence Sterne, an English clergyman and author, was born in 1713, and wrote *Tristram Shandy* among other works.'

'How the hell d'you know that, Dave?'

'I read *Tristram Shandy* at university. Well, I tried to. It was a bit heavy-going, but fortunately it didn't come up in any of the finals papers.'

'But why has he stuck it on the inside of his safe door?' I asked a little tersely. 'To remind him to return a library book?' I didn't really want a dissertation from my English-graduate sergeant on someone I'd never heard of or the book he'd written.

'It tells me two things, guv: despite his rough-diamond exterior, Victor Downs appeared to have had a liking for English literature, and he had a bad memory. If I'm right, that is the password for his laptop.'

'Surely it can't be that easy,' I said. 'Why on earth did he leave it there? Doesn't seem a very clever thing to do.'

'Easy,' said Dave. 'The safe was always locked, the keys were always in his pocket or nearby, and finally he didn't expect to get topped . . . sir.'

'All right, smart-arse. See if you can get into it.'

Dave seated himself at Downs's ornate desk and began playing with the laptop. Within seconds, he looked up and chuckled. 'We're in, guv'nor.'

I moved a spare chair so that I could sit alongside him. 'Anything interesting, Dave?'

'Yes, a link with the Cuyper murder.'

'How so?'

'Just have a look at this, guv.' Dave twisted the laptop sideways so that I could read some of the information on the screen. There was a list of names starting with Dirk Cuyper, Pim de Jonker and Anna Veeltkamp. Those three names had been bracketed together and marked with the single word 'Opposition'. 'But there are a lot more, all of which are Flemish or French.'

'It looks as though the picture is beginning to clear,' I commented. 'I think it's safe to say that there are two opposing gangs here: Downs's lot and the Flemish lot, although we don't

know who the leader of that lot is yet. And if what Dennis
Jones told us about Cuyper being scared out of his wits by
some woman, it could be any one of the names on his computer
who topped him.'

'Or it might be someone whose name hasn't yet surfaced,'
said Dave. 'It's jolly good fun, this murder investigation business, isn't it, guv?'

'Chantal Flaubert's name was on Cuyper's laptop and it
sounds French, Dave. I wonder if she could be the woman Lydia
Maxwell saw a couple of times letting herself into Cuyper's
flat, who she suggested was French.'

'I suppose it's possible,' said Dave doubtfully, 'and it's an
odds-on chance that the other names on here are Flemish or
Dutch. More likely to be Flemish perhaps, as Cuyper was a
Belgian. But there's a whole lot of other stuff on here. It'll take
some time to go through it all.'

'We'll take it back to the office and I'll get one of the team
to spend a few hours analyzing it.'

Kate joined us in Downs's study. 'There's not much in the
way of evidence on this floor, guv. Unless you think that
collecting things because they are valuable rather than useful
or beautiful is an indictable offence.'

'I said the man had no taste,' muttered Dave.

I glanced at my watch and was amazed to find that it had
gone eleven o'clock. It had been a long day.

'You can stand your team down, Kate,' I said. 'But perhaps
you'd leave a couple of them here overnight. We've got uniforms
outside, mainly because the front door was broken down to
obtain entry, but I don't want any of our light-fingered brethren
doing a sightseeing tour of the property in our absence.'
Regrettably it was not unknown for policemen to help themselves to small items of property as souvenirs of a murder, or
to take photographs that they anticipated might have a market
in one of the tabloids.

'That'll do for tonight, Dave,' I said. 'I'll stand the team
down and you and I will meet at the incident room tomorrow
morning and make our way to the post-mortem. Let's say at
about nine.'

                    *   *   *

It was gone midnight by the time I got home to my flat in Surbiton. It seemed rather empty now that Gail Sutton had walked out of my life. I missed her not being there, scantily attired and holding a bottle of champagne, or finding her underwear scattered about my bedroom. Being Saturday my precious cleaning lady, Mrs Gladys Gurney, had not put in an appearance. Gladys was an absolute treasure. She would make my bed, iron my shirts, and generally care for me as if I were an errant son. And she would wash and carefully wrap the aforementioned items of Gail's underwear in tissue paper, and leave them on the kitchen worktop with one of her charming little notes.

Perhaps I should get married. But I'd tried it once. When I was a uniformed PC, I was involved in a fracas with a group of youths I was attempting to arrest in Whitehall and dislocated my shoulder. I attended Westminster Hospital, where a delightful young physiotherapist pummelled me into shape. Her name was Helga Büchner, an attractive twenty-one-year-old German girl from Cologne. I took her out dancing the same evening, and we were married two months later. The wiseacres at the nick said such a whirlwind romance wouldn't last. They were right, of course, although it did take sixteen years before we finally divorced. It was the death of our son, Robert, that started the rot. Helga had left him with a friend while she went to work, much against my wishes, and he fell into the neighbour's pond and drowned.

That tragedy spelled the beginning of the end of our marriage. During its death throes there were extra-marital affairs on both sides, and finally Helga announced that she intended to marry a doctor with whom she'd been having a torrid affair for six months. The only benefit, as far as I was concerned, was that I learned to speak German fluently. On balance, it might have been cheaper to go to night school.

FOURTEEN

I called in at the office on Sunday morning in case any information had come in, either from enquiries made by my team or from other agencies. Alas, there was nothing. Dave was already there, and we were about to leave for the post-mortem when I received a telephone call from Linda Mitchell.

'I thought I'd let you know straight away, Harry, that one of the prints we lifted from Downs's bedroom and banister rail was identical to one we found in Dirk Cuyper's apartment.'

'Interesting,' I said. 'Where was it in Cuyper's place?'

'All over the place,' said Linda. 'The sitting room, the kitchenette area and the bedroom, but we also found an identical print on the safe. If you remember, Harry, the safe was behind a panel in the bedroom wardrobe. What's more, this particular print was on the *inside* of the safe door.' She paused to give weight to her next revelation. 'We also found the same print on Cuyper's laptop. Fortunately I examined it before Lee Jarvis put his own dabs all over it.'

That was indeed fortunate. Jarvis, our tame IT geek, was always so keen to get at any sort of computer we found that he tended to overlook the importance of it first being examined by forensic-science experts.

'I suppose there's no trace of these prints in the national database, Linda?' I posed the question tongue in cheek.

'You suppose correctly, Harry. It's fairly safe to assume, based on my experience, that someone who's careless about leaving their prints all over the place doesn't have a record and intends to keep it that way.'

'I think, Linda,' I began thoughtfully, 'that it might be a good idea to enlist the help of our colleagues in Europol. As Cuyper was a Belgian, it's possible that those prints belong to a Belgian citizen. If I remember correctly, there is some arrangement whereby we can fast-track this.'

'That's absolutely right, Harry, and we've done it before.

What's more I know a shortcut whereby we bypass Europol and send the prints straight to the Directorate of International Police Co-operation in Brussels. It's called the "old boy net", or in my case, the old girl net. I'll get on to it immediately. In fact, while I'm about it, I might as well send all the prints that we lifted from both scenes, apart from the only one we've already identified.'

'Good idea, Linda. Nothing like casting your bread on the waters.'

'Actually I was thinking of sending them by secure email,' said Linda drily. 'One set of prints I mentioned just now were found in both Cuyper's apartment and in Downs's house, and we did identify them as belonging to a convicted prostitute by the name of Irene Higgins. She has no convictions for any other type of offence.'

On the way to the mortuary to meet Henry Mortlock, I told Dave the full details of this latest development. 'I think we might be getting somewhere at last,' I was unwise enough to suggest.

'Not until we know who left those dabs there, guv. I think Linda Mitchell was right: whoever spread their dabs all over the place knew damned well that we wouldn't find a match in our database. Or probably in *any* database.' As usual Dave managed to pour cold water on what I'd firmly believed to be a breakthrough.

'One thing is certain, Dave. The prints on the inside of Cuyper's safe door weren't Dennis Jones's. The CID at Richmond took his prints after we arrested him, and Linda's eliminated them from the enquiry.'

'Oh well,' said Dave, 'that's another quick fix gone down the drain.'

We arrived at Mortlock's chop shop, and further discussion about the fingerprints had to be deferred until later.

Surprisingly, Mortlock had only just finished sewing up Downs's innards as we walked through the door. 'I don't know why anyone bothered to murder this man, Harry.' He stripped off his protective gloves and tossed them into a medical waste bin. 'His liver was on its last legs and he had lungs that look like pickled walnuts. He'd have been dead within months, if not weeks, and that's the result of too much drinking and too much smoking. Be warned, Harry.' And that was hilarious coming from a man who drank champagne to excess and smoked cigars.

'Thank you for that advice, Henry, for which you will doubtless send me a bill. But what actually killed Downs?'

'These did.' Mortlock handed me a kidney-shaped stainless-steel bowl containing two rounds of ammunition. He followed this up by handing me a second similar bowl containing two more rounds. 'And those killed Downs's manservant. Sign these bits of paper, Sergeant Poole, and you may take them away with you.'

'You are overwhelmingly generous, Doctor,' said Dave, taking out his pen and scribbling his signature on the form that maintained the chain of evidence.

'I think your killer was an expert shot, Harry,' Mortlock continued. 'Or a damned lucky one, three times over. The two rounds that killed Downs went straight into his heart, and the two with which Ram Mookjai met his end also went into the heart. Via his back, of course. And Cuyper was killed by two rounds straight into the heart. I'll write my report after I've finished my round of golf.' He glanced at the clock over the door and tutted.

'So the same murderer killed Cuyper, Downs and Mookjai, then?' I ventured to suggest.

'Oh, come on, Harry,' said Mortlock despairingly. 'I hope you're not suggesting that it's within my field of expertise to know if the same killer did for all three victims. I'm only the poor bloody pathologist. It's your job – you and the ballistics experts – to sort that out. All I can say with certainty is that in the three victims I've examined the cause of death was two rounds straight into the heart. But don't quote me until I've put it all on paper. By the way, Downs had had a vasectomy, which might explain why there weren't any condoms at the crime scene.' He took off his apron and donned his jacket. 'And now, if you'll excuse me, I have to go and fill some cavities at Richmond. If I'm not too bloody late.' Leaving us to find our own way out, Mortlock departed, whistling an air from Mozart's *Cosi fan tutte*. At least, that's what Dave said it was.

* * *

Back at the factory, Dave and I dropped into the small office that Nicola Chance had commandeered so she could have some peace and quiet while analysing the contents of the laptop we'd found in Downs's safe.

'How's it going, Nicola?'

'Slowly, sir, but I'm getting there.' Chance was in her early thirties and spoke fluent Spanish, a qualification that had come in handy on more than one occasion. She was not what you'd describe as a classical beauty, but good-looking and attractive she most definitely was. Her short blonde hair was never untidy, and she always wore a skirt. In fact, I don't recall having ever seen her in trousers or jeans.

On duty, she always wore flat shoes. Just in case she had to run, she said. And run she certainly can. I recall one occasion when we'd attempted to arrest a wanted man on the concourse of Heathrow Airport, but he suddenly broke away and made a dash for it. Nicola Chance took off and chased him for about fifty yards before bringing him to the ground with a rugby tackle that would have brought her a standing ovation at Twickenham. Despite having an air of modesty, Nicola is capable of occasion-ally shocking everyone with an uncharacteristically risqué comment or even swearing quite obscenely. The aforementioned chase was one of those occasions.

'To summarize, sir, this man Downs was up to his neck in the sex business.' Nicola leaned back in her chair, stretched and took off her glasses. 'According to the details on his laptop, he appears to have controlled a tidy empire of brothels, prostitutes and upmarket call girls, and the minders that go with that particular sort of business. There are lists of women together with their nationality, dates of birth, where they originated from and where they are now.' She looked up and laughed. 'Against each name are details of their special talents and a tariff. All in all, he's got a record system on here that would do credit to the human resources department of a big company.'

'I'm not sure whether to be pleased or horrified, Nicola.'

'Why, sir?' Chance looked disappointed, as though she'd done something wrong.

'I think the guv'nor sees an unending vista of report-writing,

Nicola,' said Dave. 'And that actually means you and I doing the writing.'

'Not necessarily,' I said. 'Given that a lot of those women's names are foreign, I think we might be able to swing the whole lot on to the Trafficking and Prostitution Unit out at West Brompton.'

'There are also the names you know about,' Chance continued. 'Dirk Cuyper and Anna Veeltkamp, who together with Pim de Jonker and a list of others are all marked down as "Opposition".'

'Yes, we saw that when we opened the laptop,' said Dave. 'It looks as though the Belgians were trying to muscle in on Downs's empire and Cuyper was the first casualty in this turf war. It looks as though our list of suspects is narrowed down to one of Downs's associates, guv'nor.'

'Yes, but who?' I asked. 'If Henry Mortlock is right about the accuracy of the shooter, it could be the same person who killed Cuyper and Downs. It was probably unfortunate for Ram Mookjai, the manservant, that he happened to be in the wrong place at the wrong time.'

'Perhaps the fingerprint search in Belgium will turn up something,' said Dave hopefully. 'In the meantime, guv, I must get these rounds across to the ballistics guys.'

'Tell 'em it's urgent, Dave.'

'I will . . . if there's anyone there, sir.'

Despite Dave's pessimism about finding anyone in the ballistics department on a Sunday, I was agreeably surprised to find a report waiting for me when I arrived at Belgravia first thing on Monday morning.

I walked out to the incident room where my team was waiting for the day's tasks to be allotted.

'We have good news of a sort from ballistics,' I began. 'The rounds taken from the bodies of our three victims were fired from the same weapon.'

'The cause of death was lead poisoning, then, guv?' said DC Sheila Armitage.

'The examiner at the ballistics lab,' I continued, once the laughter had subsided, 'states that the rounds were of 9mm calibre and most likely fired from an automatic handgun.'

'Blimey!' said Dave. 'He's going out on a limb.' It was a comment that raised another laugh.

I left DI Len Driscoll to send the team out on the various enquiries that were outstanding. We still needed to locate or get better particulars of some of the names that appeared on the two laptops we'd seized. And Wilberforce had at last located the other three names contained in the report that Pim de Jonker claimed had been sent to him by Dirk Cuyper.

However, in view of what we now knew of de Jonker and Cuyper, principally from what Nicola Chance had culled from Downs's laptop, it was possible that those three might be worth looking at after all.

The most likely suspect was Renée Hollande, apparently also known as 'the Duchess'. Wilberforce told me that after extensive enquiries from various useful informants he had finally found a West End address for the woman. But Dave was going to be disappointed: when interviewing a woman associated with prostitution it was advisable, nay imperative, to be accompanied by a woman officer.

'We'll have a trip up to the bright lights of the West End, Kate,' I said.

'Shall we take a Job car, guv?'

'What? And park it in Soho, where someone can pinch it? No, we'll take a taxi.' Given the present state of lawlessness prevailing in Britain thanks to swingeing budget cuts, it had become a new sport to steal police cars or at least let down the tyres.

It came as no surprise that the address we were seeking was above an establishment that catered for the lewd and licentious and advertised all-day live sex shows.

Standing in the doorway of this den of perverted taste was a tired-looking forty-something, trying-to-look-younger, female attired in a red basque, black fishnets – now considered passé even in Soho – and very high heels. This ensemble of unsuccessful allure was completed by a top hat and a silver-topped cane. Her job description required her to persuade the passing gullible to venture inside. And she'll succeed: these naive punters flock to London from the shires in the hope of seeing what they firmly believe to be 'life'. All that will happen, though, is that they'll be ripped off and go home poorer in pocket and no richer in anything else save the wickedness that prevails in the West End of London.

However, whatever other talents this vision of loveliness may have lacked, ability to suss out the Old Bill was not one of them, and she made no attempt to inveigle us into her tawdry establishment.

The door to the flat we wanted was an unremarkable door with only a house number on it, and from my years of experience I knew that 'the Duchess' would be the sort of prostitute whose clients booked her in advance. I also knew that it is a myth to assume that call girls, or however you like to describe them, worked only in the evenings. Some of the women I've encountered told me that they always kept office hours, and that daytime business was much more profitable. It all depends on the clientele, I suppose. Not that I knew whether Renée Hollande was a night worker or a day worker.

Bearing all that in mind, I rang the bell of this unpretentious establishment and waited. Kate stood to one side, where she wouldn't immediately be seen by whoever answered the door.

'Can I help you?' The woman who stood in the doorway was a peroxide blonde, probably nearer sixty than fifty. She was squeezed into a short black dress that was clearly a size too small for her overweight figure. She was wearing black tights and teetered on black patent shoes, which I imagined would be painful to walk in.

'I've come to see the Duchess,' I said.

This announcement evoked no surprise. 'Have you an appointment?' she asked in an Estuary accent that seemed to indicate roots in Essex, possibly Billericay, where, it is rumoured, they put ice cubes in their red wine.

'No, I don't.' I displayed my warrant card, at which point Kate emerged from beside the door.

'Oh Gawd! I s'pose you'd better come in.'

Having showed us into a rather tatty sitting room that probably looked much better in the evenings with subdued lighting, the woman went to fetch 'the Duchess'.

A few moments later a woman entered the room, her satin robe open to reveal tart's underwear as she came towards us.

Probably the wrong side of thirty, she possessed a good figure, was about five ten in height, with shoulder-length Titian hair, and could've fitted the description of the woman Lydia Maxwell had seen entering Cuyper's apartment on two occasions. Her face betrayed a common allure, and she had already applied cosmetics – a little too much lipstick and eye shadow – which seemed to indicate that she was a day worker. On the other hand, she may have been one of those women who never greet visitors without first 'putting on a bit of slap and a dash of lippy', as a friend of my mother used to describe it.

'Dominique said you are from the police, *n'est-ce pas?*' The woman spoke with a French accent that was good enough to have been genuine, or it may have been well rehearsed. But I very much doubted that the overweight 'maid' who answered the door had been named Dominique at birth.

'Are you Renée Hollande?' I asked.

'*Oui.*' The woman sat down and waved a hand languidly to indicate that Kate and I should take a seat. 'What is it that you want? I don't think either of you wants to go to bed with me, so why are you 'ere? You are from the Vice Squad, *non?*' She emitted an intolerant sigh, as though she had been visited frequently by its officers and glanced pointedly at her wrist-watch. 'I do 'ave an appointment at a quarter past eleven.'

'I'm Detective Chief Inspector Brock of the Murder Investigation Team at Scotland Yard and this is Detective Inspector Ebdon,' I said.

'Oh Christ!' Renée Hollande sat up sharply, all pretence at a French accent disappearing instantly. 'Who's been topped, then?'

'Richard Cooper. How well did you know him?'

'I've never heard of him,' said Renée, a little too quickly, and looked away.

'Well, he knows you, mate,' said Kate. 'What's your real name, by the way?'

'Irene Higgins.'

'How many times were you nicked for tomming before you got yourself set up here, Irene?'

'A few. Can't remember the exact number. But you should know. It'll all be written down at West End Central.'

It was strange that Colin Wilberforce hadn't connected Renée Hollande with Irene Higgins when she'd been identified by fingerprints. The only explanation I could think of was that for some reason the name Renée Hollande didn't appear as an alias on Irene Higgins's file. Wilberforce must've traced her through some of his contacts at West End Central police station. It was a slip that Kate for one wouldn't let the otherwise highly efficient Wilberforce forget.

'Where were you on Friday the twenty-sixth of July around midday, Irene? That's a week ago last Friday.'

'Good God, I don't know.' She turned her head slightly and screeched, 'Ma!'

Moments later, the woman previously known as Dominique appeared in the doorway. 'What is it, love?'

'Have a look in my appointments book, Ma, and see if I was working on . . .' Irene stopped and turned back to Kate. 'What date was that?'

'Friday the twenty-sixth of July, around midday.'

'See if I had a john that day, Ma. In fact, you'd better bring me the book.'

'Is Dominique your mother, Irene?' asked Kate.

'Yeah. Pays to keep it in the family. Her real name's Eileen.'

When Irene's mother reappeared she was holding an A4-sized diary, which she handed over to her daughter.

'I was entertaining a Japanese gent by the name of Takahiro Kawano,' said Irene, stumbling over the pronunciation. 'He spent a couple of hours getting laid and forked out a grand.'

'I'm in the wrong bloody job,' muttered Kate. 'And where is Mister Kawano now? Is he staying in London?'

'Nah,' said Irene, 'he's gone back home to Japan. Told me he lives in a place called Kinki, which comes as no surprise after what he got up to.'

'How very convenient,' said Kate. 'And I don't suppose he gave you his exact address there?'

'No, he never. And before you ask, he paid cash, not credit card. I don't think that was his real name anyway.'

'Supposing I was to say that I have a witness who claims she saw you letting yourself into Richard Cooper's apartment with a key, Irene. What would you say to that?' It was a wild attempt on my part to con an admission out of the woman. Lydia Maxwell said she hadn't seen the woman's face, so putting Irene Higgins on an identification parade wouldn't stand a chance. But it was worth a shot.

'I've never been to North Sheen, and I don't even know—' Irene stopped suddenly. 'Oh bugger!' she exclaimed.

'I think we'd better start again,' I said.

'All right, so I did know Dick Cooper and we had a fling.' Irene looked across the room, with what I suspected was a fabricated dreamy expression on her face. 'He liked dressing me up in some kinky gear what he kept there. Mind you, it cost him.'

I had great difficulty in believing all this. There was no doubt that Irene Higgins, alias Renée Hollande, was a well-established West End prostitute, and looking at her I should think she was good at what she did. But she had to have had a very good reason for travelling to North Sheen for what she described as 'a fling'. That would offend her business sense, and these women are very good at business, believe me. To coin an apt phrase, they don't miss a trick.

'OK, let's have the real reason now, Irene,' I said. 'For a start, who's your benefactor?'

'How d'you know about him?' Irene's eyes opened wide.

'I haven't always investigated murders,' I said. 'A lot of women in your line of business have a backer. Or a pimp.' I took a wild guess. 'And Victor Downs was yours, wasn't he?'

Irene Higgins remained silent.

'I'll take that as a yes, then. You see we found your name on a list in Cooper's possession.' I had no intention of telling this woman exactly how it came into our possession or mention the fingerprint identification, at least not yet. 'What was it all about, turf war?'

'Yeah!' Irene let out a sigh. 'Cooper was a Belgian, you see. His name was Dirk Cuyper. And Victor was convinced that he was part of a gang of sex slavers bringing girls in from Romania and God knows where else. Well, Victor don't like people muscling in, especially when they're foreigners. He asked me to get to know Dirk and see what I could get out of him. Well, I did manage to find out quite a lot before he sussed me out.'

'Did you have a key to his place?' asked Kate.

'Oh yeah. I'd got me feet well under the table there, or I s'pose I should say in his bed.'

'You know that Victor Downs has been murdered, I suppose, Irene?' I said.

'What?' Irene's face registered shock. 'When did that go down?'

'The day before yesterday.'

'Who done for him, then?' she asked, having made a quick recovery.

'We don't know yet, but we will.' I turned to Kate. 'Read out those other names we found on Downs's laptop, Kate.'

'I know that Anna Veeltkamp was one of Dirk's lot,' said Irene, when Kate had finished. 'But I've not heard of any of the others.'

'Finally, what about Bernie Stamper, Sidney Ellis – known as the Caretaker – and Charlie Chatterjee?'

Irene's face dissolved in a smile. 'You're having me on. Did you make them names up?'

'No. I've already interviewed Bernie Stamper in Stone Mill nick.'

'Don't tell me he knew me.'

'No, he didn't, but we found your name with those other three on the list that Cuyper had, that I mentioned just now.'

Irene Higgins shook her head. 'I've never heard of any of 'em,' she said.

That tended to reinforce my original view: that Cuyper had made them up to appease Pim de Jonker, or whoever his paymaster was, to justify the expense of living the high life in London.

We took our leave of Irene Higgins, otherwise known as Renée 'the Duchess' Hollande.

'What d'you think, Harry?' asked Kate as we were waiting to find a cab.

'She could have murdered Cuyper, Kate. In fact, if she was working for Downs, who thought Cuyper's lot were trying to steal his trade, the motive's perfect. And I don't like her alibi. Too convenient to claim she was having it off with a passing Japanese visitor who has now returned to Japan. But we haven't got enough to nick her. Yet.'

'But they weren't her dabs on Cuyper's safe, Harry.'

'It doesn't mean she didn't have access to it, Kate. She could have gone into it without leaving prints. After all, she'd have known that her prints were on record and it would have been useful if Wilberforce had found that out before we paid her a visit.'

FIFTEEN

It was getting on for lunchtime on Tuesday, and Kate, Dave and I were in my office mulling over what we'd achieved so far, and planning our next moves, when Linda Mitchell arrived with information that would at last move my struggling murder enquiry towards a satisfactory conclusion.

On most of the occasions when we met, Linda was attired in the unflattering coveralls and sort of mobcap that comprised her working gear. When, however, we had a conference away from a crime scene, she usually wore a smart trouser suit. Today she had excelled herself, by wearing an attractive green dress and high heels and she had disciplined her black hair into a neat ponytail. In fact, it is fair to say that she didn't look much older than thirty. But down-to-earth Linda destroyed that illusion with her opening sentence.

'If you're wondering why I'm all tarted up, Harry, it's because I've got the afternoon off. It's my youngest granddaughter's engagement party and I daren't miss it.'

'Engagement! How old is she, Linda?'

'Nineteen.'

'And she's the *youngest*?'

'Yes. However, I'm not here to have a homey chat about my family. Much more important is that I've just received the result of the fingerprint search from Brussels.'

'Is it good news?' asked Kate.

'That's for you detectives to decide, Kate,' said Linda, and glanced sideways at me with one of her impish smiles. 'The Belgian police have identified the woman whose prints we found inside Cuyper's safe and elsewhere in his apartment as Chantal Flaubert. She's a Belgian citizen who was born in Knokke-le-Zoute in Wallonia.' She handed me the Belgian report. 'All the details – date of birth and all that sort of thing – are on there.'

'That name's cropped up already,' said Dave, thumbing through a docket he had resting on his knee. 'Chantal Flaubert was one of the names on Cuyper's laptop.'

'Her prints were also found in Downs's house,' continued Linda. 'And more particularly in his bedroom.'

'I wonder if she was the woman he was having sex with,' suggested Kate.

'I'm sorry to disappoint you, Kate,' Linda said, 'but there was nothing in the swabs that Dr Mortlock took or from the bedding that was examined at the lab to indicate that sexual intercourse ever took place between Downs and his killer. But I suppose that having killed Ram Mookjai on the way up to Downs's bedroom, the murderer probably thought it politic not to hang around for too long.'

'In any event,' I said, 'if we amass enough evidence to charge this woman with murder, the question of whether she had sex with Downs is irrelevant.'

'There was one other snippet of information that might explain a lot,' Linda continued. 'I was told by my Belgian contact that Chantal Flaubert has a master's degree in computer science from the University of Antwerp. I think that's included in there, too.' She waved a hand at the Belgian police report she'd given me.

'So she could have hacked into Cuyper's computer,' I said thoughtfully. 'But I still don't understand why she didn't worry about leaving her fingerprints all over the place.'

'I think I might be able to answer that, Harry,' said Linda. 'Recently the Belgian authorities have required applicants for passports to provide a set of their fingerprints. Chantal Flaubert probably thought that those prints would be kept at the passport office and nowhere else. But I suspect what happened is that the Belgian Ministry of Internal Affairs thought it was too good an opportunity to miss, and decided that they should be placed on the national database. It may have had something to do with the Belgian government and the police being criticized fairly heavily of late about sex crimes that were not investigated. They're probably a bit sensitive about it, and the more information they can amass about their citizens the better they'll be equipped to deal with crime.'

'That's ripper,' said Kate, 'but the one thing they haven't told us is where we can find her.'

'We might get lucky,' said Dave. 'If Chantal Flaubert has a passport, the Belgians will have a photograph of her on record. If they're prepared to send us a copy, we could do worse than circulate it in the national press.'

Linda Mitchell smiled. 'I thought of that, too, Dave,' she said. 'They've agreed to send us a copy. It should be with you this afternoon sometime. But now, if you'll excuse me,' she added as she stood up, 'I've an engagement party to attend.'

'Give our congratulations to your granddaughter, Linda, and thanks for everything you've done,' I said. 'You obviously know the right people in the right places.'

'Don't you, Harry?' said Linda. And pointing silently towards the commander's office, did a back kick with one leg and winked as she swept out of the door.

I still couldn't believe she was a grandmother.

I treated Kate and Dave to lunch at my favourite Italian restaurant and even paid for a taxi back to the office, such was my euphoria at being convinced that we were going to solve the murders of Dirk Cuyper, Victor Downs and Ram Mookjai.

As we walked into the incident room, Colin Wilberforce handed me an envelope covered with important-looking seals. 'An official at the Belgian Embassy sent for the Diplomatic Protection Group liaison inspector and asked him to get this to you ASAP, sir. A DPG motorcyclist arrived with it about five minutes ago.'

'I wonder why the embassy got involved.'

'Apparently it was sent by diplomatic bag this morning, sir,' said Wilberforce. 'According to the DPG bloke it's the safest way, and these DPG blokes know about such things.'

I adjourned to my office, and called for Kate and Dave to join me. The envelope from the embassy contained an A5-sized photograph of Chantal Flaubert and all the details about her that the Belgians held in their official records.

'Well, I'm damned!' I said, and handed the photograph to Dave. 'Anyone you know?'

'The cunning bitch,' Dave said, and passed the photo to Kate.

'Bloody hell!' Kate exclaimed, and handed back the photograph.

'At least we know where to find her,' said Dave, 'but how do we go about it? Although we never thought so at the time, I reckon she'll now have to be regarded as armed and dangerous. I suppose we'll need the full circus.'

'I reckon so,' I said. 'Get this photograph reproduced urgently. I want a copy to be given to each officer on the team, but make sure that DS Carpenter and DC Appleby get one first. They're doing day duty in Cuyper's apartment.'

'I know . . . sir,' said Dave. 'I'll put it in hand straight away.'

'Oh, and get one to Mark Hodgson, the concierge at Cockcroft Lodge, also as a matter of urgency.'

Despite Dave's plea that we ought to 'nick the bitch ASAP', it would not be possible to make the arrest before the morning of Thursday, if then. The reason was the need to coordinate the various units that would of necessity be involved in the operation, and that takes time. I agreed with Kate that if our suspect was ruthless enough to have murdered three people and at once proved that she was an expert pistol shot, care must be taken in arresting her. There was little doubt in my mind that she would not be taken easily, and I didn't want any police officer or any member of the public to be killed or even wounded. Furthermore, I would prefer that this woman be taken alive and unharmed.

The main people to be involved, apart from our own, were members of the Tactical Firearms Unit. This meant liaising first with one of their inspectors, who would assess the situation. He would then pass it upwards for a superintendent to look at, and if he gave the green light we were in business. The local police would have to be informed and a request made for road closures while the operation was carried out. All in all, it differed somewhat from the 'good old days' when you knocked on a suspect's front door and told him to put his boots on because he was nicked.

But before any of these preparations and the concomitant endless briefings took place there was one vital enquiry to be made, and I sent Kate Ebdon and Dave Poole to make it. And as it turned out, it was as well that I did.

At half past eleven on Wednesday morning, Kate and Dave returned to the office.

'It was a blow out,' said Kate.

'What d'you mean, a blow out?'

'To coin an apt phrase, guv,' said Dave, 'the bird has flown.'

'Dammit!' I exclaimed. 'We've got her phone number, Dave. Give it a try.' I pushed my telephone across the desk.

Dave tapped out the number and listened only briefly before replacing the receiver. 'It's gone to a message answering service,' he said. 'I reckon she's had us over.'

'Dammit!' I said for the second time.

'I've got another line of enquiry, guv,' continued Dave. 'Give me a couple of minutes to make a phone call.'

'Use this phone,' I said.

'I need to look up the number.'

Ten minutes later, Dave returned and handed me a piece of paper. 'That's where she is, guv'nor.'

'Where the hell is Greenham?' I asked.

'It's a village in Somerset, not far from Wellington.'

'I don't even know where that is. Which police force covers the Somerset area?'

'Er, the Avon and Somerset Police . . . sir.'

'I shall make enquiries of the aforementioned police force,' I said, ignoring Dave's veiled sarcasm. 'Incidentally, how the hell did you find that out so quickly?'

'My informants are many and various,' said Dave mysteriously.

The Somerset constable assigned the task had not been a police officer for very long, and the excitement of being involved in an enquiry for Scotland Yard, albeit on the very periphery, had inflated his ego to the extent that he had become a little blasé. And the instruction that he was to wear plain clothes had only served to add to the perceived importance of what he was doing. Unfortunately, he had not yet had time to acquire those essential tools of the experienced police officer: local knowledge and the innate suspicion known as copper's nose.

He had been ordered by his inspector not to knock on the door of the house where the woman in whom Scotland Yard had an interest was supposed to be living, but to make what are known euphemistically as 'local enquiries'. He alighted from his unmarked police car at eleven o'clock on Wednesday morning, and went to the house opposite the one where the suspect was thought to reside.

'Good morning, sir. I'm a police officer.' The young constable discreetly displayed his warrant card.

'And I s'pose you've come to arrest me for summat else I ain't done. Again.' That hostile greeting came from a man some fifty years of age. He was scruffily dressed in an old tweed jacket, a torn striped shirt with no collar, moleskin trousers and heavy boots. And, as he always did, indoors or out, he was wearing an old cloth cap. This surly individual was no friend of the police and regarded the officer with grave suspicion. There was a good reason: he had several convictions for poaching, and fishing in privately owned streams, and considered that the police who had charged him on those occasions to have been overzealous.

'I'm making enquiries on behalf of the Metropolitan Police, sir,' began the constable importantly. Had he known of the man's previous convictions and reputation, he would not have approached him in the first place.

'Oh ah!' exclaimed the man. The Somerset vernacular could have meant something or nothing, depending on the recipient's interpretation. He raised a dirty forefinger to scratch at the three days of stubble that adorned his chin.

'Would you happen to know if this woman has just moved into the house opposite, sir?' the constable asked naively, and produced a photograph.

'Oh ah! I think she be there right enough, Constable,' said the man, scratching his chin again. 'Be about a week since, I wouldn't wonder.'

'Thank you very much, sir.' The constable put the photograph back in his pocket, turned and took a pace or two. Then he paused and retraced his steps. 'I'd be obliged if you didn't mention my visit to the lady if you happen to see her, sir.' Given the sensitivity of the enquiry, it was unfortunate that the constable had failed to recognize that a man who expressed anti-police sentiments from the outset was not to be relied upon. But as has been said, he was not too experienced in either police work or indeed the broader ways of the world. He scribbled a few words in his notebook, then drove back to Wellington.

Standing in his doorway, the poacher watched the policeman depart and then crossed the road to the house opposite. He banged on the door, and when the woman answered he told her what had just transpired.

Back at Wellington police station, the constable sat down and wrote a brief report for an officer called Detective Chief Inspector Brock of the Murder Investigation Team at New Scotland Yard. That done, he stared dreamily out of the window for a moment or two. Chewing the end of his ballpoint pen, he wondered whether to apply for a transfer to the Metropolitan Police.

I received the report from the Avon and Somerset Police at two o'clock on Wednesday afternoon.

'She's there,' I said to Kate and Dave. 'Now is when it begins to get complicated.'

'Are you going to let the locals arrest her, guv?' asked Kate.

'Not likely. It's not that I don't trust them to do their job properly, but there are always complications. I want to interrogate this woman when we have her in custody, but if local officers caution her just to be on the safe side, I'm stymied. If we arrest her, I needn't caution her until I decide to charge her, as I must once I'm satisfied that there is sufficient evidence to do so.'

'I rather think we knew all that . . . sir,' said Dave. 'But what do we do now?'

'We tell Somerset that we're coming down to effect the arrest, and would appreciate local firearms support as the suspect is believed to be armed and dangerous.'

'I can see why you said it begins to get complicated,' said Kate.

'I think we need to bring out the big guns,' I said.

'Like the DAC, guv?' queried Dave.

'Exactly so. I'll get across to the Yard right now.'

I made a phone call to Fiona, the DAC's secretary, and after a brief chat with the boss she told me to come over straight away.

*   *   *

'It looks as though you're near to wrapping up this job, Harry. Have a pew.' The DAC gestured to an armchair and sat down in the one facing me. 'So, what can I do?'

I explained the problem of involving the Avon and Somerset Police. It was not that I had any concerns at all about their efficiency, but more that when two police forces work together their officers have to be fully aware of everybody's role. Otherwise an operation of this sort can go disastrously wrong. And that's why I needed the DAC's intervention: to smooth the waters.

'Who do you intend taking with you, Harry?'

'DI Ebdon and DS Poole, guv'nor.'

'Good choice.' The DAC was not a man to mess about. Or to be messed about with. He buzzed his secretary. 'Get me the Chief Constable of Avon and Somerset, Fiona, please.'

The DAC had spoken to the Somerset chief, who it turned out was an old friend. I got the impression that the DAC knew most people who were likely to be able to assist him when the necessity arose.

The upshot was that the arrest had been scheduled for the following day, Thursday. It was now thirteen days since the murder of Dirk Cuyper, and five days after Downs's and Mookjai's murders.

It was 175 miles to Wellington police station, where we were due to meet the local officers assigned to support the arrest. Dave's usual 'positive' driving got us there in just under three hours and we arrived at ten o'clock.

The superintendent who was to oversee matters introduced himself and asked me to brief the armed backup officers. I told them precisely what we intended doing and told them that Kate, Dave and I were also armed, just so there wouldn't be any misunderstanding. I showed the superintendent the arrest warrant which I'd obtained the previous day from the Chief Magistrate at Westminster. We didn't really need one, but the DAC had suggested that everyone would be happier if we had one in our possession.

With the armed support team's vehicle leading the way, we

drove out to Greenham and stopped just out of sight of the
cottage where Chantal Flaubert had been reported as living.
Kate and I walked up the path and knocked at the door, while
a number of armed officers deployed themselves covertly, ready
to rush in at the first sign of opposition from the Belgian woman.

There was no reply despite our knocking several times.

'What d'you think, Mr Brock?' asked the superintendent
when we'd retreated for a quick conference.

'If you're agreeable, sir,' I said, 'I think we should break in.
The warrant empowers us to do so, and for all we know our
suspect might've committed suicide.'

'I agree,' the superintendent said, signalled to the inspector
in charge of the armed response unit and issued a number of
instructions.

Two officers in protective riot gear raced up the path and
smashed in the front door with a rammer. Another six armed
officers swarmed into the house and spread out with shouts of
'Police'.

After a few minutes a sergeant appeared and spoke to his
inspector, who then joined the superintendent and me.

'The house is empty, sir,' said the inspector, 'and according
to my sergeant it appears to have been vacated in something of
a hurry.'

The superintendent turned in time to see the man who lived
opposite standing in his doorway, hands in pockets and a broad
smile on his face.

'I'll just have a word with that chap, Mr Brock. He's one
of our local poachers.' And crossing the road, said, 'Well, Jethro,
did you think that I'd brought all these officers just to arrest
you?'

'I bain't been a-poaching, if that's what you means, mister.'

'Do you know if the woman who lives across the road has
moved, Jethro?'

'Ay, I reckon,' said Jethro. 'Yesterday afternoon it were, not
long after that young copper come here of the morning
a-showing her photey around.'

'Did he actually call at her house, Jethro?'

'No, mister. He only come here and said summat about them
police up London wanting to have a word with her. Well, I

thought I'd better let her know, being neighbourly like, so's she could p'raps give them Scotland Yard chaps a call on that funny phone of hers, the one that ain't got no wires attached to it. I mean to say, I was only a-helping the police, like.'

'Very public-spirited of you,' replied the superintendent through gritted teeth, and marched back to where the inspector was talking to his sergeant. 'Find out the name of the PC who was making enquiries here yesterday and tell him I want to see him. Like now!'

SIXTEEN

It was a despondent group that gathered in the incident room on Friday morning. I had been so sure that we were about to lay hands on the elusive Chantal Flaubert that it was a huge disappointment to find she'd slipped though our fingers.

At the far end of the room, Wilberforce replaced the receiver of his telephone just as I was wrapping up my briefing to the team and was on the point of taking Kate and Dave across the road for a cup of coffee.

'That was a call from the DAC's secretary, sir,' said Wilberforce. 'Would you ring him ASAP.'

I told Kate and Dave to come into my office in case it was something that would affect them, and tapped out the DAC's direct line number. He sympathized with me over the Somerset job going belly up, and suggested it was possible that Chantal Flaubert had now fled back to her native Belgium. He said that he had spoken to his contact in Brussels, who had undertaken to have enquiries made urgently, starting in the Knokke-le-Zoute area.

When I'd finished my conversation with the DAC, I told Kate and Dave what he'd said.

'Very helpful,' said Dave, 'but it doesn't really get us any further forward, does it?'

'Not immediately, no. But if she has returned to Belgium, I'm sure the Belgian police will track her down.'

'Then we'll have to go through the whole extradition rigmarole, I suppose,' said Kate.

'I'm glad you volunteered for that, Kate. The DAC also suggested that we start preparing an application for a European arrest warrant, just in case the Belgians find this woman.'

'How the hell do we do that?'

'I haven't a clue,' I said. 'The best idea is to ring our contact at the Crown Prosecution Service and ask her.'

'Thanks a bundle, guv,' said Kate sarcastically. In common with most detectives, she would face up to a violent criminal without a second's hesitation, but was horrified by the prospect of dealing with complex form-filling. Something detectives learn early in their career is that the letters CPS also stand for 'copious paper submissions'.

However, things were about to change.

'Can I help you, madam?' Mark Hodgson was standing in the doorway of the concierge's office at the entrance to Cockcroft Lodge, contemplating what to do about lunch.

'Oh, perhaps you can, sir.' The woman who had been walking past was about five foot ten tall and had long Titian hair. She paused and retraced her steps. 'I'm Doctor Saskia Cuyper, Mr Dirk Cuyper's widow. I've only just arrived back in Belgium from the Congo and then came straight here. I am with Médecins Sans Frontières, you see. I have come to see about removing my husband's belongings.' The woman looked immeasurably sad. A tear trickled down her cheek and she shook her head irritably as if trying to dislodge it. 'It was a terrible shock to learn that he was murdered, you know. There I am in Africa trying to save lives, and here in England my husband is shot to death. Where is the justice in that?'

'You have my sympathy, madam. Apartment E in the first block is where Mr Cuyper lived.' Hodgson pointed at a block that was about fifty yards from where he was standing. 'It's on the first floor.'

'Thank you so much.' The woman gave Hodgson a smile.

'But how are you going to get in?'

'I have a key,' said the woman and, producing it from her shoulder bag, held it up.

'That's all right, then.' Hodgson smiled and gave the woman a friendly wave of farewell.

However, his years of service in the Royal Military Police had honed his powers of observation and his innate awareness of when something wasn't quite right. Although the woman spoke with a convincing foreign accent and had been extremely confident in her approach, he was not easily fooled. He was sure she was the subject of the photograph the police had given him. He dashed back into the lodge and dialled the number of Cuyper's apartment.

'Carpenter.'

'There's a woman on her way up, Sergeant,' said Hodgson. 'She gives the name of Doctor Saskia Cuyper and claims to be Cuyper's widow. She gave me some sob story about coming back from the Congo; and although she sounded foreign, I'm not sure she is. That said, she's a dead ringer for the woman in the photograph one of your blokes gave me a couple of days ago, despite having long Titian hair. Oh, and she's got a key to the apartment.'

'Thanks, Mark. Do me a favour and ring our incident room with that info, will you?' Carpenter started to give him the number, but Hodgson interrupted.

'It's all right, Sarge, I've got a note of it.'

'And perhaps after that you'd alert the local police.'

Detective Sergeant Liz Carpenter moved to a point where she would be behind the front door when it was opened. She directed Detective Constable John Appleby to stand in the kitchen area, ready to challenge the woman that the concierge had told her was on her way up to the apartment. Carpenter was in the right position to tackle the visitor, and restrain her if it became apparent that she was about to resist arrest.

There were a few tense moments while the two detectives awaited the arrival of the woman who might be Chantal Flaubert. Or might not. Then they heard a key in the lock. The front door swung open, and the woman walked confidently into the room.

'I'm a police officer,' said Appleby, his hand flicking back the skirt of his jacket and moving towards the revolver in his hip holster.

But the woman was faster. Her right hand was already holding an automatic pistol and with no compunction whatsoever she raised it and shot Appleby twice before he had a chance to draw his own weapon. He collapsed unconscious, his face becoming deathly pale within seconds.

Realizing that she had walked into a trap and sensing too late that the concierge had probably alerted the officer she'd just shot to her pending arrival, and might even have called other officers, she turned, intent on escaping.

But she found that Liz Carpenter, in a crouched stance, her revolver in a classic two-handed grip, was facing her. The woman again raised her pistol, but this time it was Carpenter who was the faster. Suddenly, two blows like a steam hammer hit the woman's right shoulder, spun her round and toppled her so that she collapsed on the floor. Her pistol flew from her paralysed hand, skittering out of reach across the tiled section of the kitchen area, and her Titian wig fell off, revealing long black hair tightly pinned up.

Liz Carpenter picked up the pistol, then leaned over the woman who was now clutching her right shoulder and moaning loudly. 'I'm an armed police officer,' said Carpenter. 'Put down your weapon or I'll shoot. By the way, Chantal Flaubert, you're nicked.'

Standing up, she took her mobile from her pocket and called an ambulance. 'Two casualties with gunshot wounds,' she told the control room. Next she called for police assistance, but already sirens could be heard approaching Cockcroft Lodge.

Instinct told me that it must be Chantal Flaubert who had asked for Cuyper's apartment, and the moment that Mark Hodgson telephoned the incident room I summoned a traffic car to get Kate, Dave and me to North Sheen as fast as possible.

And they did. Traffic Unit drivers of the Metropolitan Police are the finest there are, but when they're driving me I always get this overwhelming fear of sudden death. Mine! It's about eight miles from Belgravia police station through the centre of London to North Sheen. Any sane person would take anything up to an hour to do the journey. The traffic guys got us there in eleven minutes.

When we arrived, the local police had already sealed off the entire Cockcroft Lodge estate. Tapes were in place and an incident officer was on post with the inevitable clipboard to record the comings and goings of interested parties.

Once we had identified ourselves, the three of us made our way to Cuyper's apartment.

'What's the SP, Liz?' I asked.

Liz Carpenter gave me a succinct account of everything that had occurred since receiving the phone call from Mark Hodgson. 'She shot John Appleby the moment she walked through the door, and he doesn't look to be in good shape. When Flaubert turned, I put two rounds into her right shoulder, so I doubt that she'll be practising marksmanship any time soon. The paramedics summoned an air ambulance and John's been airlifted to the Royal London, along with Flaubert. Local police accompanied them and they've undertaken to provide a guard on Flaubert until such time as we can set up a more permanent arrangement.'

'You did a bloody good job, Liz. Are you feeling all right?'

'Not really. It should have been me that faced Flaubert when she came in. Instead, I told Appleby to challenge her so that I could grab her from behind if the necessity arose, but she didn't stop to talk, she just opened fire.' Carpenter's decision to deploy Appleby and herself in those positions was to haunt her for the rest of her life. 'I just want to be in court when she goes down for a life-means-life sentence.'

'I'll get you taken back to the factory, Liz. Leave a short statement outlining your action today, and then go home.'

'There's one other thing, guv. My firearm needs to be zeroed. I aimed at the centre of that bloody woman's body mass, but I was well off to the right. Twice!'

Now the whole machinery of investigation swung into action. The Professional Standards Department would be involved; and because a member of the public, albeit a woman wanted for triple murder, had been shot by a police officer, the matter would also be referred to the Independent Police Complaints Commission. Just in case we'd infringed Flaubert's human rights. The only person who would be delighted by the generation of acres of paper would be our beloved commander who, since the DAC's intervention, had kept his head well below the parapet. But now he had a legitimate justification to become involved once again.

Linda Mitchell, our crime-scene manager, arrived together with her team of scientific investigators and set to work.

Detective Sergeant Tom Challis walked into the apartment. 'I thought you might need some wheels, guv. I know the Black

Rats brought you here, but they've done a runner. I've got a car outside whenever you're good to go.'

'Thanks, Tom. First port of call is the Royal London Hospital. I want to see how John Appleby is, and I also want to find out when Flaubert is likely to be fit enough to be interviewed.'

Leaving Challis to assist at the scene, Dave took the car keys and we went downstairs.

It was fourteen miles from Cockcroft Lodge to the Royal London, in Whitechapel, and after a tortuous drive through rush-hour traffic we arrived at the hospital just after five o'clock.

We were directed to an office and were immediately joined by a senior surgeon.

'Chief Inspector Brock, is it?'

'Yes, doctor, and this is Detective Sergeant Poole.'

The surgeon acknowledged Dave, then looked back at me, a grave expression on his face. 'I'm sorry to have to tell you that your detective, John Appleby, died on the operating table, Chief Inspector. He'd received two rounds straight to the heart. Even in cases like that there is sometimes a slender hope, but it was not to be so with your man. I'm very sorry, but we did our best.'

'I'm sure you did, doctor,' I said, 'and thank you for your efforts. You also have Chantal Flaubert here.'

'Yes, Chief Inspector. It was a through-and-through injury, but the collar bone was chipped and we operated to repair the damage. Nevertheless, the shoulder will still take some time to heal and she'll never have the full use of her right arm again because there was also damage to the surrounding muscle tissue, nerves and ligaments. She'll certainly need a long period of convalescence to recover fully from the injury.'

'Where she's going, she'll have plenty of time to recuperate, doctor,' said Dave.

The surgeon smiled. 'Yes, I rather thought that would be the case.'

'How soon will she be fit enough to be interviewed?' I asked.

'I would be inclined to leave it until Monday at the earliest, Chief Inspector,' said the surgeon. 'Unless you're in a desperate hurry.'

'Not really, doctor. She's under arrest, so she won't be going anywhere. Incidentally, there'll be a constant police guard on her.'

The surgeon nodded. 'It has happened before, Chief Inspector. We're quite accustomed to accommodating the occasional villain. Which is why I suggested leaving the interview until Monday.' He gave me a crooked smile. 'You don't want her counsel to suggest that she was still under the influence of anaesthetic when a statement was taken, do you?'

'I can see you know a thing or two about this business, doctor.'

'My wife's a barrister,' responded the surgeon.

As we returned to the reception area, a young woman came through the main entrance accompanied by Detective Inspector Len Driscoll.

'This is Patricia Appleby, guv'nor,' said Driscoll. 'John's wife. This is Detective Chief Inspector Brock, Mrs Appleby.'

'Oh, you're his boss, aren't you, Mr Brock? How is John?'

Patricia Appleby was a pretty young woman whose face had a classical beauty about it, surrounded as it was by stylishly cut brown hair that was not quite shoulder length. Although she was dressed in jeans and a white sweater, she managed to look like a model. Perhaps she was, I thought. In fact, looking at her, I was sure that she was a model or perhaps an actress. John had never discussed his wife or shown us her photograph, and now I had met her, I didn't blame him; coppers are a lecherous lot. The outcome was that none of us on the team knew anything about her, apart from the fact that she was a working wife, that the couple lived in Pinner, and that they had no children.

'There's a room just across the hall that I was told we can use, sir,' said Dave. This time it wasn't a sarcastic honorific. Apart from the fact that this was not a suitable occasion for irony, he always addressed me as 'sir' in the presence of the public.

I escorted Patricia Appleby into a room that was obviously set aside for such situations. There were a number of armchairs and, among other things, a water dispenser and several boxes of tissues.

'What is it, Mr Brock? Is it serious?' Patricia Appleby seemed to sense that the news would not be good, but she was about to learn that it was devastating.

'I'm afraid they couldn't save him, Mrs Appleby.' There was no other way to say it. Telling members of the public that one of their nearest and dearest had been murdered was difficult enough. To tell the wife of a police officer that he had been murdered doing his duty was even harder.

'Oh!' Patricia Appleby sat down suddenly in one of the armchairs and stared at a picture on the opposite wall. There were no tears, no outward signs of grief, just a stoic fixation on the picture. Dave handed her the box of tissues, but she just shook her head. After some minutes, she looked up at me, an appealing expression on her face. 'Would it be possible to speak to the surgeon?'

'Is that a good idea, Patricia?' I asked. 'I hope you don't mind me calling you Patricia.'

'Not at all.' Patricia's response was quite calm. 'I'd like to know exactly what procedures were undertaken. I'm a nursing sister, you see, and I understand these things.'

'I didn't know that, Patricia,' I said, thinking to myself that despite all my years of experience in assessing people it's still possible to get it wrong. I had been sure she was a model or an actress. 'Dave, see what you can do, and perhaps you could get some coffee?'

'Yes, sir.'

The same surgeon came very quickly, and Dave and I left him to explain to Patricia Appleby what he had done to try to save her husband.

Twenty minutes later, she emerged from the room, still dry-eyed and outwardly composed. In a matter of seconds in a luxury apartment in North Sheen two rounds from a pistol fired by a callous killer had completely changed Patricia Appleby's life. For her, nothing would ever be the same again.

'I'd like to go home now, Mr Brock,' she said.

I signalled to Len Driscoll, who had been waiting in reception, and asked him to see Patricia Appleby home.

'I've got a family support officer from Bromley standing by, guv,' he said, 'and local police will chase away the press.'

I now telephoned the DAC and told him of the latest turn of events, principally the death of John Appleby. The Commissioner would have to be informed immediately because it did not bode

well for any of us in the chain of command if he learned of
the death of an officer from the media. Or worse still, a telephone
call from a journalist more interested than anything else in filing
the story ahead of his competitors.

Naturally enough, my team was in a sombre mood when I
returned to the incident room. The death of one of our own is
the hardest thing for any of us to bear. Anger and a desire for
revenge were the foremost natural reactions, followed by a
feeling of utter impotence. There would be annoying little
reminders that John Appleby was no longer there. A pay slip
perhaps, a memo telling him to attend the next firearms refresher,
or a note from the Traffic Branch asking for details of his
renewed driving licence. The administrative machinery of the
Metropolitan Police is like an oil tanker: it takes time for it to
slow down before eventually stopping.

SEVENTEEN

It was common sense that I should be accompanied by a woman officer when I interviewed Chantal Flaubert, and I decided to take Kate. But I intended that Dave Poole should be there too. He was conversant with the wider picture of the investigation and could make a note of questions that needed to be asked, now or later.

It was going to be a tricky interview. I could not ask any questions about the murder of John Appleby because it was what the Americans would call a 'slam dunk'. We were in the unique position of having a witness in the shape of DS Carpenter, and Flaubert would be charged with murder the moment she was fit enough.

What interested me more was the motive behind the killings of Cuyper, Downs and Ram Mookjai, and I intended to discover what that was all about. We didn't have much in the way of evidence that Flaubert had murdered them, although I was certain she had. But assumption is not evidence. There were the fingerprints, of course, but she would probably have a plausible excuse for them being there. We also had the ballistics report proving that the pistol used to murder John Appleby had also been used to kill Cuyper, Downs and Mookjai. That evidence helped up to a point, but it didn't tell us who had actually pulled the trigger on the first three occasions.

When we arrived at the hospital, we were shown to a private room outside which a middle-aged uniformed constable from Bethnal Green police station was seated.

'Can I help you?' The PC leaped to his feet as we approached, and stood in front of the door to bar any entrance, his hand hovering over his revolver holster. This copper obviously knew his job.

'DCI Brock, DI Ebdon and DS Poole, all from HMCC.' We produced our warrant cards and I was pleased to see that the PC inspected them closely.

'Right you are, sirs, ma'am. Can't be too careful.'

'I'm pleased to see it. Any unusual visitors attempted to gain access?'

'No, sir.' The PC tapped his revolver. 'It's what you'd call an unwise course of action if they did try,' he added with a grin, and opened the door.

Chantal Flaubert was sitting up in bed reading a magazine. Her long black hair was loose and draped across her shoulders. DC Sheila Armitage, who was on the day shift, was seated nearby. She stood up as we entered.

'Everything all right, Sheila?' I asked.

'Yes, sir. Miss Flaubert hasn't said a word since she got back from the operating theatre.'

Chantal Flaubert looked up and grinned. 'Why speak to the monkey when you know the organ grinder will turn up sooner or later?' she said, and blew me a kiss.

Dave Poole set up the portable tape recorder that we used on occasions such as this, when an interview could not be conducted at a police station, and I announced who was present.

'You are entitled to have a solicitor present,' I said as Kate and I drew up chairs and seated ourselves close to the woman's bed.

'A fat lot of good that would do,' snorted Flaubert.

'May I take that as meaning you're waiving your right to legal representation at this stage?'

'You may, my dear Chief Inspector.' She actually laughed at me. 'In fact, at any stage.'

'What is your real name? Is it Chantal Flaubert? Or is it Katherine Thompson?' I asked.

'It's Chantal Flaubert in Belgium and Katherine Thompson over here,' she said enigmatically, 'but you can still call me Kat. No doubt you'll have found out from the Belgian police that I was born in Knokke-le-Zoute and I'm thirty-two years of age. My father was Gaston Flaubert, a Walloon cabinetmaker, but my mother was English. Her name was Katherine Thompson, which I used as an alias. As a result, I speak French, Flemish and English. All fluently and with the accent appropriate to whichever language I'm speaking.'

This was a good start. Kat Thompson was obviously one of

those vain criminals who could not help boasting. I hoped that she would also boast about her marksmanship with a pistol.

In her role as Katherine Thompson, former health-club manager, she had been very convincing when we'd interviewed her on the day she was moving out of her flat in Ham. She had been confident and not at all disconcerted when we had arrived and started asking questions about the murder of Dirk Cuyper. Maybe she thought that by telling us she was moving to Thames Ditton, when she knew she was not, she assumed she could not be found. She'd certainly tried to avoid capture.

What really amazed me about this woman was the complete volte-face I was now witnessing. When Dave and I had interviewed her previously, she'd been polite, open and not at all aggressive, apart from mildly berating the removal men, and had even gone as far as gently flirting with me, albeit just the once.

But I now realized that she was a consummate professional assassin, entirely devoid of conscience and convinced that she could outwit the police and retain her liberty. If only we'd had the evidence that would have justified us searching her and her flat on that occasion, we might have prevented the murders of Victor Downs and Ram Mookjai. And more importantly, the senseless killing of John Appleby.

'I'm not going to talk my way out of killing that copper, am I?' Thompson asked suddenly.

'I very much doubt it,' I said cautiously.

'So what'll I get for that?'

'I don't know, Kat,' I said, even though I had a very good idea. 'It's up to the judge.'

'Oh come on, Brocky darling. Don't piss me about. What's the going rate?' Puckering her sensuous lips, Thompson blew me another kiss.

I was about to give another cautious answer when Kate spoke. 'Let me put it this way, mate: I don't reckon you'll need to buy a new frock for at least thirty years.' She knew just how to put coquettish women in their place.

'That's what I thought. You could have told me that, Brocky, instead of letting your little Aboriginal friend open her big mouth.'

If she'd thought that an insulting comment of that nature would incite Kate to an act of violence, she was disappointed. Kate stared at her, smiled a smile that conveyed just a hint of pity and slowly shook her head. Having been the occasional recipient of one of those smiles, I knew just how indicative of disapproval they could be, carrying as they did an implication similar to Dave's use of the word 'sir'.

'Well now, Brocky,' continued Thompson, 'supposing I were to give you chapter and verse on the whole of Vic Downs's empire and tell you what Dirk Cuyper and his gang were up to, d'you reckon that might chop a substantial bit off the sentence? Cut it to twenty, say, and parole after ten?'

'You should know that I can't make any promises, Kat. What I can do is to advise the Crown Prosecution Service of the extent of any assistance you've afforded to the police.' I had no intention of forgetting that this conniving bitch had cold-bloodedly murdered one of my officers. However, if she was about to give me valuable information, I would have to avoid alienating her, even to the extent of sweet-talking her. With any luck, we'd get the best of both worlds. In common with the rest of the team, I wanted to see her serve a full life sentence without parole.

'Is that a long-winded way of saying you'll float the idea?'

'If you like,' I said.

At some time during our talk, Thompson had surreptitiously undone the top few buttons of her pyjama jacket so that it fell open to display more than was seemly.

But Kate had spotted what she'd done and knew why she'd done it. 'I should do those buttons up, sport, or you'll catch your bloody death of cold.'

'If I confess to the other murders, it won't add any more to the sentence, will it, Brocky dear? I mean, it'll be concurrent, won't it?' Thompson ignored Kate's comments and left the buttons undone.

'Once again you're asking me questions that only the judge at your trial can answer, Kat.'

'If he spent an hour in my cell with me, I might persuade him.'

'You might get a woman judge, mate,' said Kate.

'Even that might work.' This time, Thompson blew a kiss in Kate's direction. 'Oh well, nothing ventured, nothing gained.' She leaned across and filled a tumbler with water from a jug, grimacing as she put a strain on her injured shoulder. 'Here we go, then. Yes, I murdered Dirk Cuyper and Vic Downs. Unfortunately poor little Ram would have been a witness, so I'm afraid he had to go too. What you might call collateral damage.'

Over the years I'd met some callous criminals, but Kat Thompson, alias Chantal Flaubert, was fairly near the top of the list in terms of cold-bloodedness.

'Do you want to tell me why?' Her admission, recorded on tape, meant that I now had sufficient to charge her with those three murders. And that precluded me from asking any more questions, dammit. However, there was nothing to stop me from inviting her to explain her motives; and if she declined, that was that. 'If you tell me everything you know, I may have to ask you some questions, Kat, to clear up times and places and any other ambiguities. Are you prepared to answer such questions?'

'I'll answer anything you want to ask, Brocky dear, if that'll help to cut my sentence. You will tell them how helpful I've been, won't you?'

'Go ahead, then, Kat,' I said, without committing myself.

'Vic Downs was the mastermind. He owned brothels all over London and beyond, and he owned the women he put in them. They'd usually been smuggled in from abroad, Romania and the Ukraine mainly, but some Syrians and Turks as well. Then the Belgians decided to muscle in big time on the London scene, and that upset Vic.'

'But you're a Belgian,' said Kate. 'Did you have divided loyalties?'

'It's true I'm a Belgian, but I wouldn't have anything to do with their set-up. I knew which side my bread was buttered. Anyway, Vic didn't like foreigners interfering in his enterprise and that was good enough for me.' Kat paused to chuckle. 'He didn't like them grabbing a piece of the action. In fact, he was hopping mad. Well, Vic had snouts in every trough and those informants very soon sussed out that it was Dirk Cuyper, and Pim de Jonker back in Ypres, who were behind it all.'

'How did you know about de Jonker?'

'Dirk told me everything, including the secret address. I even threw a spanner in the works by sending de Jonker a list of names, pretending they came from Dirk.'

'As a matter of interest, where did you get those names from, Kat?'

'The newspaper.' Kat chuckled at the deception she'd played on de Jonker. I wasn't going to tell her that she'd also deceived me. Well, very nearly.

'Cuyper and de Jonker had been smuggling women in from the Balkans and the Near East and setting them up in whore-houses throughout Belgium.' Kat laughed outright this time. 'The people who work at the European Union in Brussels are particularly good customers, rich too, although I daresay they claim it on expenses. Well, I'm sure the MEPs do.'

'Oh, surely not,' said Kate sarcastically.

'Anyway, to cut a long story short,' Thompson began, 'Vic Downs wanted rid of Dirk Cuyper once they started encroaching on his territory. He had one particular nose who told him that Cuyper had started using the health club at Richmond. So Vic promptly bought it, kicked out the existing manager and put me in there to get to know Cuyper. It worked a treat. He came on to me straight away, not without my encouragement, of course. We started an affair, although it was actually me who started it, and I'll bet he'd never had such a good ride in all his life, even though I say it myself.' She smiled and pursed her lips at me.

'We found some kinky gear in his wardrobe: thongs, very high-heeled shoes, whips and bondage gear. D'you know anything about that?' asked Kate.

'Oh yes. Dirk told me that his wife, Inge, didn't want to know about sex, that she was dowdy and had lost interest in him. So I bought that sexy gear because he needed a kick start, but once he was under way he was not bad in the sack. After that he thought he was in love with me, and he gave me a key to his flat and a pass to use the pool at Cockcroft Lodge.'

'What went wrong, then?' I asked.

'Someone in the Flemish camp found out that I was part of Vic Downs's empire and intended to kill Cuyper.' Thompson gave an expressive shrug, and winced again. 'So Vic said Cuyper had to be eliminated. Permanently. Before his lot eliminated me. But in the meantime Cuyper's bottle went and he moved into a hotel.'

'How did you know he'd be returning on Friday the twenty-sixth of July at precisely one o'clock?'

'Oh, Brocky dear. I told you, Vic had snouts. He had Cuyper followed. Vic knew exactly where he was staying and he knew whenever he moved.'

'But it was a stroke of luck for you that Dennis Jones turned up half an hour late on that day. Otherwise you might have been caught.'

Kat adopted an expression that seemed to mock my apparent naivety. 'Good Heavens! There wasn't any luck involved, Brocky darling. Jones was on Downs's payroll. Being a school teacher, he needed the money. Anyway, I think it gave him an orgasm just to know that he was on the fringe of something involving sex, pathetic little wimp. He was bloody sex mad was Jones.'

'Why was he there?' asked Kate. 'What was the plan?'

'Jones isn't as daft as he looks. He was the one keeping an eye on Cuyper, having befriended him at the club. He actually arrived with Cuyper, and I arrived a few minutes later. The idea was that once I'd done the job and vanished, Jones would wait till one thirty and then call on a neighbour and raise the alarm. He had to tell everyone that he'd turned up at half past one and spin this yarn about Cuyper being scared witless over some anonymous woman who was out to kill him.' Kat smiled. 'And that was true, of course.'

'Are you telling me that Jones witnessed you murdering Cuyper?' I asked.

Kat smiled. 'Yes, and I thought he was going to be sick. It might just have been all right if he hadn't gone bonkers and started screwing one of his schoolgirls. That's when you showed up and nicked him, Brocky, and I suppose he squealed like a stuck pig and put the finger on me.'

'No, as a matter of fact, he never said a word about you, or about Downs's dodgy business affairs.' I didn't like to admit that Jones's involvement had all come as a complete surprise. He might've been a wimp, but he'd completely fooled me.

'Are you telling me he didn't grass?' For the first time since we'd been talking, Kat Thompson's flamboyant confidence evaporated, albeit momentarily. 'Then how the hell did you track me down?'

'By your fingerprints, Kat.'

'They're not on record.'

'Oh, but they are,' I said, with a certain feeling of satisfaction. 'When you applied for a Belgian passport, you had to provide a set of fingerprints, which went into the national database. And that's how we knew you were involved. We found them all over Cuyper's apartment and in Downs's house. You left them inside Cuyper's safe, too.'

For a long moment Kat Thompson sat in absolute silence, as she realized that she had put herself in her present predicament by applying for a Belgian passport. She eventually broke her silence with a typical British reaction.

'Bugger!' she said.

Kat Thompson went on for another hour and a half, listing in detail all of the late Victor Downs's nefarious activities. Several times I was duty bound to ask her if she wished to continue or whether she was too tired. But on each occasion she opted to continue.

When she'd finished, I asked the one question that had been nagging away all the time she'd been talking.

'Why did you murder Victor Downs, Kat?'

'Haven't you worked it out, Brocky darling? The bastard was having me over, and not only in bed. After I'd killed Cuyper for Vic, I suggested that it was about time he gave me a half share in the enterprise. After all, I was the one taking all the risks while he was sitting up in Hampstead without a stain on his character. What's more, I wasn't sure that I'd get away with murdering Cuyper. I had intended to hide away in Somerset, but then that poacher who lived opposite came beetling across the road and told me that your lot had been making enquiries. That was good enough for me, and I asked Vic to buy me a place in Mexico and fix me up with a new identity, new passport and everything. But he refused and just laughed. So I said I'd make my own arrangements, but I'd come back for one last tumble just for old time's sake. He was ready and waiting, naked and on top of the bed. But like I said, it was a shame that poor little Ram was there.'

'Why did you return to Cuyper's flat at Cockcroft Lodge?' asked Kate. 'The day you murdered our officer.'

'I wanted Cuyper's laptop. I knew he kept it in the safe, but I didn't have time to get it the day I murdered him. There was bound to be stuff on there that would incriminate Vic, and therefore me too. I knew the combination to the safe and I knew you guys wouldn't be able to get into it. And even if you did, I knew you wouldn't be able to break the password and hack into the laptop. So, I waited until you'd packed up and gone home – at least I thought you'd all gone – and paid a visit. I didn't know that some of your people were still there.'

'I've got news for you, mate,' said Kate. 'Our locksmith did open the safe and our computer expert did open the laptop for us.'

'So you found out everything about us, I suppose.' Kat Thompson made the statement with a resigned expression.

'No, Kat,' I said. 'There was nothing on it. It'd been wiped clean.' That wasn't true, of course, but I didn't see any harm in a little disinformation designed to discomfit. 'One last question, what did you do with Cuyper's mobile phone?' I was convinced that no one else could be responsible for its absence.

'It's at the bottom of the Thames if you feel like looking for it, Brocky dear.'

The funeral of Detective Constable John Appleby was held two days later at Pinner Parish Church, close to where he'd lived with his wife, Patricia, since their marriage five years previously.

The Metropolitan Police has always been good at ceremonial, probably because there is so much of it in the capital. At a quarter to eleven a black limousine escorted by two outriders stopped outside the fourteenth-century church. The Commissioner, in uniform as befitted the occasion, alighted and strode quickly up the path. Two constables standing either side of the church door saluted as he entered. As other cars arrived, more of the Yard's senior officers joined the congregation, and I was pleased to see that Mark Hodgson, the concierge at Cockcroft Lodge, was also there.

Next to arrive were the families. Patricia Appleby, all in black, was flanked by her mother and father, and followed by John's sister and their parents.

All my team were there without exception. Kate Ebdon immaculate in black suit and tights, high heels and a small pillbox hat with a veil. Dave Poole, never regarded as one of the smartest dressers, had made a real effort and wore a suit, a white shirt and, in common with all the men, a black tie. I imagine that his wife, Madeleine, had inspected him before he left home.

At eleven o'clock precisely the hearse arrived under escort and stopped in Church Road. Six pallbearers, all constables supervised by a sergeant, bore the coffin into the church. As was customary on these occasions, it was covered by the Metropolitan Police standard. The church bell began its solitary funereal toll, and somewhere a police trumpeter sounded the 'Last Post'.

The Commissioner delivered the eulogy and paid a sincere tribute to John Appleby, even though he had never heard of the detective until informed of his murder. But in all fairness, he couldn't be expected to know every one of the 30,000 officers under his command.

I have to admit that we were all rather relieved when the ceremony was over, and even more relieved to know that the cremation and the wake were to be private affairs. It was not that we were indifferent, but we all wanted to remember John Appleby as we had known him and had no desire to make embarrassed small talk with his family and friends.

EIGHTEEN

The trial of Chantal Flaubert, as the judge directed she should be called throughout the hearing, opened at the Central Criminal Court at Old Bailey on Monday the fourteenth of October.

Despite Flaubert having confessed to murdering Dirk Cuyper, Victor Downs and Ram Mookjai, the Common Serjeant of London, who was the presiding judge, ordered that pleas of not guilty be entered. When Flaubert queried this, he told her that it was common practice and designed to ensure that she had not been coerced into pleading guilty. I found that amusing. I couldn't visualize Flaubert being coerced into doing anything she didn't want to do.

The trial was a remarkably short one considering there were four counts of murder on the indictment. Prosecuting counsel, a stern-faced woman QC devoid of make-up and also, it seemed, devoid of a sense of humour, took me step by step through my investigation. Defence counsel tried chipping away at trivial points, but without much success. Then one after another, the prosecution witnesses followed. Henry Mortlock gave his opinion of the cause of death. The ballistics expert gave indisputable evidence about the automatic pistol recovered at the scene of Appleby's murder and testified that it had been used in all four murders. And Linda Mitchell, the crime-scene manager, who always knew exactly what she was talking about, gave evidence with convincing sincerity. It was a mark of her professionalism because it's easy to be blasé after so many appearances at the Old Bailey. I've seen it happen with police officers who get tripped up by a smart barrister because they have become careless.

Detective Sergeant Liz Carpenter's eye-witness account of the murder of John Appleby by Chantal Flaubert was lightened a little by a stupid question from defence counsel.

Rising ponderously from the front bench to cross-examine,

he adjusted his gown. That done, he tipped his glasses forward and peered over them at his brief.

'Was it absolutely necessary for you have shot my client, Sergeant?' Defence counsel waved his brief vaguely in the air and finally dropped it on to the desk in front of him.

'Yes,' said Carpenter.

'Would you care to explain why, Sergeant?'

'Yes, it was a case of shoot or be shot. And I didn't intend to get shot.'

'Seems to answer your question,' the judge observed drily.

The Common Serjeant's succinct summing-up took only an hour and a half. Liz Carpenter's virtually unchallenged account of the murder of Detective Constable Appleby and Chantal Flaubert's undisputed confession to the other three killings obviously caused the jury to wonder why the hell they were there. They returned verdicts of guilty on all four counts within the hour.

'It has been brought to my attention,' began the Common Serjeant as a preamble to sentencing the prisoner at the bar, 'that you have been instrumental in furnishing the police with information that has led, or will lead, to the prosecution of certain individuals allegedly engaged in prostitution and other related and somewhat distasteful matters. I have no doubt that this willingness to assist was motivated simply and solely by the hope of securing a lesser sentence, and for no other reason. However—' At this point the judge paused and glanced at the press box. 'However, I cannot overlook the fact that you murdered a police officer engaged in the execution of his duty in an attempt to prevent your apprehension for the three other murders you had committed. Whatever assistance you might have afforded the police subsequently, I cannot in all conscience lessen the sentence. Chantal Flaubert, you will go to prison for life without parole.'

The severity of the sentence caused frantic scribbling in the press box, and gasps and whimpering little cries of 'Oh no!' from among the do-gooders and chattering classes who had nothing better to do all day than sit in the public gallery at the Old Bailey.

A stunned Chantal Flaubert gripped the dock rail for support.

After a moment's pause, she glared down at where Kate, Dave and I were sitting in the well of the court.

'You bastards!' she screamed at the top of her voice. 'I've been screwed!'

'And not for the first time,' Dave observed quietly.

Immediately after the Chantal Flaubert trial, Dennis Jones appeared in the dock in the same courtroom at the Old Bailey. Looking pale and scared, he glanced around the impressive location of his trial and gripped the rail firmly.

'Dennis Jones,' began the clerk of the court, 'you are charged in that you did on divers dates in July this year of Our Lord, conspire with Chantal Flaubert, otherwise known as Katherine Thompson, and others not in custody or deceased, to murder Dirk Cuyper, otherwise known as Richard Cooper, at Apartment E, Cockcroft Lodge, Cockcroft Grove, North Sheen. How say you upon this indictment, guilty or not guilty?'

'Not guilty, sir,' mumbled Jones.

But despite a valiant effort by his counsel, the jury wasted no time in finding him guilty. There was little doubt that mention of Detective Constable John Appleby's murder may have swayed the jury in arriving at that verdict.

When it came to sentencing, the judge didn't waste any time either. 'Dennis Jones, you have been found guilty of a heinous crime. You will go to prison for ten years. Take him down.'

Whimpering and half fainting, the pitiful figure of Dennis Jones was almost carried down the steps to the cells beneath the court. It was of no comfort when one of the prison officers – an amateur historian – mentioned that Hawley Harvey Crippen, a famous murderer, had descended that same flight of steps on his way to the condemned cell in 1910.

During the course of Jones's brief trial, his counsel had become heartily sick of his client's repeated demands that he should 'get me off this stupid charge', despite being told that the case against him was rock solid. Once the trial was over and Jones asked what was to happen about the matter of his sexual liaison with his pupil Sally Grey, the barrister replied, with some sadistic pleasure, that the case would be adjourned *sine die*.

'What does that mean?' asked Jones.

'It means they'll try you for it when you come out of prison and then send you straight back again,' said counsel maliciously. But erroneously.

Every murder investigation has fall-out, usually concerning other crimes that have come to the notice of the police during the course of that investigation, and which leads to further, but unrelated, arrests.

Chantal Flaubert had provided extensive information about Victor Downs's widespread sex empire that I'd passed on to the Trafficking and Prostitution Unit, as a result of which its officers made a large number of arrests during the next few weeks.

The murder of John Appleby and the arrest of Chantal Flaubert occurred before all the enquiries into the three previous murders had been completed. But thanks to Flaubert's confession we were able to abandon quite a few follow-ups.

And so ended that particular investigation. Well, not quite. In my case, there was a consequence that had nothing to do with the four murders. At least, not directly.

It was the first Saturday in November and my first weekend off following the end of the Dennis Jones trial. I was lounging about at home trying to get some semblance of purpose and order back into my life. In short, it was a case of working out how to fill the void left by the departure of Gail Sutton to Hollywood, and the realization that she would not be returning.

Until now, my mind had been fully occupied with the two trials. As far as the police are concerned, a murder trial doesn't stop when the court rises at the end of each day. The evenings are taken up with ensuring that the right papers and right exhibits are in place for the following day's proceedings. Sometimes there are hurried conferences with prosecuting counsel in the well of the court, particularly if an additional witness is needed to plug an unforeseen gap in the Crown's case. Especially one that has been created by a wily defence counsel.

As a result, there was no food in my fridge, simply because I'd not had the time to shop. I was on the point of venturing out to Kingston to have a lonely pub lunch somewhere when the phone rang.

Please, not another bloody murder, surely, I thought. There must be another DCI available.

'Brock,' I snapped. 'What the hell is it now?'

'Bloody hell! That's a nice way to greet an old friend, I must say. You're not pissed already, are you, Harry?'

'Who is this?'

'Bill Hunter.'

I laughed. 'Sorry, Bill. No, I'm not pissed, just pissed off. Anyway, what can I do for you?' Bill Hunter and his actress wife, Charlotte, known always as Charlie, were old friends from way back.

'Thank God I've reached you at last, Harry. I've been trying to get hold of you all week. Why don't you buy an answering machine?'

'Not bloody likely!' I responded. 'You should've called my mobile.'

'I did, but you'd changed the number without telling anyone,' said Bill tersely. 'Anyway, I've got hold of you at last. Does the name Lydia Maxwell mean anything to you?'

'Yes, of course it does. She lived in an apartment in North Sheen opposite the one where a murder was committed in July and a second in August. Why d'you ask?'

'She's just moved into the house next door to ours, Harry. She knocked on the door a week or so ago to introduce herself. We invited her in for a drink and she told us that she'd moved from North Sheen because she didn't feel safe there any more, after the murders. I asked if she knew who'd investigated them, and when she mentioned your name I told her you were an old friend of mine and Charlie's. Small world, isn't it?'

'She told me she was going to move, Bill, and mentioned Strand-on-the-Green, but she later said she couldn't find anything in that area that suited her. She did mention Surrey, but wasn't specific. I didn't know where she'd gone.'

'Weren't you interested enough to find out, Harry? I'd have thought that a young and rather gorgeous wealthy widow like her would have grabbed your attention immediately. Why on earth didn't you track her down? After all, you are supposed to be a detective. But all that aside, I have to warn you, Harry, now that Gail's deserted you for the bright lights of Tinseltown, Charlie is plotting.'

'Lydia's certainly an attractive woman, Bill, but at one time I thought she was quite a strong suspect. It wasn't until after the fourth murder occurred, and we'd made an arrest, that I ruled her out completely. But you needn't mention that to her.'

'Ye Gods!' exclaimed Hunter. 'You coppers are suspicious bastards. However, Charlie and I have invited Lydia for dinner this evening and Charlie very much wants you to join us. And what Charlie wants, Charlie gets. What d'you say?'

Charlie Hunter was obviously matchmaking. Although I wasn't averse to the idea, I wasn't altogether sure about accepting. Nor was I sure that I wanted to go back to the Hunters' house where Bill and I had enjoyed summer afternoons watching Gail and Charlie cavorting in the pool while we drank copious amounts of wine. After all, the Hunters had been Gail's friends; or more particularly, Gail and Charlie were friends, having met on the stage. But the real point was that I wasn't sure I was ready to start a new relationship that might end the way the last one did.

Gail Sutton had accepted a part in a Hollywood 'soap' in February, but at the end of March she had emailed me to say that her contract had been extended indefinitely and she had put her Kingston townhouse on the market. I knew instinctively that she would remain in Los Angeles and that I'd never see her again.

'Harry, are you still there?'

'Yes, I'm still here, Bill.'

'Well, old boy, you'd better say yes or you'll have Charlie to answer to. She doesn't like having her dinner arrangements buggered up.'

'Yes, of course, Bill, thank you. Tell Charlie I'll be delighted to come.' Nevertheless, I was still a little apprehensive. If I was honest with myself, I didn't really know Lydia Maxwell at all.